*For Parakletos. And Rashee.*

# 1

Opening his eyes, Baba yawned and scratched his nether regions. With another gusty yawn, he got up from the wooden bench where he'd spent the night, and stretched his thin arms above his head. He was a wiry man, no more than 5'5, with a bald head and grey hairs sprouting from his chin. His large eyes held a haunted look in them and were more often than not red from chewing kola nut, a local bitter fruit that also acted as an appetite suppressant. Under the weight of a certain sadness that wilted his eyelids dragging them down, his haggard worn out face had become a local fixture in the community.

It was 6am, his favourite time of the day. That time in the morning when it wasn't quite dawn, but wasn't quite the pitch dark of the night. The dark where, typically, at first sight, the good people of Palemo, Lagos where he lived, scurried away inside, to bring out their solar lamps and light their candles.

At 6am, the air was "freshly laundered" as he liked to call it. At 6am, before the inevitable smell of decayed and decomposing human detritus that permeated the neighbourhood rose up, the air was fresh, smelled earthy, and, dare he think it, was filled with hope.

Baba coughed up a particularly hearty mass of phlegm from his lungs. Turning his head slightly he heaved the whole lot, *en masse*, into the decomposing heap of rubbish outside his building. He gave a satisfied grunt and reached into his trouser pocket for his *pako*, chewing stick, quickly returning it there when he remembered he had no water to rinse out his mouth. He spotted the neighbourhood cobbler across the road, setting up his roadside stall. Before Baba could greet him, the cobbler held up his hands.

*No water*, he mouthed.

Baba's chest momentarily slumped in defeat, before he remembered he had options. Namely, the two useless boys at the auto-repair shop he frequented. He waved goodbye to the cobbler and started making his way there. But not before taking a backward glance at his building, his hellish hole of a home, and shuddering at the possibility of spending yet another night on the bench outside.

There was a slight breeze as he made his way to the auto-repair shop. He noted the snake-like queue of people waiting patiently at the end of his street to buy water. He couldn't help but notice that half of them were schoolchildren. As he rounded the corner, a water company tanker appeared and stopped at the head of the orderly line of people waiting patiently for this life-giving commodity. As if on cue, all order disappeared, replaced by a scrum. A man jumped out of the passenger seat of the water tanker with a whip in his hand, with which he began lashing out at the crowd.

Baba heard a few schoolchildren cry out in pain. Resolutely, he turned his face away, and carried on walking. Towards the auto-repair shop. Towards Mama Seyi and her famous, *dundun*, fried yams, and away from this scene that by chipping away at his Lagos armour threatened to make him care.

Truth be told, Baba himself did not know why he went to the mechanic's auto-repair shop every morning. It certainly wasn't for the company; two layabouts with mashed yams for brains who also doubled up as mechanics, did not count for company. Sometimes, as he watched the shop television, typically perched on the roof of some poor bastard's car, wires protruding down its backside, all the way to the poor bastard's car battery, he thought he only went there to save the two layabouts from themselves.

Other times, he and the two layabouts wondered why he was deluding himself; they all knew he had nowhere else to go. As Mr Sowemimo, the auto-repair shop owner, who loathed and tolerated Baba with an equal, visceral, passion put it, "He's like their adopted grandparent and stray dog in one."

Baba was not a man who wasted his time thinking about, or dwelling in self-reflection. So whenever he heard Mr Sowemimo talking about him in such dismissive and belittling terms, which he noted was with increasing frequency, he would turn his head away from the auto-repair shop owner and face the street. This being Lagos, there was typically some drama unfolding, which was always more interesting than the useless drivel coming out of Mr Sowemimo's mouth.

Sometimes, Mr Sowemimo would scream and yell at Baba to leave his auto-repair shop, only to be told by the layabouts that if Baba wasn't allowed to come there anymore, then they would leave as well.

And for another day, Baba's stay in the auto-repair shop would be secured.

His daily routine was simple. He arrived at the gates by seven in the morning, sometimes, a little earlier; it all depended on the situation at home. Some mornings, one of the layabouts would just be opening up. Other times, he would have to wait a little for them to arrive and be let in. Upon entering, he would be handed a glass of water, so he could brush his teeth with his trusty pako, chewing stick.

Occasionally, if the layabouts were feeling particularly gracious, they might hand him half a bucket of water, so he could wash his "shrivelled parts" and "mouldy armpits" in the shop backyard. Consider it a service to humanity, they would say, laughing like the idiots they were.

They were full of insults, the layabouts. Most times, he didn't mind. When they started on their "useless nonsense", as he liked to call the insults, he simply turned his face away from them, and towards the street, and sure enough, some drama would unfold under the glare of the scorching sun.

Today, he sat on his chair, a rickety bench on its last legs, looking up at the television, now on the hood of another poor bastard's car, and found himself staring at a man wearing dark red, wraparound sunglasses, their bulging lenses making his square, pale, face look just like a mosquito's. On the screen, surrounded by jostling cameramen and photographers, he saw the man waving while giving the British prime minister a firm handshake. As the Mosquito Man waved, the cameras exploded, bathing the room in bright flashing lights. A few seconds later, the camera panned to a journalist on the edge of the fray speaking animatedly, his voice loud and barely containing his excitement.

"That was Bono with the British prime minister. He will be at the All African Summit taking place in Abuja in a few weeks, on October 24, to campaign for access to healthcare for all Africans. The highly anticipated summit will be attended by all 54 African leaders. And now, back to the studio..." The newsreader's voice faded away.

Baba turned to layabout number one; Dauda, a young man in his early twenties, with the swagger of the particularly ignorant.

"Who's that man?" Baba asked him, pointing to the television. Dauda looked at the television. All he saw was the newsreader, a woman with the moderately bleached skin and modulated tones of the expensively educated.

"I only see woman," he replied.

"Not her, stupid. The man that was on the television before her. The one with the dark red glasses that makes him look like a mosquito."

"Na Bono," layabout number two, Dimeji, shouted from under a car. Dauda went back to the car he was repairing.

Only he wasn't repairing it, he was evidently destroying it. Baba shook his head in despair as he watched him trying to yank one of the car parts from its nether regions.

"Dauda! Come here!" He summoned him. He saw Dauda roll his eyes before swaggering towards him again.

Baba had been coming to the auto-repair shop for as long as everyone could remember, offering his opinions on everything from what he saw on the television to the micro-dramas that were played out every day on the street outside. His ponitifcations notwithstanding, his primary job was, essentially, to survive each day preferably with food to eat and water to quench his never-ending thirst.

In fact, if Dauda was to describe Baba to people who didn't know him, he would say that Baba excelled at being the very best version of himself, which was as "a useless man, and one that was incapable of malice".

"Has it ever occurred to you that someone could die because of what you're doing?" Baba asked him. "You're stealing car parts from people who trust you to fix their cars. I shudder to think how many people's blood you've got on your hands."

Dauda shrugged. "Have you finished?" he asked Baba in that particular way he knew would drive Baba mad and no doubt would incur another lecture on Dauda's insouciant approach to life.

Baba shooed him away, shaking his head, whether in grief at Dauda's ignorance or the headache that suddenly came upon him, he wasn't sure.

"Oladimeji, you said his name was Bono?" He asked the other mechanic.

"I've told you to call me Dimeji. There's no need to draw out my full name when you talk to me," Dimeji grumbled from under a car.

He slid out, wiping his greasy hands on his overalls. "And yes, his name is Bono. He's a famous singer in London."

"I see," Baba said, although he didn't. If he was a famous singer, why was he coming to Nigeria to tell the government to give people healthcare? Furthermore, why would the Nigerian government listen to him?

Baba voiced his opinions aloud.

"He does a lot of things for poor people everywhere," Dimeji said. He quickly slid back under the car before Baba started one of his sermons. Baba was a fool, but he was an old fool, so they all tolerated him.

But not this morning, Dimeji thought. It was way too early for a sermon.

"And everyone listens to him? Oladimeji, I'm talking to you. Get out from under that car!"

Yes, Baba was an old fool, but he was harmless, and quite possibly, the nearest thing to a father that he and Dauda had, and in his own way was often the wisest among them. Long after the fact they found themselves recalling his words, like having tuned out a parent whose admonishments were, in the end, prophetic and surprisingly wise. Dimeji slid out sighing with exaggerated patience before talking.

"Baba, of course they listen to him. He's a white musician

11

from London. You saw how the British prime minister was listening carefully to what he was saying. That means that he will do whatever Bono tells him to do." Dimeji slid back under the car.

Baba thought some more about what Dimeji said. He stood and stretched. It'd just gone past 7am and already, the heat was becoming oppressive, the earlier freshness of the day a faded memory. The auto-repair shop's steel corrugated roof, which was supported by concrete pillars, and nothing else, didn't help matters. If anything, it made things worse, condensing the heat and making its inmates sweat. When it rained torrentially, as it thankfully did in Lagos, loud cheers would reverberate around the neighbourhood. This would be followed by an exodus of people from their homes armed with buckets, bowls and any container they could get their hands on, to collect the rainwater. The containers would be lined up strategically, to ensure they captured every drop.

In the auto-repair shop, at such times, first the roof would rumble under the force of the torrential rain, and then it would sway. It had even been known to shudder, at which point, Baba, a man not given to the whims of religion, would briefly contemplate his life, and what awaited him in the next. But those moments never lasted. Inevitably, the rain would stop. And the people of the neighbourhood would lift their hands to the sky, whispering prayers of thanksgiving to God above for the gift of water.

The aftermath of the rain also provided welcome shelter from the blazing heat for them all, for which Baba was especially thankful. In fact, whenever Baba thought about his days as a peddler on the streets of Lagos, he didn't think about the *area boys*, the local gangsters who often harassed him and stole his money, not the policemen who roughed him up and took his money, simply because they could, nor the crazy drivers who navigated the roads as if it was their own personal fiefdom. No, he didn't think about any of that whenever he thought of his street-peddling days. What he thought about was the sun and its merciless rays beating down on his sweat-stained clothes and bald head, as if it was on a mission to remove him from Earth in liquid form.

Outside the auto-repair shop gate, Mama Seyi, the roadside food stall owner, fried some *akara*, finely grounded bean paste, in a vat of cooking oil, sending the delectable aroma in the air. Baba's stomach rumbled. He thought the layabouts would buy him food, but he daren't hope. As he sat back down on his bench his stomach rumbled again. The layabouts ignored him. His hunger was becoming unbearable. He stood up, yawned and sat down heavily again on the bench. He put his head in his hands and thought about his wife Munira; then about the Mosquito Man, how *he* could get anyone, even the British prime minister to do his will, and then, his thoughts went back to his wife; her rolling, ample buttocks and voluminous breasts, the often overwhelming desire they inspired in him, that made him want to bury his head in her cleavage, never to come up for air again. He'd always thought that if he died, her chest would be his head's perfect resting place. Miserable, he sighed theatrically.

"Oh, for the love of God, I can't take this anymore," Dimeji said. "Mama Seyi!" he called out. "Please give Baba some rice and beans. I'll pay for it."

"Next time, even if you pay for it, I won't give him anything until he pays me what he owes me. Old fool," Mama Seyi said, crossly. She scooped some rice and beans onto a plastic plate and told her ten-year-old son, Fela, to give it to Baba.

"Oladimeji, you will live a long and prosperous life," Baba said as he took the food off Fela and started eating.

"And me? What about my life?" Dauda teased.

Baba spoke with his mouth full. "You are a lost cause," he said, smiling.

"But at least I can read," Dauda retaliated, with a kind smile.

That evening, after the auto-repair shop closed, Baba roamed the streets trying to delay the inevitable. Eventually, about 11pm, dripping with sweat in the humid night, he made his way home. For a few moments he stood across the street from his building; a face-me-I-face-you, rectangular bungalow with individual rooms on opposite sides separated by an open corridor. There was no electricity, and the building was dark, although he spotted a candles burning dimly through a few of his neighbours' windows.

Once satisfied that his landlord, a local mogul, was not going to come out of the building and find him loitering there, he entered. Outside his room, he reached to unlock the door but stopped when he heard sounds of moaning and grunting emanating from within. Leaning in to hear better, he recognised his wife's laugh, followed by the landlord's. Whereas his wife's laugh had been edgy, the landlord's was triumphant and malicious.

Baba stood still. From experience, he knew it would take at least a full minute for the pain in his chest to subside. So he waited. When he was finally rendered mobile, he staggered away from the door and went back outside where there were several benches lined up under the small windows along the exterior of the bungalow. He chose one, laid down across it and closed his eyes. That night, he dreamed of a white man wearing bulging mosquito-eyed sunglasses in which his wife's luxurious breasts loomed in reflection.

Baba shot to his feet. The shock of cold water on his face startling him awake. Standing over the bench was his wife, Munira, holding an empty cup in one hand. Water dripped from his face down his neck and onto his clothes. Squinting at the sun he averted his eyes from her heaving bosom. He estimated it was about 7 o'clock in the morning. Idly, observing that he'd missed the morning freshness, Baba wiped his face with a corner of his vest ignoring the other tenants who were sniggering at him from their windows.

Baba looked at the cup as it dripped with water.

"Did you have to waste the water?" he asked her, not expecting an answer.

Munira drew herself up in front of him, with her magnificent breasts. Baba steered his eyes away with difficulty.

"So, this is where you slept," his wife sneered. Baba ignored her and his now hardening loins, consoling himself with the fact that if his wife wasn't sleeping with the landlord, they would be homeless, and what good was that?

"Didn't you hear me?"

He ignored her. Sidestepping her he headed into their 10 x 10 square metre home. As he entered, he averted his eyes from the bed, only for his knee to collide with the frame causing him to reel back onto the wretched object with a groan.

The bed took up most of the space in the room and a small wardrobe holding Munira's clothes took up the rest. On top of the wardrobe were Munira's cooking utensils, for when she did cook. Baba nursed his throbbing knee and tried not to think about his wife and the landlord's activities the night before. Once again, he reassured himself with the thought that whatever Munira did to keep the roof over their heads was none of his business. Munira had her own dreams and motivations for their marriage and he never really knew what motivation would win out on any given day.

There were some days when she felt magnanimous towards him and they would spend the time together like any normal couple. They would make love for hours. Afterwards, she would prepare his favourite dish—she really was a terrific cook when she deigned to cook—and then they would go for a stroll around their neighbourhood where she never failed to spend a few minutes talking to the cobbler across the street. The natural disdain she had for most people did not extend to him. She enquired about his health and was genuinely upset if he said he felt unwell. Before continuing their walk, she would dip into her purse, give him some money and tell him not to forget his dream of going to night school. His reassuring head nod would be the only way they would be able to continue on their path. Then, and only then, would they lock arms and move on.

Baba loved those times. His heart would swell with pride that he was the husband of such a beautiful lady, even if she had a viper's tongue. On those walks, Munira would talk to him about her dreams and he would catch a glimpse of the real Munira, the person behind the viper's tongue and rhinoceros skin. This person was compassionate: "I don't care how bad things are. It is not right for a ten-year-old to be selling cigarettes at 11pm." This person had ideas about Nigeria and its people: "There is nothing wrong with Nigeria that cannot be fixed by a female president." Above all, this person genuinely wanted to make a difference in people's lives: "I want my movies to inspire people to do things that they never thought they could do."

When she spoke like that, he felt inadequate, for he had never had such dreams. *His* dreams had never extended beyond getting through the next hour, preferably with food in his stomach. Yes, he preached at Dauda and Oladimeji all the time about changing their ways, but none of his so-called preaching had an iota of the common sense that Munira dished out on her magnanimous days.

When they eventually finished their strolling, they would

go back to their one-room home and he would make them both tankard-sized cups of Lipton tea, with plenty of condensed milk and three cubes of sugar, which they would wash down with Jacob's cream crackers. Afterwards, they would usually have a nap or Munira would perform scenes from her favourite Nollywood movies for him, which never failed to thrill him.

As an actress, he felt she was majestic. He didn't know how she did it, but between getting up from their bed and standing, she would morph into the character she was playing. No silly caricatures for Munira. No, she became the character. Her facial features would change, as would her voice and overall deportment. Baba often thought that she played Nollywood characters better than the actresses themselves.

As much as he loved her performances, what he hated more than anything else was the inevitable come-down. At the end of each performance, a mixture of loneliness, fear, disappointment and sadness would flit across her face and she would look at him with such despair, whether at him or at the situation she found herself, that she would head for the bed, weighed down by an invisible darkness and refuse to leave, sometimes for days after. He dreaded those episodes because Munira wouldn't speak. She would just lie in bed, her eyes blank. Other times, she would weep uncontrollably. If anyone asked him what the worst thing about those episodes were, he would tell them that it was the fact that his Munira was gone, and he didn't know where.

He tried to comfort her during one of the episode, once. He took her hand and covered it with his. Munira didn't say a word. She withdrew her hand from his and continued staring past him into space, with her blank eyes. And then, just as suddenly as it began, the episode would lift. He had no way of knowing when. All he knew was that she would suddenly jump out of bed and take a shower—which she wouldn't have done in days. Then, she would get dressed and go out to he knew not where. One thing he did know was that her tongue became even more waspish after each episode and her behaviour more belligerent.

They never discussed those episodes or made reference to them. However, they were becoming increasingly frequent. From a few episodes a year, Munira was having one every other month and with each one, recovery seemed to be taking that little bit longer.

Baba took his toothbrush but abandoned it when he remembered that he—not Munira—was out of toothpaste. He put the toothbrush back on top of the wardrobe and took his chewing stick instead. Anyway, he didn't even like using toothbrush and toothpaste. He'd only started using them because he thought it would make him more appealing to his wife. Dauda said that it would take an act of God for that to happen. But then, that Dauda was an ignoramus.

Baba got off the bed. He took a furtive look at the door, grabbed a plastic cup and filled it with water, his shoulders tense. He had to be quick. If Munira found him helping himself to the water, she would not be pleased. He opened the door and stuck his head out, towards the building's main entry. Munira was still holding court. He vaulted to the backyard as quick as his wiry legs would allow, where he expertly brushed his teeth with his beloved chewing stick. When he finished, he gargled and spat out the water into the rubbish heap. As he turned to go back into the building, he met Munira's eyes. She watched him with undisguised contempt.

"You're such a foolish man," she said. "You are a worthless, foolish old man," she repeated.

Baba ignored her and went back into their room. A few moments later, he came back out again with a change of clothes.

"If you come back here tonight and you don't see me..."

"You say that all the time, and yet when I come back I see you." Baba said. "Like you have anywhere else to go." Baba kissed his teeth and shook his head, as if talking to a silly teenager.

"Why don't you go and watch your stupid television at the mechanic's? God knows, you're not fit for anything else!" Munira screamed at him.

Baba walked off. He took perverse pleasure in knowing that it made her even madder when he did that. He made his way to the auto-repair shop, a thirty-minute walk away. He knew it so well, he could probably walk it in his sleep.

The sun was just about bearable; there was even a slight breeze. He saw a water tanker pulling away from his street, surrounded by a group of people and some children of school age with empty containers. A few of them tried barricading the water tanker, but jumped out of the way when they saw the driver had every intention of mowing them down.

Baba wondered how many of the kids would get beaten by their parents for coming home with empty containers. He didn't blame the parents; the lack of water in Palemo made monsters of them all. Thinking about water made him think of his wife, Munira, and once again, the landlord. He steered his mind and feet back towards the auto-repair shop and continued.

Already, there was traffic, but not the mind-numbing, frustrating mass of vehicles that was sure to come later, resulting in frayed tempers, a few scuffles, and if the area boys had anything to do with it, victims to extort.

The layabouts weren't around yet, so Baba waited outside, on the bench. Mama Seyi met him there. They greeted each other warily, she muttering about how much he owed her, and how people like him were trying to drive her out of business. Baba watched as she set out her cooking utensils by her road-side stall, outside the auto-repair shop gates. Soon, the smell of fried akara filled the air. His stomach rumbled. Dauda arrived and opened up the auto-repair shop. He watched Baba's eyes follow Mama Seyi's hand as she scooped up the bean paste with a ladle and dropped it into the vat of boiling oil. The paste bubbled, and rose to the surface turning a golden brown.

"Mama Seyi, please give me akara and *dundun*, fried yams," Dauda called out to her.

"No problem," she answered, but not before giving Baba a baleful glare.

Inside the auto-repair shop, Dauda brought out the television and connected it to one of the car batteries. He messed around with a few wires and soon it spluttered to life.

"Baba, the television is ready," he said.

"Dauda, come and take your food," Mama Seyi called out.

Dauda left the auto-repair shop and went to collect the steaming plate. He smiled wryly to himself when he re-entered the auto-repair shop.

"Baba, come," he pulled up a chair alongside Baba's bench and held out his plate. "Let us eat."

"Dauda, you will live long," Baba said, eating heartily. Baba made sure he kept his eyes on the television. The morning news was on. Heavy rainfall had washed away a settlement in Ibadan, southwest Nigeria. University lecturers and students were on strike, and one of the country's politicians had been assassinated.

"Baba, this is depressing. Let's have some music," Dauda said.

"No, don't change the channel. Leave it. How else will we find out what's going on?"

"I'll leave it for one more minute and then, I'll change it," Dauda said.

Baba knew it wouldn't be the last time that day that he would despair about the brain cells—or lack thereof—in Nigeria's youth.

"And now for the international news. Celebrity, Bono, is today in Nairobi, lobbying the Kenyan president on his plans to raze Kibera, the biggest slum in the country, and turn it into a national athletics training academy, complete with stadium and luxury golf course. Bono believes that the president's plan to convert the land—an area of almost three square kilometres—needs to be considered further as Kibera is home to almost one million people who will most certainly be displaced. Despite assurances from the Kenyan government that alternative resettlement plans have been made for the Kibera residents, Bono is going to press the Kenyan president to delay the razing until the resettlement plan has been certified viable by Kibera residents and local NGOs..." the television panned to a video of the Mosquito Man talking to whom Baba assumed was the Kenyan president. He had his arm around the president, who was smiling like the cat that had got the cream.

"See, it's that Bono man again," Dauda said.

The screen faded back to the newsreader. "Bono will be in Abuja later this month at the All African summit to campaign for healthcare rights for Nigerians and all Africans."

Dauda changed the television channel. A young girl in miniscule shorts and a string top gyrated in front of a popular Nigerian rapper. Dauda put on his greasy overalls and started singing.

"You see that girl? The day God grants me the know-how, I will sleep with someone exactly like that. The real thing. We'll go to a nice hotel with air-conditioning and a shower, like those ones you see in films. Then, we'll go to the hotel swimming pool to relax and float in those floaty things to cool down even more. Imagine, all that water, just for us *to relax*," he laughed to himself at the incongruity.

"That's your ambition?"

Dauda slid under one of the cars. "Baba, the problem with you is that you think too much."

Baba heard Dimeji greet Mama Seyi. Dimeji came inside the auto-repair shop, said "good morning" to Baba and Dauda, then changed into his overalls.

"Baba, how body?"

"We thank God."

Outside, food vendors carrying plastic trays on their heads called out.

"Iced water!"

"Buy fried yam!"

A mobile cobbler, known locally as 'shoemaker', walked past, clicking his toolbox. "Shoemaker! Bring your shoe. Shoemaker is here!"

Baba turned his attention back to the girl on television. Only she wasn't on there. She had been replaced by a young man in low cargo trousers showing his boxer shorts. His teeth were gleaming white, the head clean-shaven. A lone diamond stud earring glinted in his right earlobe. His T-shirt fitted snugly around his muscular frame. The man emanated youth, vitality, success and all those other things that Baba, in his fifty-odd years on Earth had never had. Baba snorted to himself as he heard the young man speak.

"Yo, this is MTV Africa, coming to you live and direct from the Motherland. Fresh from his successful visit in Kenya where he managed to persuade the president to hold off his razing of Kibera, the second largest slum in Africa, Bono is due in Johannesburg where he will meet the South African president to talk about environmental issues on behalf of poor people. Bono will be in Abuja, Nigeria, later this month at the All African Summit to talk to African governments about access to healthcare for all Africans. And now, for more music." The screen panned out and another gyrating girl and a young black man with blonde cornrows filled the screen.

"What did I tell you about this Bono person? He makes things happen!" Dimeji said.

A plan was forming in Baba's mind. A plan so ridiculous he wondered out loud if God was talking to him directly.

"You think God doesn't have anything better to do with his time than to listen to you?" Dauda said from underneath the car. He wrenched something from the car and slid out, a part in his hand.

"Dauda, please put that thing back," Baba pleaded, gesturing to the object he was waving around. "How many more people's blood do you want on your hands?"

"I didn't hear you complain when I bought you akara and fried yam this morning with the money I got from selling these car parts. The rich don't need our help. They have carpeted hospitals with 60 inch televisions in patients' rooms that they can go to. So please, stop worrying about them and focus on your own life," Dauda said.

Dauda might have spoken the truth, but that didn't make what he was doing right, Baba thought irritatedly.

"Baba, Bono, the one you call Mosquito Man, is a good man, not so? If he comes to Abuja for this

25

healthcare-whatever-thing he's doing, maybe everyone in the country will have free healthcare. Who knows, we might even have drinking water in Palemo!" Dimeji laughed at this own joke.

Baba sat up straight in his chair. Dimeji's words swept over him, first as a tiny whisper then quickly rose to a crescendo. *Who knows, we might even have drinking water in Palemo!*

And just like that, his idea to reach out to the Mosquito Man to help aid in changing the water fortunes of the people of Palemo, and he and Munira's specifically, suddenly didn't seem so ridiculous anymore.

"Oladimeji—"

"I've told you, my name is Dimeji—"

"I want to meet this Mosquito Man when he comes to Abuja. If he tells everybody what to do and they listen to him, don't you think he'll want to hear from us, the people he's meant to be helping?"

Dimeji looked at him as if he'd grown two heads.

Baba continued. "I can tell him all the problems we're facing in Palemo, primary of which is lack of drinking water, and he'll tell the people in Abuja and who knows, maybe everybody in Nigeria will get clean water."

Dimeji decided to humour him. "And Bono will listen to you, because...?"

"Who better to advise someone trying to solve a problem than the person experiencing the problem himself?"

Dauda and Dimeji burst out laughing. In fact, they laughed so hard tears came to their eyes. Baba ignored them.

Their laughter seemed to confirm that he was on the right track.

In between his laughter, Dimeji spoke. "Ahem, Baba, you haven't told us how you'll meet the Mosquito Man."

"Yes, please do tell us," Dauda echoed.

Baba didn't know and he said as much.

"When you find out, let us know, eh?" Dimeji said before collapsing again in laughter. When he spoke again, it was to order some food. "Mama Seyi, I don laugh today. Bring me and Baba something to eat!"

"I am not bringing that man anything until he pays me what he owes me! And how many times in the morning does he have to eat?" Mama Seyi hissed.

"Dimeji, please, what is the time?" Baba asked him.

"Why? Have you got an appointment with the Mosquito Man somewhere?"

"Just give me the time and stop being stupid."

"It's 9 o'clock," Dauda said.

"Mama Seyi, where's my food?"

"Dimeji, I have no problem bringing you food. It's the man who owes me money I have issues with," Mama Seyi said.

Baba got up. The street glistened in the scorching heat. He was hot, sticky and probably smelled. He needed a bath—he hadn't had one for several days now. Munira refused to let use him the buckets of water she stored in their room, claiming that as he didn't pay for the water, he had no right of access. There had been days when she would snatch the cup of water from his hand and empty it on the dirty ground, just because she could. Even this morning, she'd barely let him brush his teeth with it. He absentmindedly rubbed his behind remembering the contemptuous look she'd given him and the shrill screech of her voice as she sent him packing to the layabouts.

He stepped out of the auto-repair shop and into the street, making noises about seeing Dauda and Dimeji later. From experience, he knew he wouldn't get any food from Mama Seyi, even if Dimeji was paying for it. In truth, he had nowhere to go, but a man could only take so much insult at that time of the morning.

"Say hello to Mosquito Man when you see him," Dimeji said.

Baba ignored him. Outside, the roads bulged with people and cars. As he walked, Baba didn't notice the decomposing refuse on the streets. He didn't notice the acrid smoke belching out of the patched-up cars. He didn't notice the beggars with mangled limbs scooting between cars on two-wheeled skateboards, ready to showcase their withered limbs to anyone who gave them more than a few seconds look, for money. And neither did he notice his wife and the landlord buying trinkets a few stalls away from him as he passed through the popular market.

Baba didn't notice any of these things as he made his way back to his one-room home. He knew Munira wouldn't be home at that time. Truth be told, he didn't know where she went or what she did during the day, and he was loathe to ask.

When he got back to his room, he sat on the bed and

pondered how he could get through to the Mosquito Man. Water was important for Palemo residents. Without water, they couldn't cook, eat or drink. As far as he was concerned, electricity was convenient, but it wasn't paramount. Everyone in their 'face-me-I-face-you' cooked with either kerosene or firewood every day without fail. In addition, they had candles and solar powered lamps, so they didn't need electricity. Granted, there had been some hairy situations with tenants' rooms catching fire from unattended candles, but that was an acceptable fact of life in Palemo. In any case, they didn't own anything that required electricity to function. Bono could talk about healthcare and all those things, but without water, people couldn't drink the medicine that the doctors prescribed. Without water, they couldn't cook, bathe, wash their clothes, or do anything.

In essence, water was life, and it was sorely lacking in Palemo, and much of Lagos. If they had free running water, half of people's health problems would disappear. It was because they didn't have water that people were using newspaper to wipe their behinds after defecating in their pit latrines. If they had water, they could wash their hands properly with soap. If they had good, clean water, they wouldn't suffer from cholera.

It all came back to water.

Not everybody had it, and those that did paid handsomely for it and charged those who didn't, highly for it. It was not uncommon for house owners to charge their neighbours a fee for using their outside taps.

So, it was all about water. And somehow, he had to make Bono see it. After following the man for little more than a few days on television, Baba had no doubt of his ability to make people listen to him and, most importantly, get things done.

Suddenly he heard voices in the corridor. They were his wife's and the landlord's bidding each other goodbye. He sat still, his heart racing and stomach churning, though he wasn't clear if it was because he was happy to see her or sickened by the thought of seeing her. The key turned and Munira stepped inside their home, taking in the room at a glance. She was wearing trinkets that Baba had never seen before.

"You're back here?" She asked, not really needing an answer.

Baba's eyes followed her as she began undressing in front of him. Despite himself, desire rose within him. She knew what she was doing, the witch. Munira changed into a kaftan and patting the trinkets on her wrists she turned and stood in front of him.

"I suppose those boys kicked you out?" Then, making exaggerated sniffing sounds, "You really do need a bath." Suddenly, her voice changed. "Why don't you do something, you useless old man!" she raged. "I will die here in this filth, this room, and you will still be going to the mechanic's, and talking nonsense as if anybody is interested in what you say or think. God, I loathe you!" Tears of frustration filled her eyes.

Despite himself, the words came rushing out of Baba's mouth. Her semi-naked, magnificent, corpulent body always did that to him; unhinge his mental faculties and slacken his jaw. "Things will change. You'll see, I'm working on a new plan. I'm going to meet Bono, the white musician from London. He's coming to Abuja to talk to the president and I'm going to tell him to give everybody in Palemo and the whole of Nigeria, water."

Munira sat on the bed. The room was sweltering. Flies buzzed around the two of them. Baba watched a trickle of sweat disappear down Munira's chest. He had a sudden image of himself sinking his head between her breasts and losing himself there enraptured.

Munira followed his eyes.

"You are going to meet a white man in Abuja and tell him to provide water for us in Palemo?" She spoke slowly.

Baba diverted his attention away from her chest with difficulty. Suddenly, he wanted her approval. He wanted her to believe in him.

"Yes, the Mosquito Man. His name is Bono. He'll help us. He helps everybody. He'll be in Abuja in a few weeks and I'll meet him there and tell him that we need water."

Munira nodded as if in understanding. And then she spoke.

"Have you lost your mind?"

"No."

Munira stood up and went to the door. She opened it and spoke through clenched teeth. "Get out," she said.

Baba opened his mouth to speak, but when he saw her face, he got off the mattress and walked out. She thought he was mad. He understood that. Truth be told, he didn't really understand what he was doing himself. However, he was convinced that he was on the right path. He would meet Bono and tell him to tell the Nigerian president to give Palemo residents, and perhaps the whole of Nigeria, water. The Nigerian president would listen because everyone listened to Bono. He was a miracle worker. Everyone knew that. Baba made his way back to the auto-repair shop, his desire for Munira receding with each step.

# 2

Munira sat on the bed after her husband left. She swatted a few flies and played with the trinkets on her wrist. The landlord would be round soon, she knew. He would have waited for Baba to leave, and like a reptile, present himself in her cage of a home with his spare landlord's key. Idly, she wondered who else he was sleeping with. He had two other properties in the neighbourhood and a few stalls in the market, which he sublet. All these made him financially attractive to the young sluts in the neighbourhood, who fluttered around him like virulent butterflies.

Sometimes, she wished he would leave her alone. In fact, she wished everyone, including her husband, would leave her alone. She glanced around the room and immediately felt depressed. She was sick of it all. The hovel they lived in; her old, spineless husband; and of course, the City of Dreams, Lagos, the city that seduced millions of innocents from all over West Africa with its bright lights and promises to fulfil people's dreams. No, she wanted to cry out to passersby. Don't believe it. This city will chew you up and spit you out, like masticated kola nut.

Ever since she could remember, Munira had dreamed

about being an actress. In her village in Ibadan, southwest Nigeria, on her parents' farm, she would recite lines from Nollywood films using withered cassava and yam tubers as supporting actors. *But the child is yours! Yours! You took my virtue and now you want to abandon me*, she would recite, her head in her nine-year-old hands. And she would wail, in the way she'd seen Nollywood actresses do in their films. Occasionally though, she pulled back. Sometimes, as an actor, one could do a lot with a line, by not doing anything at all. It was all in the eyes. A glance, a storm, a certain stillness. That said a whole lot more than any loud wailing or exaggerated body movements ever could.

Once, her primary school teacher asked her what she was doing after school. Her classmates had sniggered. Some of them pointing to her tattered uniform and rubber slippers that were so worn down they had receded to half their length, revealing her cracked heels.

"Buying another uniform," someone had twittered, to more sniggering from the class.

She didn't hear them. In her mind, she was already on her parents' farm, trying out new lines from a Nollywood film she'd seen at the electrician's workshop the day before.

In secondary school, the sniggers became louder and more cruel. One day, she approached one of her teachers. *She wanted to go to Nollywood. Did he know how to get there?* The man had said yes, but first, she had to do something for him. He gave her directions to his house and told her to meet him there after school. Later that day, when she left his house, she was no closer to knowing where Nollywood was, nor how to get there. But her teacher reassured her that he knew, and as long as she kept coming to his house after school, he would help her get there. He also said that he knew other people who had contacts in Nollywood, and she would meet them all in his house.

After secondary school, the sniggers became hostile calls for her to leave her village. They called her a whore because by then she had slept with all the male teachers who taught there. She'd denied them, all the vicious accusations, as did the teachers who had also been on the receiving end. Desperate to prove their innocence, they each failed her multiple times, forcing her to repeat classes, year in, year out. Her parents were deeply ashamed. Her mother stopped speaking to her. Her father said she was no longer his daughter. Though the family continued living together, she, keeping to her side of the hut, (her parents, the other), spent her days contriving ways to avoid their broken-hearted judgements, centred on how far she had fallen. And after all that she still never got any directions to Nollywood; it remained no more than a tantalising fantasy, that now gripped her with even deeper fervour.

The years went by. No one asked for her hand in marriage. They said she was damaged goods. Eventually, she worked out that Nollywood was in Lagos. At night, she would plot her escape to Lagos, the City of Dreams. She pictured herself arriving in the city and running into a Nollywood director as she disembarked from the interstate coach. She imagined the newspapers writing about how wonderful she was. She saw herself going up on stage and receiving awards for her work. And, in the morning, when she opened her eyes to find herself on the sleeping mat, and her parents a few feet away, on their side of the hut, she would close her eyes and allow herself to dream again for a few more seconds, before getting up and going to their meagre farm. Out there, she would pretend she was playing a farmer's wife in a Nollywood film, and her co-actors, the yam and cassava tubers, would give her applause. Or, so she imagined.

And then, she was thirty. She still hadn't left the village. The catcalls had stopped, replaced with pitying looks. She hadn't married. She didn't have children. She was cursed. One day, in the market, she overheard one of the young girls talking about someone called Baba. Munira found herself listening hard. The young girls ignored her. She was Munira, the strange prostitute who spoke to herself and the vegetables on her farm. They said Baba, who left the village many years ago, was now back, and looking for a wife to take back to Lagos with him. He had done very well for himself, despite being illiterate. Even if he was over fifty and from what everyone said, had hygiene problems, (which the young girls discussed and concluded between themselves they didn't mind, because he was a way out of the village); bad hygiene was a small price to pay for the opportunity.

The girls also talked about the way he spent money at the beer parlour, buying bottomless bottles of Guinness and Star for everyone, every night. A sure sign that the man had made it big in Lagos. The girls laughed to themselves as they promised each other that whichever one of them married Baba and moved to Lagos—the big 'L'!—they would make sure to look out for another "rich, old, illiterate man in Lagos like him," for the other girls to fight to marry.

"Or someone even older," one of them said, "so he'll die early and leave me his money."

Munira went back to her hut. It hadn't changed much in the time since her parents died. She waited until nighttime and made her way to Baba's parents' house. Climbing into his room through the open window she hid behind the door. Later, when Baba opened his bedroom door, right there, from behind it, stood a naked, magnificent Munira.

The young girls of the village didn't understand it. Munira was old and fat. How could Baba have chosen her? The rest of the villagers didn't understand it either. Rumour had it that all the men, at one point or the other, had slept with her. Baba's elderly parents pleaded and begged. Couldn't he see that Munira was soiled goods? Couldn't he see that she was cursed? Otherwise, why would she be unmarried at thirty? And could she even have children? Why not one of the young, supple, girls in the village, who were positively lined up to marry him, despite his rather obvious shortcomings?

Baba did not listen.

They got married and Baba took her to Lagos.

She cried on her first night. Because she had finally made it to the City of Dreams, and because Baba had lied to her. He was not a businessman. He didn't have a job and didn't even have enough money to get her a bottle of mineral water to quench her thirst on that humid first night. He lived in a damp room, in a festering tenement, in a Lagos slum. And he owed money to loan sharks who hammered on their door just as they were falling asleep, demanding payment. She paid them off, in the only way she knew how.

And now, she was 35, with a Nollywood age of 25.

Munira fanned herself, as if to shake the memories away. She hated the memories. They made her weak. And she had to be strong, if she was ever going to achieve her dream of making it in Nollywood.

It was this room, she decided. It was like a sweltering prison. She hated it. It made her think of all the men who had lied to her about helping her to become an actress. It made her think of the things she'd done because she had believed them. It made her think of her husband, and how he had tricked her with his lies when he came to the village all those years ago.

She resolved not to think of her husband and his deluded idea about meeting some white man and bringing water to Palemo. No, she wouldn't think of him, because whenever she did, she felt red-hot anger, pain and frustration. All at the same time.

There were times that she felt some affection for him, though. In much the same way that one would feel affection for a dog one vaguely knew. Deep inside she knew that he was a good, albeit, weak man. He couldn't help himself. He just was, and that was all there was to it. Nonetheless, right now, she felt frustrated. Towards him, towards the landlord, towards their hovel and this dream of Nollywood that refused to let her go, even with each cursed year that added more girth to her body—not that her husband nor the landlord have complained. If anything, the few extra kilos seemed to have had the opposite effect.

No, she thought. She would not think. Thinking just brought back painful memories that had no right of abode in the present. She got off the bed and walked the few steps to the mirror. Reflected in it, behind her own looming presence, was a sliver of a view of the bed, which at that moment, she decided she hated more than anything else in the world.

Tears ran down her cheeks. Munira wiped them away, furiously. She needed to distract herself, so she turned to her favourite pastime: worshipping her image. She took off the kaftan she was wearing and stood naked, in front of the mirror, liking what she saw. She was reaching out for the hair brush to use as a microphone to recite some lines from her favourite Nollywood film when she heard the key turn in the lock. She didn't turn round, but continued standing in front of the mirror. The landlord came inside the room a moment later. He came up behind her, cupped her breasts in his hands and squeezed her nipples hard. Munira grimaced in pain and killed the flash of anger and helplessness that rose within her.

She moved away.

"When are we going to see the director you told me about?" She asked him.

The landlord sighed and attempted to draw her back to him. Munira allowed him to, because she wanted an answer. Soon, she thought, she wouldn't have to put up with him. As soon as she got her part, she would dump him and get a young lover, just like the famous Nollywood actresses she admired.

The landlord led her to the bed and began undressing.

Munira took her kaftan from the bed and put it on. She sat down and looked at him.

"What are you doing? Take it off!" the landlord said.

"Not until you tell me what's happening with the director. You said you could get me an audition. It's been three weeks and nothing has happened." Munira's eyes narrowed. "Or, has it all been a lie?"

The landlord stopped undressing and sat on the bed, in his boxer shorts, next to her. He began caressing her face. His breath stank. Munira averted her face.

"Of course not," he said. "You know what creative people are like. They have no perspective of time. Anyway, the man has travelled. He's in London—"

His right hand slid up her left thigh. Munira clamped her thighs shut. "That's what you told me last month. If filming is meant to start within the next few weeks, surely he should be here, in Lagos, getting everything ready?" she said.

The landlord returned his hand to his lap. He had at least five girls on call in their neighbourhood, ranging much younger in years of age. But they all paled in comparison to the magnificent Munira. She stirred him in ways that those stupid young girls never could. And he wanted her now. Suddenly, he felt a flash of anger for the way she made him want her. Who did she think she was?

"What do you know about Nollywood, you village girl!

Listen, I've known these Nollywood people far longer than you've been in Lagos, which is all of five minutes. If you don't trust me, then let's finish this thing here and now..."

Munira looked at the mirror, which was directly opposite the bed. The landlord's spindly legs protruded from his boxers like matchsticks. She sighed, took off her kaftan and lay down on the bed. When he thrust into her, Munira closed her eyes. Her mind wandered. She thought back to her days on her parents' farm, spent acting out scenes from her favourite Nollywood films, in front of her faithful audience—the yam and cassava tubers. She hadn't realised then, that those would be the happiest moments in her life. She turned her face to the side, so she wouldn't have to inhale the landlord's foul breath or see his ugly face, as he grinded into her. When he squeezed her nipples, she didn't cry out in pain, because she knew that's what he would've liked. Instead, she focussed her mind on those days on the farm and even allowed herself a smile, as she pictured herself as a child bowing down to the applause of the yam tubers after a particularly emotionally wrenching performance.

What a lonely child she'd been. Tears dripped down her cheeks. At the sight of her tears, the landlord squeezed her nipples even harder.

As Baba approached the auto-repair shop, Mama Seyi gave him her customary glare before going back to her fried akara. Baba pretended he didn't notice. At first, he thought about greeting her, but decided against it. Knowing her foul morning moods, she would most likely slap him. He quickly walked inside the auto-repair shop, and headed straight for his bench in front of the television.

Dimeji slid out from under a car. "Baba! Your mosquito friend was on the news a few minutes ago," he said.

"What did the news say?"

Dimeji shrugged. "I didn't really catch it because the car Dauda was working on caught fire—"

"It didn't catch fire—" Dauda interrupted.

"Yes, it did. Because of the car part you tried to remove from it," Dimeji said.

"Is the car okay now? I mean; you're going to tell the owners, aren't you?"

Dauda fixed Baba with a blank stare. "There's nothing to tell. The car's fixed now."

Baba ran his hands over his bald head in despair. Dimeji wiped his hands on a rag and turned on the radio.

"It's 11.30am. Time for *Na So Dem Say*," he said.

*Na So Dem Say* was a popular current affairs programme co-hosted by a man and a woman who spent more time arguing with each other than talking about current affairs.

Baba sat back. Listening to the show allowed him to forget for a while about his troubles, his self-appointed mission to find the Mosquito Man and his impossible plan to bring water to Palemo.

"Good morning and welcome to this week's instalment of *Na So Dem Say*. I am your host, Oladipupo, with my co-host, Sola. Today, we want to talk development. We dey ask why

42

it is that 50 years after independence, Nigeria still no dey the development level it should be. We dey ask why. Make call our number and give us your opinion..."

Oladipupo reeled off a number and an advert came on.

"Baba, it looks like God is on your side. See, even *Na So Dem Say* is talking about development," Dimeji said.

Dauda took out his mobile phone and punched a number. He turned his back to Dimeji and Baba and started speaking quietly into it.

Dimeji rolled his eyes at Dauda. "Na woman go kill this boy," he said to Baba.

"That's if God doesn't punish him first for all the stealing he does," Baba replied. Dauda shot the two of them filthy looks.

"And we're back. E be like say you all get plenty to say about development." The radio co-hostess, Sola, was now live on air. "We have a caller. He say his friend, one Baba person, has something to say about development. He say his friend believe that one white musician from London called Bono go help bring water for Palemo. The guy, Dauda, dey on phone now. Dauda, how body?"

Dimeji and Baba looked at each other, and then at the radio, and then back to Dauda, who had turned around to face them, a smirk on his face.

"Yes. I dey here. I want talk about my friend. He believe that because our government corrupt and eat all our money, that is why Nigeria not develop. He believe that the answer now lies in Mosquito Man Bono. He call Bono that because of his glasses. My friend say because everybody dey listen to Bono, he go Abuja this month to meet Bono, to tell him to tell our president to give us water." Tears of laughter rolled silently down Dauda's cheeks as he spoke.

Dimeji and Baba watched him, aghast.

"Dauda, your friend dey there?" Sola asked him.

"Yes."

"Put him for line. I want talk him," Sola said.

Dauda held out his mobile to Baba who took it like a man in a dream.

"Baba, this is Sola from *Na so Dem Say*. Your friend say you wan go Abuja to meet famous musician, Bono, to tell him to tell the Nigerian president to give Palemo people water. Not so?"

Baba wasn't sure, but he thought he heard a whoop of stifled laughter from Sola's co-host. He cleared his throat. "Yes, Ma."

Was that really his voice he was hearing on the radio?

Mama Seyi had come inside the auto-repair shop with her son, Fela. They both stood incredulous, listening to the radio.

"My brother, because today is Thursday and you make me laugh today, I'll tell you something. I say, this radio station will give you money to reach Abuja. You go take airplane— you take airplane before?—go there. Hello? Hello? You dey there?"

Baba was having trouble breathing. Dauda took the phone from him.

"Hello? Sola? My friend still here. You give him shock.

44

He no fit talk. You go buy him plane ticket go Abuja to meet Mosquito Man? The man is illiterate—"

Baba took the phone off him. "Hello Sola? I come back. I do it. I go Abuja to talk to Mosquito Man. I go tell him that we need water for Palemo. I go take plane. Thank you. Thank you—"

"We never finish. Hold on and we go tell you how to get your plane ticket..."

A few moments later, Baba handed the phone to Dauda. On wooden legs, he walked to the chair next to Dimeji and sat down.

"I'm going to Abuja," he said in wonder. "I'm going on a plane. I'm going to meet Mosquito Man."

Mama Seyi planted herself in front of him. "You're not going anywhere until you give me my money," she said.

The loud banging on the door shook them out of their stupor. Munira and the landlord looked at each other askance. Munira got out of the bed and went to the door. She opened it a crack. It was her neighbour, Mama Jide.

"Yes?" Munira's voice was hostile.

Mama Jide lived in the room opposite theirs. A widow, she sold pepper in the local market.

"You can stop with the attitude. I came to tell you that I've just heard your husband on the radio. They say he's going to Abuja to meet a white musician who is going to bring water to Palemo." Mama Jide stopped and attempted to peer through the crack. Munira narrowed it even more.

"Baba?"

"It was him. I heard him myself," Mama Jide said. She attempted to peer through the crack again. "Funny, I could've sworn I heard the landlord go inside your room an hour or so ago." She paused, "I didn't hear him leave."

Munira didn't bother responding. She slammed the door in Mama Jide's face and stood there for a few moments, deep in thought. There was another bout of knocking on the door.

"Munira! Your husband is going to be a big man! He is going to Abuja to meet a white man. Remember us when your fortune changes!"

It was the local cobbler who traded in a stall across the street. Munira waited for him to leave, and sure enough when he didn't hear a response, he started walking away. Mama Jide's door opened.

"She's in there. Already, she thinks she's better than the likes of us," she hissed to the cobbler, in a voice loud enough to carry her disdain to Munira, who was still standing behind the door, in her room.

"Either way, Munira, remember us when the good times come! Remember us!" The cobbler laughed good-naturedly and left the building.

Munira didn't know what they were talking about, but she made up her mind to 'remember' the cobbler. He was a kind person, good-natured and, unlike everybody else in the neighbourhood, did not look down on her or call her names behind her back. Sometimes, she would go to his stall and sit with him, and they would chat for hours. She, about her dreams of making it in Nollywood, and he, about his dream of learning to read. The last time they spoke, he told her he had saved nearly enough money to go to night school. Jokingly, she had told him not to forget her when he met all the young girls in his class, who would no doubt be throwing themselves all over him.

He knew about her and the landlord, and did not judge her for it.

"This is Lagos," he had said. "We all do things that we don't necessarily want to do, to survive."

Munira thought about her husband and his apparent adventures on the radio. She wondered which of the mechanics had put him up to it. Probably Dauda, the boy was a miscreant.

"What has your husband got himself into now?" the landlord sneered from the bed. Munira wanted to slap him. If anyone had the right to mock her husband, it was she, his wife, not a spindly-legged landlord with bad breath.

Before Munira could answer him, there was a loud banging on the door.

"Munira! Your husband has done it this time!" Someone cried loudly from the corridor.

It was only a matter of time before the corridor filled with people. Palemo was like that. News spread really fast. And news such as her husband's latest adventure meant that people would rush to be the first to congratulate them, not because they meant it, but because they thought it meant being the first in line to be rewarded for their 'kind' wishes. It was the

Lagos way.

Munira glanced towards the bed. "I think you should leave," she told the landlord. The landlord got dressed.

There was another bang on the door, a whoop of celebration and then, receding steps. Munira tightened her wrapper around her chest and peeked through the keyhole. The corridor was empty. She opened the door a bit wider to let the landlord out. He paused by the door and grinned as he caressed her breast. Munira didn't smile, she turned her face to the corridor. Opposite them, Mama Jide's door opened, she stood in the doorway, arms akimbo and watched the two of them with undisguised contempt.

The landlord put his hands in his pockets.

"So," he said. "Let me know when your husband comes back so we can discuss the rent issue."

Mama Jide hissed and went back inside the room. Munira knew she was watching them through the keyhole. She didn't answer the landlord but instead, slammed the door shut. She went to the unmade bed and sat down. Could it...was it... possible, that her husband had indeed done what he said he was going to do this morning? It had to be those mechanic boys, Munira decided. Baba lacked the imagination and testicles to do something like this himself. She clapped her hands in delight. As if it mattered who got her husband on the radio. She was going to be famous!

Munira pictured herself being interviewed on television with her husband on one side and a white man on the other. She saw herself in Abuja, dining with the nation's finest and wealthiest, all of them hanging on her every word. She saw a queue of directors clamouring to work with her. She saw herself on the billboards advertising her own chat show, dispensing words of wisdom to her guests, and by extension, the country, as the chat show streamed all over the country. Suddenly, she felt thankful. She was going to be famous. God had finally decided to answer her prayer.

She got to work on the bed.

# 3

A steady procession of people trooped into the auto-repair shop. Every time the Mosquito Man came on the television, which was turned up as loud as it could possibly go, the crowd cheered and saluted Baba, who accepted the offers of free food and drink. He felt good. He liked seeing the respect in people's eyes when they looked at him. It made him feel heady with pride.

"Everybody, shush! It's the Mosquito Man again!" Dimeji shouted above the din. The television was showing the Mosquito Man in a slum in South Africa. He was surrounded by a coterie of people.

"You see, very soon, Baba will be one of those people with the Mosquito Man," someone said to loud cheers.

"But how? The radio just said that he was going to Abuja. They didn't say how Baba will meet the man," another person said.

It was a question Baba had been pondering himself.

"It doesn't matter. When he woke up this morning, did he know that he would be on radio, much less go on a plane to Abuja?" Dauda said. "Look at him. He can't even read."

"It doesn't matter. Baba, what time did they tell you to go

and pick up your ticket at the radio station?" Dimeji asked.

"About now," Baba replied. "They said they'll also take picture."

The television images panned back to the newsreader. "Bono will be in the Nigerian capital, Abuja, in the next few weeks."

Another loud cheer went up in the auto-repair shop. Again, Baba received some hearty slaps on his back.

"Come on, let's go to the radio station," Dauda said. "I want to make sure they give you the real plane ticket, not a fake one. This is Nigeria. Anything is possible."

Just then, Dauda's mobile rang. He picked it up, listened for a minute, then laughed before handing the phone to Baba. Baba held the phone to his ear. When he heard who was on the other end of the line, he handed the phone back to Dauda with a pleading look on his face. Dauda pretended to listen intently.

"Baba, your wife says that you are taking her to Abuja. That it is only right for a woman to be with her husband when he is meeting important people." Dauda paused for a minute before speaking again. "By the way, she says she's on her way to the radio station," he said, before hanging up the phone. He grimaced.

Baba saw the look on Dauda's face. Munira tended to have that effect on people; those she wasn't sleeping with.

"Come on, we don't have much time. Let's just go and pick up the ticket," Dauda said, to Baba, hoping they would get there before the wife.

51

It all seemed like a dream. Was it only 24 hours ago that he was sitting in front of a television watching a white man with dark sunglasses? Now, he was on his way to pick up a plane ticket to meet him in Abuja. He, a 55-year-old unemployed man who could barely read. Who stank at the best of times, because his wife hoarded water and denied him access to it, so he couldn't bathe. He looked at Dauda with his confident swagger and youthful ebullience. Not for the first time, he envied him. They all thought he went to the auto-repair shop every day to watch television and share his views about the world. But that wasn't the reason. He went there to drink out of the elixir of Oladimeji's and Dauda's youth. When he spoke to them, he felt useful, even if they ignored him most of the time.

They left the auto-repair shop to loud cheers and salutations. As they walked down the street, Baba saw people giving him the thumbs-up. A few rushed over to him to tell him, "Remember us when you meet the white man."

By the end of their 45-minute walk to the station, Baba's clothes were drenched in sweat. He wasn't sure, but he thought his smell was definitely worse.

"Dauda, is this really happening?" Baba asked him, grabbing his arm.

Dauda gave him a sideways look. "Baba, yes, it is real. And it is a good thing," he said, smiling.

At the radio station gates, Dauda gave their details to the security guard who let them through. As they walked through the gates, the security guard gave Baba the thumbs-up sign.

Baba didn't know what to do, so he returned the gesture, although he felt stupid when he did it. He didn't know why, but something told him that his thumbs-up sign would come in useful in the foreseeable future.

"You see, you're now a superstar. Everybody is saluting you," Dauda said.

Then they heard a familiar shriek and Baba's legs turned to water.

"Baba, tell this foolish security guard that I am your wife. If you don't let me through this gate—"

Baba kept on walking. If he walked for just thirty more seconds, he would be in the building.

The shriek got louder.

"Baba, Dauda, I'm telling you. If I don't get through this gate, heads will roll. Security guard, open the gates!"

Baba made it to the building's lobby. The doors opened and Dauda took a step inside. Baba turned around and with deep resignation walked back to the gate. He spoke with the security guard who opened the gate. Munira stomped in, marched up to the guard and slapped him. She was gearing up for another slap when the security guard stopped her mid-motion. An argument ensued. Baba left them and walked back towards the reception.

Why did she have to slap the security guard? Most normal people would've let bygones be bygones and just walked through the darn gate with their pride intact. But not his wife. Inwardly, he prayed that she wouldn't cause a scene and destroy his chances of meeting 'The Mosquito Man' as he fondly now thought of the white musician, however which way the event happened.

"You should've left her outside the gate," Dauda said.

"She's my wife," Baba replied.

The cool, air-conditioned air of the lobby hit him like a welcomed breeze. Dauda strode to the receptionist and said a few words to her. She gestured to them to sit down. Baba noticed everyone looking at him. *Bono. Abuja.* The whispers reverberated around the room. Baba found himself standing taller, and more erect as pride welled within him. The room was wide and airy with marble floors. A few people were sitting on sofas. Baba looked at their clothes and looked down at his own faded, patched *agbada* and battered rubber slippers. He wondered if his smell was noticeable. Suddenly, he felt deflated. He didn't belong here with all these people, with their clean clothes, posh accents and marble floors. His place was in the auto-repair shop, with people who knew and understood him. People like his wife.

Her voice brought him back to the present.

"You think you can forget about me now that you're going to Abuja?" Munira screamed at him.

Baba quailed in face of her fury. The lobby went quiet.

"I told you, you should've left her behind the gate," Dauda said.

"Shut up," Munira screamed at him.

Just then, a lady came up to them. She gave Munira a hostile once-over before turning to Dauda and Baba to announce brightly. "I'm here to take you upstairs. We're going to take a couple of pictures. Just so you know, the local newspaper is also here. They're running a front page news story of you this evening. They've said that they'll pay for your accommodation in Abuja. They believe in your cause— as we all do. Palemo needs water." She looked at him with the fervent eyes of a convert.

Dauda nudged Baba. "Don't worry," he said, giving him a wink. "Baba will sort it all out when he gets to Abuja."

"It's all a joke to you, isn't it?" Baba said.

Dauda flashed him a toothy grin.

"And I'll be going with him as well," Munira said. Baba looked at her corpulent body. Desire rose within him again along with the image of her undressing in front of him that morning. He also remembered the contempt in her eyes when she told him to get out of their home after telling her his idea about meeting Bono.

"No," he said.

Munira stood a step towards him. "What do you mean, 'no'?"

Baba quailed again, but stood his ground. "No," he said, his voice a little louder.

Munira took another step towards him, her breathing heavier.

"Security!" called out the lady that was supposed to take Baba and George upstairs. As if by magic, two burly men materialised and grabbed Munira by each arm.

"Baba! It's not over!" she shouted as they dragged her away. "You will suffer for this!"

"Shall we?" the woman said casually, to Dauda and Baba.

Dauda nodded and they both followed her. They went up in the lift. It pinged and the door opened. As it opened, they heard a round of applause, and then, a booming voice said, "This is Baba!" There was another round of applause, and then, a man in his thirties came up to them and gave Baba a hearty slap on his back. Baba saw him wriggle his nose.

"I assume you're Baba," he said. "And you," he turned to Dauda, "are the one who called us?"

Dauda nodded.

"I'm Oladipupo," the man said.

Baba realised why the man's voice had sounded so familiar. He was the co-host of the radio show. He took a look around the room. To his right was a glass-sealed room with microphones extending from the ceiling. A woman was speaking into one of the microphones. Baba guessed that was where the radio show was recorded. The woman gave him the thumbs-up when she saw him looking at her. He realised that she was Sola, Oladipupo's co-host. He returned her thumbs-up gesture. A few moments later, she came out.

"Baba! I'm Sola. So happy to meet you. Bono doesn't know what's going to hit him in Abuja," she said, with a huge smile.

The photographer stepped forward. There was a flurry behind them and then a man ran inside the studio breathing heavily.

"Baba? Thank God you're still here. I'm from the local paper. You wouldn't believe the trouble it took for me to get in here. There was a woman at the gate...never mind. Anyway, I'm from the local paper. We were listening to you this morning and we think you have a case. We want to interview you. Your talk with Bono is of local, even, national significance..." The man turned to the side and called out. "Photographer?"

Another man carrying a camera stepped in front. He held it out. Oladipupo and Sola went to stand on either side of Baba.

"Smile," the photographer said.

Baba tried to. The camera clicked. Baba looked dazed.

"Now, if you'll just come here and sign these papers, we'll give you the tickets and you can be on your way," Oladipupo said.

"He can't read," Dauda said.

"Not a problem," Sola replied. "Just put an 'X' and your thumb print where your signature is meant to be."

Baba allowed himself to be led to a marble table, on top of which several papers were laid out. Dauda guided his hand. As he negotiated the biro and drew the X, the cameras clicked again. Sola clapped.

"Isn't this exciting?" she said.

"The tickets are for you and your friend," Oladipupo said. "They're first-class tickets, donated by the airline. The only thing we ask is that you mention our radio station when you meet Bono. And the airline would also like to meet with you when you land in Abuja. They believe in what you're doing—"

"Of course," Dauda said. "He doesn't even know where

the airport is, much less what it looks like."

"Mr Big Mouth, we're relying on you to give us updates on his progress," Sola said.

"No problem at all," Dauda said, flashing her a sexy smile.

After the newspaper interview, on their way back to the auto-repair shop, Baba was quiet. He was thinking of the radio station, its air-conditioned rooms and the radio hosts. He compared their clean clothes to his faded *agbada* and two-sizes-too-small trousers. He remembered the smell of Sola's perfume when she stood next to him, and the discreet way she wriggled her nose and held her breath while she waited for their picture to be taken. When she spoke, he caught a whiff of mint on her breath. It came to him that he was mad. Dauda was right. He could barely find his way to the airport. What made him think he would be able to even get on the plane? When he thought of how Dauda held his hand so that he could sign 'X' on the papers, he felt embarrassed, ashamed, even. For all he knew, everyone at the radio station was probably laughing at him right now. To think that he, an illiterate old man, would dare think about going to Abuja to meet Bono, a world famous white musician, who had no idea if he existed, and probably didn't care if he did. Yes, it was ridiculous. Things like this did not happen to people like him. He was a smelly nobody.

He wanted Munira. There was a familiar comfort in her contempt of him. It was a contempt that was perfectly warranted, bearing in mind what she'd had to do to pay off his debts when she had first arrived in Lagos, all those years ago. They had never really spoken about what she had to do to pay off the loan sharks, but it was there, all the time, between them. He wished he could tell her how sorry he was. He also thought about how he would court her forgiveness for everything, including the way he had treated her arriving at the radio station. And when she had forgiven him, he would try his hardest to get a job, and find a way to make her a Nollywood actress. Yes, that's exactly what he would do. And it was the right thing to do. This Bono business was foolishness.

"Baba, you're very quiet," Dauda said.

"Dauda, I've been thinking. This is not a good idea. I'm sorry, but you'll have to take the tickets back. I'm not going to Abuja. This has gone far enough," Baba said.

"We're doing no such thing. We're going to Abuja. We'll meet Bono and tell him to give us water, and he will speak to our president who will provide it. And that is all there is to it."

"I'm saying that the joke has gone far enough—"

"You think it's a joke?" There was irritation in Dauda's voice. "You have a great opportunity to do something, not just for yourself, but for this country, and you want to back out now? I'm going to talk to you, not as a son to a father, but man to man. I think it's time you be a man and do something with your life, and this is the perfect opportunity to do it. Or do you want to spend the rest of your life coming to the auto-re-pair shop, watching television, giving sermons that nobody is interested in, and being serially humiliated by your wife? Don't you want more out of life?"

Dauda's voice had risen by this point. They stopped walking and looked at each other, causing those walking behind them in the densely packed street to run into them.

"Watch where you're going! Did your father build this road?!" A pedestrian hissed at them both.

Dauda and Baba ignored him and continued looking at each other.

"I've never seen or heard you speak like this before," Baba said.

Dauda looked away for a few moments. "I'm just saying that this is a chance for us to do something with our lives. People are relying on us, because they think we can actually help them with this ridiculous water situation we have. If it started out as a joke, it certainly isn't now..." he said gruffly.

They both continued walking again in silence. As they neared the auto-repair shop, they saw a crowd of people loitering outside. From the look of things, Mama Seyi was doing a roaring trade. When the crowd spotted Dauda and Baba, there was a roar of approval.

"Baba, Palemo Man!" someone shouted. Dauda gave him a look and disappeared through the throng of people into the auto-repair shop. Baba waited, unsure what to do. He gave his new admirers a wave, turned round and started walking to his house, ignoring the disappointed moans from the crowd. He hoped they wouldn't follow him. They think I'm stupid, he thought. They probably wanted him to take them to the local beer parlour and buy them drinks and food. Mama Seyi should be happy. Thanks to him, she was doing a brisk trade.

You would think that she would offer him a free meal or something. But no. She still glared at him when she saw him, and even mouthed that she wasn't done with him, yet, before turning her attention back to her customers with a beatific smile. Witch, he thought. As if on cue, his stomach grumbled.

It was lunchtime and blistering hot. His sweating did not help matters, that and the heat only accentuated his smell. He slowed down as he approached his *face-me-I-face-you* building. A swarm of people were gathered outside and in the midst of them all was Munira, all dressed up, preening before a camera. When she saw him, she grimaced briefly and announced in a bright voice.

"Baba, my husband! There you are!" and the next thing he knew, she had crossed the road, and was stood beside him by the roadside. The crowd erupted with cries of "Baba! Baba!"

"You smell," Munira said, through clenched teeth. She smiled at the crowd and put her arm around his shoulders. She part-pushed him and they both crossed the road. Now they were standing in front of their building, watched by the media and the crowd.

"Baba is just going to take a shower," she said, with a tight smile.

"Of course! Now he's an important man meeting important people," someone said.

Munira smiled and spoke to Baba through the side of her mouth. "I've put aside a hard-earned bucket of water for you, and the landlord has said that you could use his private bathroom in the backyard to have your shower. I still haven't forgotten what you did to me this morning at the radio station. But, this is not the time." She pushed him, rather forcefully towards their building.

Baba's stomach growled loudly. "I want some food waiting for me when I come out," he said.

"Then go and buy it yourself," she snapped. She looked back, and smiled at the crowd surrounding them before coming back to him with a lacerating stare.

"I mean it. I'm hungry. If you want me to do this, that is, perform in front of these people," Baba waved his arm airily towards the crowd, "then you must buy me some food."

"You are a spineless man," she spat out.

"Just buy my food," Baba said.

They made their way through the throng of people and went inside their building. A crowd had gathered outside their room. Some were their neighbours, others had come, because they knew that there would be ample opportunities to steal.

The crowd parted like the Red Sea when they saw Baba and Munira approach. Munira unlocked their room and nudged Baba inside. Then she turned around to their spectators.

"This is it for today. Baba must rest now. Thank you all!" She announced brightly.

"All hail Baba!" Someone shouted.

"Baba is the man!" Someone else said.

"Yes, yes, now go," Munira said, closing the door behind her firmly. "Thieves," she said, leaning against the door.

In the ensuing silence, she and her husband sized each

other up. Munira sighed, and went to sit on the bed.

"Munira..." Baba began.

"Don't talk," Munira said. She threw a hand towel at him and jerked her head towards the door. "They will be there for a while, until they realise that we're not coming out. Wipe yourself down. You know where the water is, and make sure you clean yourself in the place that matters. Then join me on the bed." She proceeded to take off her clothes.

Baba averted his eyes, knowing there was a barrage of abuse still to come. Munira went to stand in front of him and guided his hands to her breasts. In spite of himself, Baba squeezed them. He made to sink his head on her chest, but she stopped him.

"Wipe yourself down first. You can shower later, when your new fan club outside have all gone."

The next day, they were woken by a loud banging on their door.

"Baba! Someone is asking for you," a voice Baba recognised as his landlord's, said.

Baba's instinct was to ignore him. From the bed, Munira hissed. "Go and open the door, fool."

Baba got off the bed and opened the door. A man and woman were waiting in the corridor, next to the landlord. Baba took in the woman's appearance at a glance. She was wearing a pair of silver 4 inch heels, which easily took her height to about 5'9. She had on a pin-striped shirt that stretched across her pert breasts, which were no match for his wife's, he noted absent-mindedly. The shirt was tucked into a pair of trousers that screamed 'NOT made in China'. Her hips had that well-rounded edge he liked in women. His eyes travelled upwards to her arms. They were toned, but not in that horrible way of those professional weight lifters he'd seen on television. Hers were just the right level of slender-toned. His eyes then travelled up to her face and he met the cool gaze of the woman. Embarrassed, he looked down at his shoes, but not without acknowledging the fact that A), she was stunning, and B), her perfume was like a drug that threatened to confound his senses.

"Baba?" she asked.

"Yes?" He mumbled, his eyes still on the floor. She made him feel how rich people made him feel; exposed and ashamed of himself, for being poor. And seemingly, for choosing to *stay* poor. He wanted to hide. The woman should go away. Her refined presence corrupted his tenement building. He wished Munira would get off the bed and make the woman go away.

"I'm from WfN, Water for Nigerians, an NGO campaigning for water rights for Nigerians. We heard about your meeting with Bono..."

Munira was by the door in seconds. She gave the lady a quick assessment and coolly announced, "I'm his wife."

Baba looked at Munira, and then at the landlord. "If you can wait outside the building, I'll be with you in a few minutes," he said, although he had absolutely no intention of doing so. It was beginning to dawn on him what had happened in the last 24 hours and the expectations that were required of him. This sweet-smelling lady had just reminded him that he had no business doing this Bono stuff. He wanted to turn the clock back and go back to the way things were. His life had been simple. Now, half of his neighbourhood milled around his home hoping for whatever they thought they could get from being associated with him. The other half just wanted to rob him, plain and simple. And then, there were people like this lady and the radio DJs; rich and educated, who made him feel worthless. As if all that wasn't bad enough, they were even turning up outside his front door. Whatever and however this had started, he wasn't interested; he'd had enough. He wanted it all over.

Dauda's voice rang in his ears, admonishing him for his selfishness and the need for him to think about doing this for other people. Baba shrugged inwardly. What did he know about doing anything for other people? He was just an illiterate old man trying to find his way in Lagos. After he got rid of the sweet-smelling lady, he would go to the auto-repair shop and tell Oladimeji to flog the airline tickets on the black market for cash. Dauda can keep his youthful idealism. When he got to Baba's age, he would realise that idealism would only get one so far. The only thing that mattered in life was money.

A few seconds passed.

"Yes, we'll be with you in a few minutes," Munira said.

"Very well," the lady said. "We'll wait outside."

She made her way to the front of the building, the young man in tow. The landlord cleared his throat.

"Ahem, remember how I've been nice to you even though

you owe me almost six months' rent. Don't forget the people who've helped you when you meet all those important people in Abuja," he said to Baba, taking care not to look at Munira.

What Baba wanted to do was to punch him.

"I'll remember," Baba said, closing the door in his face. Like the man said, he owed him six months' rent. Any attempt at bravado and he would surely be the loser.

"I'm going with you when you speak with them," Munira said as soon as the door closed. "I don't trust that woman. She thinks she's better than us. And, I don't trust you, either," she added. "I'm your wife, but I know that if you had the chance, you would screw me over and deny me what's rightfully mine."

Baba was silent. Munira sat on the bed. The wrapper she tied across her chest came undone, revealing her left breast. Baba looked away. Munira tugged lightly at the wrapper and it came undone completely. She was now naked. She parted her legs. Baba sucked in his breath.

"I am your wife," she repeated.

An hour later, they met the woman and the man outside. It was swelteringly hot. Munira waved to the cobbler across the road. He gave her a thumbs-up and waved back.

"Sorry to keep you waiting," Baba said. "My wife had to get ready."

And ready she was. Munira's face was layered with thick make-up. She was dressed in yellow *iro*, top, and *buba*, wrapper, traditional Yoruba clothes that accentuated her ample body. Her neck, wrists and fingers were covered in costume gold jewellery. Baba had never seen any of the clothes nor jewellery before. And he refused to think about where she had gotten them from.

"No problem," the woman said smoothly. As if she was accustomed to waiting for people every day for an hour. Baba knew she wasn't.

"Where is the cameraman?" Munira asked.

The woman shot her an irritated look. "There isn't one. We're an NGO. We believe in your husband's cause and we want to help—"

"We're not saying or doing anything without a cameraman. And money," Munira said.

"Perhaps we should start from the beginning. My name is Olabisi Thomas. I'm the founder and Director of WfN. We campaign for water access for Nigerians. We work with international NGOs, and when we heard about your meeting with Bono, we thought a partnership with you would be of mutual benefit—"

"I understand that. But we're not doing anything until you give us money. And get a cameraman here," Munira said.

Olabisi gave an impatient sigh. "Very well. I understand a mechanic called Dauda is accompanying you to Abuja?"

"Was," Munira said. "I'm the one going with him now. I'm his wife."

Baba opened his mouth to speak, but Munira spoke instead. "I'm also his manager, so everything has to come through me."

Baba closed his mouth. It didn't matter where Munira thought this was going. He had his own thoughts, chief of which was that he'd had enough of this Bono madness.

"Very well then," Olabisi said. "Come on. I think we're done here," she said to the young man. They walked a few yards to a 4x4 emblazoned with Water for Nigerians (WfN) and got in. A few moments later, they drove off.

"Don't mind them," Munira said. "Other people will come. You see, this is our time to shine. You just leave everything to me and I'll take care of it all."

Munira spoke as if she knew what she was doing. Baba had no doubt she did —she could do anything. He just wished that Dauda's words about doing something for the good of others weren't coming back to haunt him at that very moment.

"Munira, I don't even know what's happened." he said. "One minute, I'm watching a man on television and the next, *this*," he pointed to the disappearing WfN 4x4.

"And that is why you need me to help you," Munira said soothingly. "This is also about us starting afresh like a normal couple. Or, have you forgotten all the promises you made to me last night and this morning?" She glared at him.

A few moments of silence passed. Baba shifted, then announced that he was going to the auto-repair shop.

Munira looked at him with narrowed eyes. "To do what?"

Baba spread his arms wide. "To do what I do everyday; watch television. Talk to the layabouts."

"And that's all?"

"Yes."

"I don't trust that Dauda," Munira spoke as if talking to herself. She drew herself up. "I'll come with you," she said.

Baba's shoulders slumped. "Very well then," he said.

They began the thirty-minute walk to the auto-repair shop. By the time they got there, Munira was panting and sweating heavily. Rivulets of sweat-infused make-up ran down her face and neck. She dabbed her face with tissue, which only made her look worse, as tiny slivers of white tissue marbled her fully made up brown cheeks.

A crowd of people were standing outside the auto-repair shop gates, which were locked. Baba's heart sank. Mama Seyi spotted them, smiled, and waved them over. Baba was taken aback. Mama Seyi had never smiled at him before.

"Baba is here! Baba is here!" She shouted sweetly.

The crowd turned. Munira beamed. She looked like a clown with all the melted make-up on her face. Despite himself, Baba felt guilty. He couldn't knowingly let her near the crowd looking like that.

He grabbed her arm. "Wait," he said. Tenderly, he dabbed her face with the soft cloth of his clean shirt and picked out the strays bits of tissue stuck there. They smiled at each other.

"Baba, is that you?" Dauda's voice came from behind the auto-repair shop gates.

"Yes," Baba said.

The gates opened and they rushed through the crowd and inside the auto-repair shop. Dauda gave Baba an exasperated look when he saw Munira.

"What do you want?" he asked her.

"I should be asking you that question. Do you really think you'll be going to Abuja with him? I'm his wife. I should be the one to go!"

"I'm the one who called the radio station, and I don't recall your husband saying that he was going to take you!" Dauda shot back.

"I'm his wife."

"I don't care. I called the radio station!"

With each exchange their voices rose higher and higher. Baba looked at Dimeji for help.

Dimeji shrugged. "Instead of arguing, I would do something about those people outside. We've had to lock the gates to prevent the crowds coming in. Some of them were even waiting for you when I opened up this morning," he said.

"But what do they want?" Baba asked.

Dimeji shrugged. "What does anyone want when they hear that someone in the locality is going to Abuja to meet a famous white person?"

"But—"

Suddenly the opening sounds of the morning news on television drowned his words.

"Today we're hearing reports of a man from Palemo called Baba who is going to Abuja to meet Bono, the famous musician, at the All Africa conference taking place in a few weeks, to ask him to provide water from Palemo residents."

The camera showed the photo Baba had taken the day before with Sola and Oladipupo, only they'd been cropped out. Baba's face was the only one left in the picture.

Baba looked round the auto-repair shop. He sat on his chair and put his head in his hands. Munira clapped her hands in delight.

"Baba, do you know what this means? When we go to Abuja, those Nollywood directors will beg to see me!" she squealed.

"Because they're looking for the likes of you in Nollywood," Dauda muttered sourly.

There was a shout from outside the gate.

"Look! Baba is on television!"

A huge cheer went up.

"The Nigerian News van is here," someone else shouted.

"Where?" Munira pushed through the auto-repair shop gates. "Hello! I'm Baba's wife. Come in! Come in!"

Dauda and Dimeji both shook their heads in disgust. Baba went through the shop to the backyard and slipped out of the auto-repair shop compound through a crack in the yard's fence. As he escaped, he took a backward glance. The crowd in front of the gates had grown. He saw Munira talking to a woman who was holding a camera. He kept on walking. In the next street, as usual, a water tanker was parked by the road-side, confronted by a winding queue of local people waiting patiently in the sun to buy some water, resignation etched on their weary faces. He became aware of a vague honking, and then he heard someone call his name. He started walking faster. He didn't want to talk to anybody. He wanted to watch television in the auto-repair shop and be abused and cursed by Mama Seyi. That was his life. Not this. This feeling of being watched, almost like he was an experiment, a germ under a microscope, like he'd seen in those films he watched on the shop television. It was all too much.

All he wanted to do was walk down the street without someone watching him, following him or, even slapping his back and congratulating him. *For doing what, exactly?* He wanted to scream. At this rate, it was only a matter of time before the area boys found out about his Abuja trip and start harassing him for money, because, he "was a big man, now".

He wasn't a big man. He was an illiterate 54-year-old man who smelled and was obsessed with his wife's breasts. That's who he was. He didn't want to go to Abuja. He didn't want to get on a plane. Human beings were made to walk and drive cars. If God wanted man to fly, he would've given them wings. He didn't care what Dauda said. He wasn't going to meet Mosquito Man. He decided to walk as fast as he could to put as much distance as possible between him and Palemo. Where he was going, he didn't know.

A large vehicle slowed down by him, it was a 4x4 and a woman popped her head out through the window. It was Olabisi Thomas looking triumphant at having cornered him away from the crowds and more importantly, away from Munira and her insistent interference.

"Baba, I really think that we can achieve a lot more in Abuja if we partner together," Olabisi said.

Baba kept on walking.

Olabisi spoke again. "Water for Nigerians doesn't want anything from you. We want to partner with you, so that you can achieve what you had in mind all the while—clean water in Palemo and, eventually, all of Nigeria. Is that so bad?"

Baba stopped walking and took a step closer to the window, almost defiantly. He looked at her exquisitely made up face, peering at him through the opened window. He caught a whiff of her sweet perfume and the cool air radiating from the air-conditioned jeep caressed his sweaty face, like a long-lost lover. Olabisi's left hand rested on the car's window pane. The gold gemstone rings on her fingers glistened in the harsh sunlight. The price of one ring could probably provide enough water for his own building for a month, he thought resentfully. She smiled at him, flirtatiously, he thought. A quiet rage came upon him. He hated her and other rich people like her. They were the reason Nigeria had gone to the dogs. Everything about them was deceitful or poisoned, his wife would say. Look at her, with her smile, he thought resentfully, looking at Olabisi. For all he knew, her flirtatious smile was really her way of mocking him.

It probably was.

He looked down the road, in the direction of the auto-re-pair shop. It seemed to him that the crowd had swelled. The sun beat down on his exposed back and shoulders, while the cool breeze emanating from the air-conditioned Jeep continued seducing his face. His rage dissipated. He looked back at Olabisi.

"You can get in the backseat. It's opened," she said.

Baba got in the backseat

"Kayode, take us to the office," Olabisi commanded her

assistant and driver.

"Yes, Ma," Kayode said.

From the front seat, Olabisi turned to him at the back. "I see your wife is not with you," she said.

"No," Baba said. He proceeded to look out the window.

"Baba, I know this is all very strange for you. But, I want you to know that I appreciate what you're doing and I know that between us, we can get water to every Nigerian who needs it," she said.

Baba didn't answer. He wished she could be quiet, so he could enjoy the ride. This was his first time in such a car. He wasn't sure where the chaos of the Mosquito Man's Abuja visit would take him, but he hoped that it involved lots of trips in cars such as this. For a second, he wished that his wife was with him. He pictured her face lighting up as she entered the jeep, her left hand waving away the driver, like an imperious empress. She would make sure she was settled in the jeep, rump, breasts, rolling hips and all and, in all probability, ruin the experience just by virtue of opening her mouth. No, he decided. He was glad she wasn't with him. He let out a deep breath, threw his head back and inhaled the moneyed scent of the leather seats.

"Baba, we're going to order you some breakfast when we get to the office. Is that okay with you?" Olabisi asked.

"That would be very okay with me," Baba said. He yawned loudly, without covering his mouth. In the front seat, Olabisi and the driver twitched their noses, before succumbing to the inevitable and covering them altogether.

The 4x4 rumbled on.

Thirty minutes later, they pulled up inside a driveway in Ikeja and got out of the Jeep. The contrast between the cool air in the Jeep and the scorching heat outside hit him in the face.

"Baba, follow me," Olabisi said. Baba gladly followed her into an office. The cold blast of the air-conditioner hit him again like a much-missed friend. Baba wondered how he would ever get used to an non-air-conditioned life after this.

In the office, there were two women typing away on a computer and a man on the telephone. They exchanged greetings with Olabisi, who gave them a wave and led Baba to a smaller, also air-conditioned office. She closed the door behind them and sat on the sofa. Baba started speaking, but she held up her hand, and reached for the phone on the desk.

"Toyin, can you please go next door and get some yam and fried eggs for Mr Baba, please. You want tea?" Olabisi turned her head to Baba.

"Big cup of tea," Baba emphasised.

Olabisi nodded and repeated the request to Toyin. Then, she hung up the telephone and clapped her hands.

"This is good, is it not?" she said.

Baba looked at her. Against his will, he thought of his wife at the auto-repair shop. He imagined her looking for him, giving the television crew a tight smile as she told them to wait just a little bit longer, that he would be out soon, and then, her shame, which would be followed by swift fury that he had once again, humiliated her. He didn't mean to. But, she had pushed him. She and her hunger for fame. He didn't want it. He just wanted to bring water to his community. That was all. Everything else that had happened in the last 24 hours was madness. And Munira was fuelling the madness, so she shouldn't be surprised if he abandoned her at the auto-repair shop. She was the one who left the sanctity of the auto-repair shop to go outside and stand in front of the cameraman, like a witless woman.

Despite his rationalisations, Baba still felt nervous. He should leave. Munira would kill him. And he was at fault, because he had humiliated her—again. He started getting up, then, he remembered the breakfast Olabisi had ordered for him, and sat back down.

"So, how did the idea to meet Bono come to you?" Olabisi asked him.

"We were watching television, and it seemed that every time he came on, he would speak to a president about something, and then, the next time we listened on the news, the thing would be done," Baba mumbled.

"I see," Olabisi said, although she didn't. "But how did you know that you were going to meet Bono in Abuja?"

"I've never met him before in my life," Baba said. He watched the uncertainty that flitted briefly across Olabisi's face, before it was replaced with what he thought was a forced smile.

"But he knows you're meeting him in Abuja in a few weeks?"

"Yes. No. I don't know!" Baba then fell into what had

become his mantra. "Look, I'm just an old man. I don't know anything. I've never been to school. I saw a man on television that I thought was a good person, because he got things done. I mentioned it to Dauda, the mechanic, that it would be a good idea if I met up with him—exactly how I was supposed to do this, I don't know—so I could tell him about our water problems in Palemo. The next thing I know, Dauda is calling the radio station to tell them about what I said, and then, the newspaper got involved, television people started talking and now, you're telling me about WfN and partnerships. I don't know anything about all this stuff. I just wanted to tell the man to tell our president to give us water. That's all!"

Baba let out a deep breath when he finished talking. It felt good to be able to let everything out. Olabisi was an educated woman. He wasn't sure how he knew, but he could tell that she was well-travelled. For all he knew, she'd probably met the Mosquito Man or others of his ilk on her travels. Perhaps, she would be able to make sense of this madness. He certainly didn't.

"So, when did all these things happen?" She asked.

"About two days ago," Baba replied.

"Two days?!" Olabisi reeled herself in, irritated that she'd let him see her surprise. She wouldn't let it happen again—she had higher odds at stake. "Not that it's a problem," she continued smoothly. "In fact, from now on, I think it'll be better if WfN did all the public speaking and managed your appearances from now on. We've been doing this for many years now; talking to international donors, raising money to get water for Nigerians, so we know how things work..."

"I don't know...maybe I should be getting back to the auto-repair shop. Dauda and my wife are waiting for me..."

They both knew he wasn't going anywhere until he'd had the promised yam, fried eggs and large cup of Lipton tea. Olabisi continued speaking as if he hadn't spoken.

"Baba, I was thinking, after this, that maybe we'll go to the shopping centre and get you some new clothes. You can't wear the same thing every day. And seeing as many people will want to talk to you now...I mean, you want to be taken seriously, don't you?"

Baba thought that what he wanted was to be at the auto-repair shop with his friends, Dimeji and Dauda, watching television and telling them off, the way he used to before his life got complicated.

There was a knock on the door and Toyin came in bearing a tray laden with piping hot dishes. She put the tray on the table. Steam rose from the yam and eggs, assailing his senses.

"Your breakfast is ready, sir," she said, holding out a bowl filled with warm water. Baba rinsed his hands and immediately tucked into his meal.

"No cutlery?" Olabisi's eyebrows were raised.

"What for?" Baba spoke with his mouth full.

Olabisi watched him eat with an amused smile on her face. Between him and Bono, they held the key to making her charity a worldwide name.

"Baba, it is a wonderful thing that you are doing, meeting Bono and asking him to help Nigeria with drinking water," she said.

Baba scooped some yam and fried eggs in his mouth before speaking. "Without water, we can't survive," he said.

Olabisi smiled. He really was stupid, she thought. Which was exactly how she needed him to be.

***

He'd humiliated her again. Munira kept the smile on her face and tried to quell the sickening feeling in her stomach. She'd hoped the director their landlord was talking to about her Nollywood audition would catch her performance on television.

"You're lying. You don't know where your husband is," the female reporter pointing the microphone at her said. She turned to the cameraman behind her. "Turn it off. He's gone." She brought out a card from her handbag and gave it to Munira. "When you find him, let's talk." She gestured to the row of ten or so cameramen lined up a foot or so away from the auto-repair shop's gate. In turn, they were surrounded by a motley crowd of about two hundred opportunists, idlers and the plain curious.

"Wrap it up. He's gone! Even the wife doesn't know where he is," she said.

Munira snatched the microphone from her hand. "Of course, I know where my husband is. He's taking time out. He'll be back in an hour..."

"Maybe he's left her for another woman already,"

79

someone called out from the crowd.

"Maybe you should shut up," Munira snapped. Behind her, the auto-repair shop gate opened and someone pulled her inside roughly. It was Dauda.

"I think you should leave the camera alone, for now," he said quietly. Dimeji pulled out a battered armchair, the most comfortable chair in the auto-repair shop. Munira sat down.

"Dauda, I know you're behind this. You want to go to Abuja with him to meet the Mosquito Man, but I won't let you. He's my husband. Wherever he goes, I go. I won't let you frustrate my dream," she screamed at him.

Dimeji gave her a glass of ice-cold water. Mr Sowemimo, the auto-repair shop owner, would surely kill him if he knew he was handing out water supplies to people, most especially Munira. He watched as she took a slug of the ice cold water. For a few seconds there he thought she would say, 'thank you'.

"Stupid boy! Are you trying to kill me?!" she spluttered through her brain freeze.

U*ngrateful cow,* Dimeji thought to himself, looking at her in distaste. He hoped the ice cold water would freeze her brain and tongue forever, so they would all be free of her. But then, Baba would probably blame himself for her death and sink into depression, because for all his lamentations about his harridan of a wife, he loved her, for reasons they all had yet to unravel.

While he had no intention of getting married, if by any chance he did find himself married, he hoped that his own marriage would be normal, because nothing about Baba's and Munira's was.

There was a short silence, until Dauda spoke.

"Don't you get tired of this?" he asked her.

"Shut up," Munira said. She heard the pity in his voice and hated it. It reminded her of those years in the village when she walked past people and they would shake their heads and give her pitying looks. She didn't need anyone's pity. She was going to be a famous Nollywood actress. She drank the rest of the ice-cold water in another gulp and regretted it immediately when she got *another* brain freeze.

"Do you know where he is?" Munira asked, when she couldn't bear the second silence that followed after.

Dauda shrugged. Dimeji slid under a car and slid out again.

"I think I saw him get inside a Jeep with 'water' or something emblazoned on it," he said, before sliding back under the car.

Olabisi. She knew it. Munira shot up and gestured to a side door. "This is the back way out, right?"

Dauda nodded. Munira went out through the backdoor. She had pushed her husband too hard. The cameras, the crowd and loud cheers would've rattled him. He hated being the centre of attention. Next time, she would make sure that she didn't let him out of her sight. As she left the auto-repair shop compound, through the opening in the backyard wall, she turned sideways to the front of the auto-repair shop. The crowd had dissipated and there were a few cameramen loitering around. She started walking, hoping that nobody would recognise her. A few hundred yards later, she reached into her handbag, took out a pair of flats and exchanged them for the punishing heels she was wearing. She sighed in relief. And then, for the first time that day, she smiled. Of course, everything was going to be alright. Baba will come back home. He had nowhere else to go.

Dauda opened the front gate and peered through the crack. It was about 4pm and he hadn't heard from Baba since he'd slipped out the backyard that morning. However, he wasn't worried. Baba would be back. If not that evening, then, the day after. The auto-repair shop was his natural habitat—he had nowhere else to go.

He stepped through the iron gate, which, right now, was sporting a particularly heinous shade of green, with cracked, rusting red undertones. Idly, he wondered why he and Dimeji hadn't been ordered by Mr Sowemimo to repaint the gate, in view of the media attention they were getting. Dauda looked around. The crowd had all but dispersed, although a few people loitered. The cameras had left as well. He waved at Mama Seyi, who gave him a wide grin. He smiled back and wondered how much she'd made that day. Enough for her to smile at him, he figured. In all the years he'd been working at the auto-repair shop, he didn't think she'd smiled as widely and as happily as she did just now.

"Mama Seyi, I beg, give me some akara," he shouted across the road.

"I'll bring it to you," she shouted back.

Dauda decided to take a stroll. Dimeji wouldn't mind. Although it was still hot, the temperature had cooled a little, not like the hellish heat of the morning. A young lady, carrying a tray of sweets walked past him. He struggled not to make an unsolicited comment to her.

As he walked past a house, its security guard waved to him in greeting. Dauda waved back and walked on. He dared not stop. If he did, he would be cornered into giving the guard money he didn't have. Baba might have thought he was under siege from Munira and the Nigerian media, but as his friends, he and Dimeji were also under siege from people who knew that they knew Baba, and thought all three of them were rolling in cash. Munira, security guards, Nigerian media... They were all the same—vultures.

He turned round for one last look at the sweet seller and her romping buttocks. Suddenly, she stopped and turned around. Dauda didn't bother looking away. He gave her what he thought was his sexiest smile.

"God will punish you!" the lady shouted across the distance, before turning around again.

Dauda and the security guard both laughed. Dauda, ruefully, the security guard, with the unrestrained glee that came from seeing a fellow man put in his place by a woman.

"Will you ever learn?" he asked himself, slapping his thigh in mirth.

Dauda decided to go back to the auto-repair shop and wait for Baba. Wherever he'd gone, he was sure to be hungry when he got back. He was also equally sure that Baba wouldn't have a *kobo* to buy even one kola nut to ward off the hunger pains. He made a mental note to get him some food when he did eventually turn up. No doubt, he would get a lecture from Baba, as he scoffed down the food, about his ill-gotten money.

Dauda laughed to himself as he pictured the scene. Yes, Baba was a useless, complicated old man with a natural aversion to hygiene. He was opportunistic, selfish even, with a marriage that still made little sense to him, Dauda. But he was also someone who tried to do the right thing, even if it usually ended up being a disaster. Like this Mosquito Man business.

And now, as he approached the auto-repair shop, he saw a man about his own age loitering in front of the building. When the man saw Dauda, he nodded to Mama Seyi across the street, who nodded back to him.

"Dauda, Baba has really struck it rich. This young man is from the BBC. Baba is going to London!" She shouted to him across the street.

# 4

As the Jeep pulled up outside the auto-repair shop, Olabisi smiled brightly at Baba. He had asked her to drop him there, as he was intending to spend the night on a bench outside. It wasn't like it was the first time.

"Thank you for today, Baba. As discussed, we'll come back tomorrow morning and start making arrangements for Abuja. My regards to your wife."

Baba looked at her, his eyebrows raised.

Olabisi gave him an innocent smile. He'd barely got out of the Jeep before it began moving and soon sped away. He hoped he would see them tomorrow. Nothing was certain in Lagos, especially promises made at 10pm.

It was a humid night. The street was deserted, except for a few lone security guards sitting on benches outside the factories they were guarding. Even better, there were no crowds or lurking cameras nearby. Usually, he liked this time of the night. It made him think of his childhood in Ibadan and the clear skies. The blanket of stars would twinkle so brightly and seemed so close that, sometimes, he felt he could just reach out and swipe a hand through them, causing them to ripple and sway at his touch. The night would also resonate with the sounds of dogs barking, monkeys making a racket and the latest mental case either howling at the moonless sky or speaking gibberish to himself.

But he didn't miss it. If he had stayed, he would've been a drunk, a complete failure. Just like a lot of the men in the village. Stuck sitting in the shade of the trees, in the centre of the village, whiling away the time with useless talk and copious amounts of alcohol, all the while bemoaning the lack of opportunities in the village and the lack of respect they got from "today's generation." Once in a while, a nimble girl would walk past and they would fall silent, recalling *their* nimble youth and their present pathetic existence.

He was glad he left when he did. Even if he was now in his mid-50s, poor, a failure and still illiterate. At least, he was illiterate, poor and a failure in Lagos. Much better than being poor and being a failure in Ibadan. At least, he'd tried. He'd gotten out of the village and out of Ibadan. The men he'd left behind hadn't.

He heard a rustling. Across the road, something stepped out of the shadows of Mama Seyi's stall. Baba started. He thought about running, then concluded it wasn't much use. Where would he run to?

"Baba, please don't be afraid. My name is Muyiwa. I'm from the BBC, and I would like to talk to you about your visit to Abuja and meeting Bono," the person said.

Baba relaxed. The person had spoken to him in Yoruba. His manner had been non-threatening. He was safe.

"It's 10pm," Baba said.

"Dauda said it was fine for me to wait here for you," Muyiwa said.

Dauda. The boy would be the death of him.

"What do you want?" he asked him.

"To talk, that's all," Muyiwa said.

"It's 10pm," Baba repeated. "Don't you have a home to go to?"

"I just want to talk to you," Muyiwa said.

"Come back tomorrow. I'm tired."

"Baba, I know you're tired. Like I said, I just want to talk to you. That's all."

The man had said that he was with the BBC. He didn't know much, but he knew the BBC was 'good'. It was in England and Dauda had mentioned something about it belonging to the Queen of England.

There was a silence. If Muyiwa worked for the BBC, then he would have money. And if he had money, that meant that he, Baba wouldn't have to sleep on the bench outside the auto-repair shop, and be attacked by rabid mosquitoes, all the while fearful of what Munira would do when she showed up at the auto-repair shop the next day, screaming blue murder for humiliating her in front of the whole nation. And there was the small matter of him coming to the conclusion that life in an air-conditioned room was much better than one spent outside in the humid night being devoured by mosquitoes. Slowly, a plan formed in his mind.

"I need somewhere to sleep, tonight. But first, you must buy me some bottled water to drink," he said.

Muyiwa threw out his arms as if this was the most natural thing in the world. "Ah! Baba, you should've said! I told you I was with the BBC. Of course, we'll put you up for the night. The only thing I ask is that you don't talk to anyone about your meeting with Bono until we've talked. Is that fair or what? Now, how does the Travellers International Hotel sound to you?"

Baba didn't know what the Travellers International was and, at that particular moment, didn't much care, either. He wanted water, a cold shower, an air-conditioned room and a bed, preferably in that order. Even if the boy was not from the BBC as he said, Baba figured he had nothing to lose by following him. He gave Muyiwa his perfected woe-is-me-I'm-a-poor-man look. It was a look that enraged Munira no end, because she claimed that it was dishonest as it cheated the fools who fell for it out of their hard-earned money. As if she was one to talk, he thought sourly to himself.

He shook his head, as if to banish any thoughts of Munira away.

"Come," Muyiwa placed his hand lightly on Baba's shoulder and led him to a car that had definitely seen better days. Muyiwa saw Baba grimace.

"Baba, this car will get us to the Travellers International safely. No armed robber would want to steal this car and no police man would harass us for money. Isn't that what we want?"

Baba nodded and got in and they moved off. He was asleep in minutes.

Munira applied a layer of lip gloss to her lips. It stung a little. The beauty shop she got the lip gloss from had reassured her that it wasn't made in China. Munira hoped so. If it was a fake and made in China to boot, she knew her lips would melt.

Baba hadn't come home the night before. Neither had he spent the night on the bench outside the house nor the auto-repair shop, as was sometimes his custom. She told herself she wasn't worried. She would finish applying her make-up, go outside and he'll be sitting on the bench with that stupid smile of his that made her want to slap his face, or cry in frustration.

As the stinging on her lips subsided, Munira puckered up at the mirror and then dropped her gaze to take in her whole frame. Her ample bosom, layered stomach and rolling thighs looked back at her. Draping a wrapper over the mirror she went to sit on the bed.

She put on her favourite kaftan. The market trader said it was from Senegal. It was bright yellow, with traditional Senegalese patterns woven into the neckline, the hem and sleeves. The kaftan flowed around her body, skimming her curves before landing just past her ankles in elegant waves. It made her feel beautiful, which despite what the mirror said, was what she was. What's more, the landlord and other men said it too.

It was 8am. In all their five years of marriage, she had never not known where her husband was. Even when their arguments got physical, with her pushing him around, he would raise his hands up in the air and say, "Enough". Then, he would leave their room and spend the night outside their building or outside the auto-repair shop. How he's never caught malaria from the swarming mosquitoes outside, she would never know.

It was 08:05. She knew it was only a matter of time before her neighbourhood descended on their building again and started clamouring for Baba. Vampires, all of them, she muttered to herself.

Munira got off the bed and began pacing up and down their pigeon-hole home like a caged tiger. She was sure Baba was fine. He was a wily goat. No harm ever came to people like him because he always managed to find his way out of any situation. He was canny like that. Munira had often thought that Baba would've been a brilliant businessman if only he'd learnt to read.

But what if he wasn't fine? What if he was lying in a ditch somewhere?

Munira squashed the thought. Not Baba. He would never allow himself to die in such an undignified manner. In fact, Munira concluded, Baba would probably outlive her, for no reason other than to prove to her that he could.

There was a coded knock at the door. It was the landlord. Munira ignored it.

"Muni, I know you're in there," he spoke, quietly through the door.

She suddenly hated the landlord calling her Muni, only her husband should call her by that name. It felt sullied, coming from someone else's lips.

Munira heard Mama Jide's door open, and her voice like a

slithering snake in the passageway. "The two of you should be ashamed of yourself," she hissed. "You wait until Baba meets that white man. The two of you will be history." She kissed her teeth. "Some people have no fear of God," she said before going back to her room and slamming the door behind her.

Munira flung the door open. "What do you want?" she said.

The landlord came inside the room and shut the door behind him. "Come on, that's not the way to talk to a friend who's gone out of his way to get you an audition with, quite possibly, the most famous director in Nollywood."

She'd heard it all before. "Please leave. My husband didn't come home last night..."

"So, maybe he slept outside. It wouldn't be the first time," the landlord said. He winked.

Munira sighed and went to sit on the bed. "He didn't sleep outside, because I checked this morning and also spent half the night coming in and out of this building. If anything ever happens to him..." she drew in a deep breath, surprised by the tears rolling down her cheeks. She wiped them off. "He's all I've got," she sniffed.

The landlord placed his hand on her thigh. Munira didn't beat him off. Instead, she stood up. "I'm going to look for my husband," she said.

The landlord stood up with her. He had been hoping for a quickie before the hordes descended on his building, but obviously that was not going to happen today. He put both his hands on Munira's shoulder.

"You know your husband. He's probably at the auto-re-pair shop, trying to dodge Mama Seyi's curses," he said.

Inwardly, Munira cursed *him* with impotency. Nobody had the right to speak about her husband like that, except her. She walked to the door and opened it. As if on cue, Mama Jide opened hers as well.

"I know Baba did not come home last night. God is watch—"

Munira didn't hear the rest. She slammed her door shut and dialled Dauda's mobile. He answered at the first ring. "I told you that I haven't heard from him, but I'm sure he's fine."

"How do I know you're not lying to me right now?" Munira asked. "For all I know, he's probably standing next to you as we speak. This is not just about Abuja anymore—"

"Well, he's not with me," Dauda said. Just then he felt Dimeji poke his ribs and nod his head towards the television. Dauda turned to face the television. Baba was on the news. Baba *was* the news. Baba was on the BBC World Service.

Olabisi watched the interview with Baba silently, seething. The interview obviously took place in a hotel. She bet that it was the Travellers International. Baba was wearing the new *agbada*, robe, that she'd bought him yesterday. She was equally sure that he was also wearing his new shoes as well. He even looked well. He'd bathed, she noted.

She knew the BBC reporter, Muyiwa, well. He always turned down her pitches for Water for Nigerians to be featured on the BBC Africa website, because they weren't 'news'. Yet, he'd gone and stolen her exclusive from right under her nose.

How did he do it? She'd dropped Baba off at the auto-re-pair shop at 10pm, the previous evening. In the space of 12 hours, he had tracked down her protégé, squirreled him away in one of the most exclusive hotels in Lagos and nabbed the interview of his career. She had the mind to call his editor and accuse Muyiwa of unethical reporting. Not that the editor would care. Baba's story was dynamite. Olabisi knew the editor wouldn't care how Muyiwa got his story.

On the television screen, Muyiwa started his interview with Baba.

"So, Baba, tell us how the idea to meet Bono came about," Muyiwa asked him.

Baba spoke through an interpreter. "Well, I go to this auto-repair shop every day..."

"And where is this auto-repair shop?" Muyiwa asked.

"In Palemo, where I live."

"So, you go to the auto-repair shop every day?"

"Yes, to watch television and, to talk to the two boys."

"The two boys?"

"Yes. Dimeji and Dauda. They're like my sons, you see."

"Go on," Muyiwa urged him.

"So, one day..."

"Three days ago. Is that correct?"

"Yes. I was watching television in the auto-repair shop when Mosquito Man—"

"The Mosquito Man?"

Baba glared at him and spoke in Yoruba to the interpreter.

"He says he'll stop talking if you don't stop interrupting him," the interpreter said.

Muyiwa looked at the camera with an embarrassed smile. Idiot, Olabisi thought. You shouldn't have made this a live interview. Even I knew that Baba was a live bomb.

Baba gathered his agbada and started talking again. "Yes, the white man who sings. He was on television in Kenya and South Africa, and everyone does what he says. So, when I heard he was coming to Nigeria, I thought I would ask him to tell the President to provide water for the people of Palemo."

"Which president?"

Baba glared at him, turned to the interpreter and said something to him in Yoruba. The interpreter gave a small cough.

"He said that Nigeria has only one president and he doesn't know why you keep on repeating everything he says," he said.

The camera panned to Baba. Very clever, Olabisi thought. The BBC does protect its own from embarrassment. She gloated for a few seconds at Muyiwa's discomfort.

"Apologies, Baba. We just want to make it clear to our international viewers which president you were referring to. So, why do you think Bono, the Mosquito Man, would want to do this?"
"I don't know. I just know that people listen when he speaks. Maybe our president will listen to him."

Muyiwa turned to the camera. "Unfortunately, our time is up. But, just to let you know, we've received a message from Bono himself saying that he can't wait to meet you in person when he comes to Nigeria. This is Muyiwa Abraham, Lagos, Nigeria for the BBC World Service."

The camera panned back to the newscasters. Olabisi pointed the remote control towards the television and turned it off.

Seven years. That's how long it'd taken her to build up Water for Nigerians, and just when she thought her work would get the recognition it deserved, some fool named Muyiwa thought they would mess it up for her. Well, she wasn't having it. She had ambitions, great plans for WfN. In her mind's eye, she could see WfN's offices in all regions of Africa. The ones outside Nigeria would be called Water for Africans (WfA). In fact, she'd gone so far as to register the charities' names in the UK, South Africa and Kenya. She'd been told she need not bother with North Africa, but she wasn't deterred. She knew there was a demand for Water for Africans in Tunisia.

In the seven years she'd launched WfN, other local water charities had come and gone. Some had come and resurrected themselves under new names, but with the same personnel. And yet, WfN still remained. Campaigning, lobbying, cajoling, threatening... She'd done them all—because she cared.

People could talk about access to health and education until the cows came home. But, without water to drink, cook and clean, all of it was hogwash, as far as she was concerned. What good was medication if one didn't have water to wash it down? What was the point of education if children went to school sick from drinking polluted water?

Her friends thought she was mad, even obsessed. They wondered why she wasn't like the other 'international NGOs' who swanned around Lagos and Abuja, in 4x4s and went to international conferences, with bulging suitcases. Well, she'd lived that life and decided that she would be of more use to her fellow Nigerians and, by extension, Africans, if she travelled less, focussed more on writing better funding proposals, to get more money, so she could do the work she wanted to do.

She hated those funding proposals. Every one of them. They sucked the life out of the urgent need to provide water and eradicate waterborne diseases like cholera, typhoid and hepatitis A, which unfortunately, had a high number of child casualties. And it didn't matter how many children she'd seen with those diseases, because she would never get used to it. And that's why her resolve stiffened with every funding proposal that was rejected.

Still, she had no choice but to keep on writing the proposals. They were WfN's lifeblood. But until she had a global celebrity to front their campaigns and keep the money coming in for their projects, that was all she could, and would keep on doing, until the day the Nigerian government and its African counterparts made clean, drinking water a reality for their citizens.

Discovering Baba's meeting with Bono was a stroke of luck. She'd been in the Jeep, playing around with the radio frequency when she'd heard Dauda speaking to the DJs and, right then, she knew her prayers had been answered. By aligning herself with Baba, her beloved WfN would get the global recognition it deserved and funding would pour in for their work.

Baba was an international donor's dream. His withered-looking face, tired body and haunted eyes all added to this beaten-down image of Africans that donor agencies liked to put in their marketing materials. And she intended to milk it for all it was worth. The fact that Baba seemed pliable had been a definite bonus, because the last thing she wanted was to get some savvy person who would've insisted on getting a cut of everything out of their partnership. Someone like Munira, Baba's wife.

At the thought of Munira, Olabisi flicked her head as if shooing away a pesky fly. Her thoughts returned to Baba. She was beginning to wonder if there was more to his woe-is-me manner than she'd previously imagined. In fact, she concluded, Baba was a wily, old man who'd obviously used her to get a free meal and new clothes, and had maybe even, outwitted her.

Well, he was also a man who'd met his match. She flipped the remote control she had been gripping onto the coffee table and picked up her phone.

She didn't care much for Bono, nor any other celebrity for that matter. But, she did care for what WfN stood to gain by associating with them. Celebrities opened cashflow doors. They did try getting a well-known Nollywood actress once. When she demanded US$250,000 upfront, Olabisi showed her the door. As far as celebrities went, Bono's celeb cred was stratospheric, and whatever his thoughts may be about being 'charitably used', she bet he would be piqued by Baba, especially after his performance on BBC World Service this morning. She hadn't checked her social media feeds yet, but she was sure they would've exploded with mindless chatter about Baba, *her* protégé and all the goings on.

Once again, her mind turned to Munira, Baba's wife. Olabisi decided that Munira was the secret sauce to her accomplishing everything she was planning. Yes, there was potential for fireworks where she was concerned, but it was nothing that she, Olabisi, couldn't handle. The most important thing was making sure she got what she'd worked so hard for all these years: exposure for WfN. And nothing and no one, not even a harridan like Munira would get in her way. She flicked on her mobile and punched in Muyiwa's number.

Baba watched as the camera crew wrapped up their equipment. He was hungry and wondered if he was going to be fed. Muyiwa walked over to him.

"Thank you, Baba. That was good. Next time, just try answering the questions, okay?"

Baba kissed his teeth irritably. He had the mind to slap Muyiwa to oblivion and back. *His* behaviour during the interview had been reprehensible. Was it really necessary for him to repeat everything that he, Baba, had said? And look at him now, telling him to just answer 'the question'. That was the problem with Lagos and young people nowadays. They had absolutely no respect at all. At least, Dauda and Dimeji occasionally showed him a little.

"You know, in my day, young people did not interrupt their elders," Baba said.

"Yes, Baba. And now, we have to leave this room. I may work for the BBC, but our expenses budget is not as big as everyone thinks." He wrapped his left arm around Baba's shoulders and strong-armed him out of the room. "I say, we go downstairs, have a meal and call it a day," he said.

"How am I going to get back to Palemo?" Baba asked. He didn't have any money on him, and now that the enormity of what he did—leaving Munira behind (and overnight for that matter) and not telling her where he was—was dawning on him, he felt more than a little bit anxious. He knew—if Munira allowed him to live—he would be sleeping on the bench outside the auto-repair shop, for the rest of his life after today—if Munira allowed him to live.

"Baba, you don't need to worry about that." Muyiwa said, patting his shoulders affectionately. "I'm sure we can sort you out."

Baba sighed in relief. He would ask to be dropped off at the auto-repair shop. Dauda and Dimeji would take care of him. Perhaps, Mama Seyi would even repay the good fortune his sudden fame has had on her business by giving him a few meals. Even as the thought flitted through his mind, he knew it was unlikely. He shrugged and allowed himself to be led by Muyiwa to the hotel restaurant.

Muyiwa watched Baba wolf down a steaming plate of rice with vegetable stew and, from what he could count, at least six pieces of choice meat. Baba ate like a man who didn't know where his next meal was coming from. He ate with wild abandon, as if expecting to be thrown out of the restaurant at any second. Baba ate with both hands. Baba ate like an animal.

Muyiwa averted his eyes when Baba started speaking with his mouth full.

"So," he chewed noisily. "When you take me back to Palemo, you'll tell my wife that it was too late for me to come home. What with armed robbers and everything rolling around Lagos at that time of the night, yeah?"

Muyiwa nodded. He picked up his fork and found that the sight of masticated food in Baba's mouth had killed his appetite. He pushed his plate away. Baba pulled the plate towards him.

"You really shouldn't waste food," he said. "It's sinful."

Muyiwa scrolled through the emails on his smartphone. He looked up at Baba, as if seeing him for the first time. Suddenly, he got up.

"Baba, I need to make a telephone call," he said. "Don't go anywhere."

"Where can I go? You're taking me back to Palemo, aren't you?" he replied, his mouth full. He felt a momentary guilt. He shouldn't be eating such wonderful food without his wife. It wasn't right. As he ate the remnants of Muyiwa's food, he wondered how she was doing. He shouldn't have left her last night. She was his wife. She should be with him to meet the Mosquito Man.

His thoughts went to her first night in Lagos and how she had to pay off the men he owed money to. He squashed them immediately. He would not dwell on the past. It was too shameful. He now had a great opportunity to do something good for his local community and Palemo as a whole. And possibly, maybe, redeem himself with Munira, which he would very much like. He would make use of this opportunity to do something right for once, and he won't embarrass himself. Who knows, maybe he would even go to night school and learn how to read, just like their local cobbler. Yes, he was in his fifties, but it wasn't too late to try. Perhaps, he could even ask the Mosquito Man to help him pay his school fees... It was a perfectly reasonable request. After school, he would learn a trade and open up a business. Perhaps he and Munira would have a baby...

His thoughts were going to dangerous waters. He turned his attention back to Muyiwa's abandoned plate and attacked it with vigour.

In all their years of working in the auto-repair shop, Dauda didn't think that he'd seen their boss, Mr Sowemimo, more than once a month. And, when they did, he came rant-filled with curses and flinging accusations at them as being cheaters who robbed him.

Mr Sowemimo was right in that Dauda cheated and robbed the auto-repair shop blind. However, as far as Dauda was concerned, Mr Sowemimo ought to be thankful that his thieving and robbing was at best, quite low-key. Mr

Sowemimo owned three other auto-repair shops and Dauda knew that the mechanics in those auto-repair shops did far worse than he did. Last he heard, they were stealing car parts to order. He was no angel, but, as far as he was concerned, that was plain wrong. At least, his own stealing was for his own use. Anyway, what did Mr Sowemimo expect? He barely paid their salaries, if at all, and told them they should be grateful for even that. He didn't even bother to hide his delight at keeping them in employment servitude. He got away with it, because he knew his mechanics had nowhere else to go. For every job at the repair shop, there were a few hundred apprentices waiting to take the existing mechanic's place. And people thought Nigeria's youth were the problem: it was Mr Sowemimo's generation, the bloodsucking vampire generation that leeched Nigeria of its resources and ensured the same politicians that had been in power since the 1960s, were still ruling the country from behind the scenes.

Baba was worth a million of them all.

As he watched Mr Sowemimo give yet another interview to a local television station, lies spewing easily and sweetly from his *pomo*, thick lips, a slow rage built up within Dauda.

"Oh, yes. We've always made Baba welcomed in this auto-repair shop. In fact, he has his very own special seat," Mr Sowemimo held up a newly upholstered chair to the camera.

He was lying. He hated seeing Baba in the auto-repair shop. He called him a "useless old fool." In turn, Baba called him an "evil menace to society", who should be teaching Dauda ethical, professional values, instead of telling him to use fake car parts from China on their customers' cars.

Baba wasn't a particularly religious man, but he was convinced that Mr Sowemimo was going to hell. Dauda wondered what Baba would say if he heard the way Mr Sowemimo was now singing his praises.

"So, where is Baba now?" the journalist asked Mr Sowemimo.

Mr Sowemimo hesitated for a second before replying quickly. "He's taking a well-deserved rest in a secret location for his good. You know, he's a simple man and not used to such attention." He laughed good-naturedly. "As you can see, we are like a family in this auto-repair shop. And we extend that level of care to the cars that we service, so if you're looking for a reliable, trustworthy mechanic, be sure to come down to our repair shop..." As he gave the address, the reporter hastily cut him off.

Dimeji watched Mr Sowemimo in silence. He turned to Dauda. "Do you know where Baba is?" He asked him. The two of them were standing at the edge of the crowd.

"I don't know. The security guard next door said he saw him get into a car about 10.15pm yesterday," Dauda responded. "Munira hasn't seen him either. I think she's on her way here."

Dimeji blanched.

"She thinks I'm hiding Baba from her," Dauda said with resignation.

"But, we don't even know where he is!" Dauda shrugged. "Wherever he is, I'm sure he's giving everybody laughs. You saw the way he put that young reporter in his place?"

They both laughed raucously, happy for the sudden change in atmosphere between them and all the craziness.

"That man won't kill us," Dauda said, wiping tears from his eyes. His fleeting rage now gone. There was no point getting angry about things he couldn't control, like Mr Sowemimo and his ilk. "But his wife will. Probably. I just hope he's okay. I don't want anyone taking advantage of him," Dauda said.

The Water for Nigerians Jeep pulled into the Travellers International Hotel, Ikeja. Olabisi's plan had been to get Baba away from Muyiwa that morning and set him up somewhere that she could control access to him.

She sighed and chewed her lower lip. She had to get to him before anyone else did. He was her ticket to making Water for Nigerians a global name. The driver had barely parked the Jeep before she opened the door and scrambled out.

The Travellers International billed itself as a premier hotel in Nigeria. Built in 1985, it has survived four coups, the odd robbery attempt and the curses of the local and international visitors who believe the hotel was past its sell-by date, but still felt forced to use its facilities, because of a lack of alternatives in Lagos.

It wasn't that the Travellers International Hotel was a bad hotel. It had all the things that a functioning hotel should have: swimming pool, well-tended gardens, constant electricity—powered by generators naturally—and the kind of puerile customer service that turned a blind eye to the bulging suitcases, fat sugar daddies and nubile teenage girls thronging through its reception every day.

Olabisi nodded good morning to the workers and made her way into the hotel foyer. Once inside, she headed straight for the restaurants—there was no point in pretending that Baba would be anywhere else—and found him with two recently massacred dishes on the table. She glanced away quickly and held her stomach.

"Baba."

Baba raised his head. Olabisi saw the uncertainty that fleeted across his face. And then, he broke into a wide smile.

"Oh, there you are!" he said.

She wanted to be mad at him. She wanted to go up there and tell him in no uncertain terms how much he'd humiliated her. But, she couldn't. She might not have known him a long time, but she felt she understood him. He was who he was, he couldn't help it. Baba didn't plan for the future. He lived by the day, taking opportunities as they were presented to him, often without thinking of the consequences—to himself or to others. In any case, she needed him more than he needed her. So, in actual fact, she was at his mercy. At least, he was alone, which was good.

She strode up to his table.

"Baba." She said his name quietly, looking into his eyes with the part-pleading, part-stern facade she'd perfected over the years, to deal with situations just like this. "What happened? I thought we agreed that I would come and pick you up from the auto-repair shop this morning? So, why did I wake up to find you on the BBC? You have treated me badly. You know you have."

Baba shifted a little uncomfortably, then his face brightened. "Well, I'm here, now. So, we can do whatever it is you wanted me to do."

Olabisi knew she had to get him out of the hotel before Muyiwa appeared. Wherever Baba was, she knew Muyiwa wasn't far off. She had to move quickly. She shifted gears.

"Baba, I'm glad you said that. Because it tells me that you're still serious about the work. If we leave now, I can take you and your wife to our office, where we will prepare you for Abuja, so that you can look your best and also make use of the opportunities that come your way. We will, of course, make sure that you and your wife are well catered for. In fact, the people at *Masobe* Clothing, the most exclusive clothing boutique in Lagos, are waiting for you and Munira as we speak."

Olabisi watched his face. She knew that Baba would pick up on the shopping trip for his wife. It didn't matter that she had no such shopping trip planned—it was easily remedied by picking up the telephone.

Olabisi's proposal was music to Baba's ears. Munira loved shopping. With a shopping carrot dangling before her eyes, she would forgive him for abandoning her at the auto-repair shop and appearing on the BBC without her.

"Then, what are we waiting for? Let's go!" Baba gathered himself and got up from the table. But not before swiping his fingers across the remaining meat, and stuffing the last few pieces down his throat. A trail of palm oil dribbled from his mouth to his chin. Baba wiped it off with the back of his hand and continued chewing the meat noisily. Olabisi looked away in disgust.

When Muyiwa came back to the restaurant five minutes later, Baba was nowhere to be seen. Muyiwa sat down at the now-vacated table and wondered how he let the biggest coup of his career slip between his fingers.

# 5

Michael Li was a man of few principles. He was driven by two things: making money and then making even more money. The son of ambitious Chinese immigrants to the UK, he was sent to boarding school from the age of seven to eighteen to ensure he would have lifelong relationships with the finest of English society.

Michael mingled with the finest, all right. He mingled with the finest offspring of Burmese army despots. He mingled with the children of English aristocracy whose education was mostly funded by their grandmothers. He mingled with the sons of Bollywood royalty and with the sons of Africa's finest. Somewhere, in the midst of all his mingling, he concluded that he preferred his African connections. At every opportunity, he wheedled and cajoled his parents to spend his holidays with his friends in Kenya, Ghana and Nigeria.

By the time he finished university, he'd spent enough time in Nigeria to speak Yoruba fluently and to know that his financial future was in Africa. In the early 2000s when China began making noises about developing Afro-China relationships, Michael emerged as the natural middleman to negotiate the vital contracts that would secure Chinese interests in the region. He didn't ask for much, just 1% of the contract worth. His biggest haul was a £10 million commission on what was supposed to be the tallest building in Africa, a 60-floor behemoth to be built in Lagos, Nigeria. Building work commenced. Five years, £200 million, several corruption cases and ten local builders' deaths later, work had yet to be completed on the building.

But Michael Li wasn't too concerned about all that, because he knew what would happen. The corruption case would drag on until infinity and the building would lie barely completed, until the deal would be bought out by the very same government officials who negotiated the original contract. He would be hauled in to negotiate the new contract and, in the process, earn himself another couple of million. It was the African, and the Chinese way. But, that was then. Right now, he had other, bigger dreams; he wanted to develop the gambling industry in Nigeria.

A few people had told him that it couldn't be done; Nigerians might be religious and concurrently, amoral, but gambling was a step too far. Michael Li knew that to be a lie. As a second-generation Chinese, he knew that the pursuit of money and the lure of winning would appeal to vain, prideful Nigerians, in much the same way it appealed to wealthy Chinese people.

Michael Li wasn't interested in the lottery. Every country had a national lottery, which, for Michael, was the lowest form of gambling. It lacked finesse and glamour. His dreams were much bigger. To start his project, he wanted to build the kind of casino that would attract people from all over the world. He envisioned a kind of Vegas, but bigger and better. And he knew exactly where he would build it. Somewhere in the northern part of Nigeria, where the air was fresh and the land and the people still relatively untouched, compared to their counterparts in the south. He batted away security concerns with a single sentence: "Even terrorists worship money."

Michael Li had known Olabisi for a long time. Since their university days, some ten years ago. He admired her commitment to providing water to the neediest of communities, even if he did think that she was deluded. Lagos was the greatest city in the world, where anyone could make money from anything, including water. So, when he looked up at his television screen and saw her van outside an auto-repair shop, where it seemed, some impoverished old man was saying that he was going to meet Bono the musician, Michael Li had to take notice. He also called his associates immediately.

"I have an idea," he said gleefully into the mouthpiece. And as his associates listened, they couldn't help but agree with Michael that the idea was genius. If it went according to plan, they might possibly escape the threat of a manslaughter case that was casting a shadow over their latest contract.

After his phone call, he called Olabisi.

"What?" Her tone was dour.

Michael Li laughed. "No, 'how are you?'"

He tried to connect the dour voice to the beautiful face and failed. Even if she was at her worst, for him, she would always be beautiful, irrepressible, selfish Olabisi. *His* Olabisi.

"What do you want, Michael Li?"

"I saw you on television. I think I can help you."

"I'm not buying," she said and she hung up the phone.

Michael Li wasn't concerned. He knew she would come round. She always did.

The room was oppressive and hot. Munira listlessly fanned herself listlessly with *Showcase*, the latest society magazine to hit the newsstands in Nigeria. She wished she could read all the articles in the magazine properly, but contented herself with looking at the pictures. Adamu, the cobbler, who worked across the road, had promised to help her improve her reading as soon as he was able. He'd finally started night school. Although, he'd only had two classes, she could see the change in him. He was happy. The first time he came back from night school, he found her sitting outside their building to escape the stifling heat inside. She beckoned to him to keep her company on the bench, and asked him to tell her what he had learnt. He told her, and she soaked up the second-hand knowledge from him.

"Adamu, you must continue with your education," she told him.

"Madam, how can I not continue with you lecturing me every day that I must continue?" he replied, with a smile.

She didn't know much about him. Sometimes, snippets would come out. He told her that he was 30 years old. Or so he thought. That he'd come from Kaduna, northern Nigeria. His family had been killed in a raid by herdsmen. The only reason he was spared was because, he'd gone to help his uncle on his farm in another village, and decided to spend the night there, so he could spend more time with his nieces.

Munira didn't like listening to those stories, because they made her sad, and also made her think of her own past: her school days; her parents; those days in the farm, practising her lines with tubers as her audience. She wondered why life was so hard. Surely, a bit of happiness wasn't too much to ask?

Now, Munira stood up and peeked through her tattered curtain. The cameras had left. She had no doubt they would be back soon, to catch their beloved Baba.

Baba, her husband. Munira didn't want to think about him too much. Where was he? She went to the door and turned the lock, quietly, so that the landlord would not hear, and come bothering her with his shrivelled penis. Ever since Baba had been in the news, he'd become more demanding, as if he owned her and had a right to her.

The only person who had a right to her was herself, she told herself fiercely. No one, absolutely no one, owned her.

She tiptoed out of the room. As she went past Mama Jide's room, she heard movement. She was sure the witch was listening at her door, recording everything Munira did, so that she could relay it to the fools who were stupid enough to listen.

The heat outside was even worse. She spotted Adamu across the road and gestured for him to join her on the bench, outside her building. Perhaps today, he would continue the story of Nigeria's independence and how it was said that the Queen of England's cousin came to officiate at the occasion.

She would also ask him if he knew where she could get pictures of that day. It would be good to see what the Queen's cousin had worn. Maybe she could even ask her tailor to create something like that for her, but more updated and with a Nigerian twist. Her spirits sank when she remembered how much she owed to said tailor.

She sat on the bench, folded her hands on her lap and once again, wondered where her husband was. And then, she prayed inwardly to God to protect him. She hoped that his newfound fame hadn't gotten him in trouble. She didn't think she would cope if she found out that he was lying in a ditch somewhere and needed help.

She watched Adamu cross the road to sit on the bench beside her. He had a textbook with him. "I thought you would like to see pictures of the Queen's cousin when she came to Nigeria for the Independence Day celebrations," he said.

She smiled at him, trying to keep her mind off Baba. Adamu opened the textbook.

The maid went about fluffing the pillows, picking things up and putting them back down again, as Baba watched her warily. Olabisi had put him up in her 'boy's quarters', a bungalow at the end of her garden, usually reserved for the house helps. The accommodation was basic, but clean. He tested the bed, first by laying his hands on the mattress and pressing them down. It felt firm. Then, he sat down and stood up again.

The maid stood by, silent.

"Do you need anything else, sah?"

Baba did not understand what she meant. What was it to her if he did?

"Madam said I should make sure you were okay," the maid said, gathering from his expression that having a maid, or indeed, a servant, at his beck and call was something of a novelty for the man. Her boss, Olabisi, said the man had showered, but she wasn't sure. He still smelled. There were streaks of palm oil on his agbada, and she was pretty certain that he'd also farted.

"The bathroom is through there," she jerked her head pointedly towards the half-opened door, where he could see a bathroom. Just to make sure he got the message, she added, "There's a fresh bar of soap in there and a raffia sponge as well."

The raffia sponge was hard, but it left the skin feeling like new, if rather bruised. And after spending a few minutes with Baba, the maid thought the soap and raffia sponge were exactly what Baba needed.

"And will you join me?" He leered at her. The maid shook her head and left the room.

Baba sat on the bed and patted it. It was firm, not like the lumpy one they had at home. The one Munira complained made her back ache. To shut her up, he'd got Dauda to slip a large, flat board between the mattress and the bed frame, which made a great difference to Munira's disposition; she'd become so happy. In turn, he'd been happy to be able to do something that she appreciated. It made him feel ten feet tall.

If she saw this room, she would be beside herself in ecstasy. He couldn't believe that a houseboy had a room and bathroom facilities to himself. Was this how the rich lived?

He got off the bed and paced around the room. He wondered what his wife was doing. Probably cursing him with every fibre of her being, if she hadn't already consulted with the local witchdoctor and cursed him with erectile dysfunction. As if he could sleep with anyone else but her. Not that he hadn't tried, and failed, repeatedly.

The maid came back. He guessed she was about Dauda's age. She didn't even knock.

"Madam says she will go and pick up your wife in an hour, so she can take you both shopping. She apologises for keeping you waiting, but says that she had to take care of some business, first."

She stood by the door, as if she was undecided about something. He saw a look of distaste fleet across her face, before it was replaced by what could only be described as gritted determination. She took off her dress in one fluid movement and stood in front of him, naked, and a bit harried, he thought.

"Is this how you service all your madam's guests?" Baba asked her.

"Only the ones that have money," she said, walking slowly towards him. She didn't even bother hiding the grimace on her face.

Baba decided there and then that she was a witch.

"What's your name?" he asked her, as she started pulling

at his trousers.

Whether she decided to ignore him or perhaps didn't hear him, he didn't know, because he didn't get an answer. Ten minutes later, her clothes were back on and she was muttering to herself, "The witchdoctor said it would work... That you would leave your wife and I would be rich..."

In the meantime Baba was looking at his resistant penis and wondering why it refused to work with anyone but his wife.

He looked at the girl still muttering to herself.

"I'm old enough to be your grandfather," he told her.

"Then you should know better, shouldn't you?" she snapped. "And if you even think about telling my boss about this, I'll say that you tried to take advantage of me, an eighteen-year-old girl, from the village," she said.

Baba shook his head sadly. She reminded him of Munira, except in Munira's case, she *had* been taken advantage of. And he himself was no better. In fact, he was one of the very people he railed about that was causing Nigeria's decay. Olabisi's young maid did not know any different. She'd been taught that sex opened doors, and in the past, it probably had opened doors for her. But not *his* door.

He wondered how long she'd been offering her body to her boss' guests on the sly before deciding that it was none of his business. In Lagos, it was every man for himself, which was what he should be doing, not trying to have sex with someone young enough to be his granddaughter.

"I'm assuming that your *oga*, boss, would like Munira

and I to stay here while she helps us with this Mosquito Man thing?" he asked.

The girl nodded. Baba sat on the bed. Munira would never agree; people like Olabisi played havoc with her inferiority complex. Once again, Baba made a decision: Olabisi and Munira's issues were not his problem. In fact, he'd had enough of the two of them. Let them fight it out. The maid interrupted his thoughts.

"Please put on your clothes. Nobody wants to see your old, tired penis," she said.

Munira pursed her lips when she saw the WfN 4x4 pull up outside her building. She recognised the driver and noted that Olabisi, the no-good, scheming witch was not in the vehicle, and neither was her husband. Yet, she knew the witch had something to do with his disappearance.

She tapped the cobbler lightly on his arm, indicating that she would talk to him later, then walked up to the vehicle. There were a few people milling around, hoping to catch a glimpse of Baba, even after she'd told them that he was in seclusion for his own safety.

The windows slid down.

"Good morning. Madame Olabisi says that your husband is with her and that she would like you to join them, so you can all discuss how the Mosquito Man can help the two of you."

Munira gave Olabisi points for strategy. By sending her driver, instead of coming herself or even, bringing Baba, she knew Munira would have no choice but to come with the driver.

She turned and waved to the cobbler, then got inside the 4x4. The cool air instantly calmed her anger. By the time they reached the end of her unpaved street, Munira was firmly leaned back on the leather seat, had kicked off her shoes and was idly planning endorsement deals with SUV car companies. She wasn't worried about Olabisi; she'd battled women—indeed people—like her all her life. They thought they were better than her, but she'd proved them wrong, always. Today was the last day of battle. She was done with fighting. Now, it was success all the way, with or without her husband.

# 6

Baba did not know which he feared most; Munira's anger or this person, who was smiling at him the way a tiger watched its prey. But either way, it made him nervous.

"Munira, there you are!" he said when his wife entered Olabisi's office, which had been wisely chosen as a neutral area.

Munira gave both him and Olabisi a catlike smile.

She directed her question at Olabisi. "So you were the one that took my husband?"

Olabisi met her venomous look with a cool air. "He came with me by himself," she said.

"Muni, it was too late to call you and I didn't want to disturb you—" Baba started.

"I'll get to you, later," Munira cut off her husband and turned her attention back to Olabisi.

"There's a word for people like you who kidnap other people's husbands," she pointed a manicured hand at Olabisi. "Have you no shame—"

"Oh, please. As if anybody would be interested in your husband. Look, enough of this pretence. There's work to be done. There's an opportunity for all three of us to make money here, and the sooner we can start work, the better. So let's start from the beginning again: what do you want to get out of this?"

"I just want to be an actress," Munira blurted out, waiting for the scorn that would inevitably appear on Olabisi's face.

Olabisi did not know what being a Nollywood actress had to do with Baba meeting Bono, and she wasn't much interested in finding out either, but she filed away the information, for future use.

"But of course you do!" she said smoothly.

Munira searched Olabisi's face. There was no scorn.

"You see, Munira! I knew Olabisi could help!" Baba said, clapping his hands in delight.

Michael Li looked at the text he'd just received from Olabisi's maid. *Dey are in madame's office*, it said. He decided to pay Olabisi a surprise visit. He walked out of his house and signalled to his driver. As they pulled through his security gates, he felt the same tingle of excitement he did whenever he thought he was close to making a business deal.

"Sunday," he called to his driver. "You think we'll miss the traffic today?" knowing full well the answer. Like most Lagosians, he'd resigned himself to losing at least two hours of his day to the Lagos traffic, known locally as 'go-slow'.

"We'll see," Sunday replied, smiling at his boss in the car mirror.

Chino-Centric was one of the most powerful companies in the

world, and it got there by trading in one of its most precious commodities: water. From Azerbaijan to Zanzibar, Chino-Centric's trademarked logo—a drop of water suspended in space—was a sign of comfort and reassurance to governments and private companies alike that the billions of dollars worth of contracts they awarded every year to the company, to develop and maintain water systems and infrastructure, was being put to good use. So when the CEO took a call from Michael Li, about an opportunity to get some good PR for their company via a Nigerian man and international superstar Bono, the CEO listened to what Michael had to say.

Two hours after leaving his office Michael pulled into Olabisi's parking lot. An oil tanker had overturned on the Third Mainland Bridge, causing a 10-mile tailgate. Despite the blistering heat, frayed tempers and the area boys weaving their way between the stationary cars, trying to intimidate drivers and their passengers to give them money, Michael felt positive. The area boys didn't scare him. They were victims of their circumstance, and he had been known to employ one or two to pack some heat on his competitors. However, there was a time and a place. If he found himself at the mercy of a so-called area boy after a night out in town, he used his gun. Lagos was a great city, but living there was not without its risks, security being one of them. That was why people built fortresses, not houses, with eleven feet tall perimeter walls spiked with broken glass, and also kept arsenals on their premises. Not that any of them would ever admit to that publicly.

Olabisi's maid came out of the office as he pulled inside the driveway and turned off the engine. Grimly anticipating the rush of hot air as the car's air conditioning died he wondered how she had wrangled a visit to the office. He came out of the car and gestured to his driver to go wait under the shade of the tree, opposite the office building.

"Good morning, sah," she said, looking like butter wouldn't melt in her mouth, which was ridiculous, because he knew very well what she could do with butter.

"Madam is inside," she said. She made as if to take his briefcase, and spoke from the side of her mouth. "When will I get my money?"

Michael ignored her and made for Olabisi's office. Behind him, the maid, Funmi, fumed. Then, she straightened her back and, still livid, stalked back into Olabisi's office. As she approached the receptionist, Michael's briefcase, which she was carrying, collided with the receptionist's table and it burst open, its contents spilling out on the floor. Funmi made a great show of distress and thrust the contents of the briefcase, mostly papers, back and forth with false urgency. Michael didn't even turn around.

"Your madam will hear about this," he said, speaking over his shoulder.

The receptionist looked at Funmi and Michael, and shook her head.

"Be careful, Funmi. You're playing with fire," she told her.

"I think you should mind your business," Funmi hissed, shoving the contents back into the briefcase.

Olabisi heard Michael before she saw him. Indeed, he was such a familiar sight at her office, and had been for years, that her PA simply waved him in whenever he came. His meeting appointments, which were duly noted in Olabisi's diary, were a formality; Michael came and went as he pleased. Which was fine, most of the time. Today was not one of those times. So when Olabisi heard him talking to her PA, she signalled to Baba and Munira to excuse her, and to Munira's irritation went outside to the reception area to meet her visitor.

"Did you just see the way she told me to shut up?" Munira turned to Baba, chest heaving.

"When do you think we can eat?" Baba said. They'd been in Olabisi's office for just an hour, and he was tired, bored and hungry. He wondered what Dauda was doing. Then, his mind wandered to Funmi, the maid and their attempt to have sex that morning. If he ever needed proof, once again, that Munira had done juju, witchcraft on him, that morning's non-incident with Funmi was it.

He'd accused her once, during one of their fights, of using witchcraft over him. Munira had simply clapped her hands and cackled—exactly like a witch he'd thought with a shudder, and then with fury, she had pulled down his trousers to reveal his penis. To this day, he didn't know why he did not wear underpants.

"See," she pointed disdainfully at him. "You're not even with other women, and it's still shrunken."

She took two steps towards him and he cowered. She cackled again then left the room.

Later that night, when she got back home, she got into bed with him, and proceeded to give him the best sex of his life. As he drifted off to sleep, he thought he heard her say.

"You cannot get it up with other women, because you're my husband, no one else's. I don't need juju."

He wasn't sure he believed her, but still he kept on trying. This time though, he was glad nothing had happened with Funmi, the stupid maid. No one was a match for his wife.

"Baba, be quiet. There's a Chinese man outside."

Munira was no longer sitting down. Instead, she was peering through a crack in the door in Olabisi's office, that looked out to the receptionist area. She could tell from Olabisi's body language that her Chinese visitor wasn't welcomed. She saw Olabisi look back over her shoulder at her office, and begin walking... towards her. Munira ran back to her chair. She'd barely sat down when Olabisi reached the door, and shut it firmly. When Munira heard her footsteps receding from the door, she tiptoed back to the door and attempted to open it a crack.

"Munira," her husband's voice was cajoling. "Let it be."

Munira looked back at Baba. She knew he was right. She sighed and sat back down on the chair. "Then, how will we know what's going on?" she asked him, although she wasn't expecting an answer.

"Let. It. Be."

They both leaned back on their chairs and waited for Olabisi to come back.

Michael noted the secrecy with the way Olabisi shut her office door. As she drew closer to him he flashed her what he called his "sex smile". Olabisi sighed; already on unsteady ground with all the shenanigans of Baba and Munira and the possible threat of Muwiya, one look at Michael's handsome, lopsided grin and bright white teeth and she knew she'd been beaten.

"No tricks," she said.

"I promise," he said.

Olabisi gestured towards her office as they both began walking down the hallway. As Michael opened the door to Olabisi's office, the receptionist heard him say to her, "By the way, you need to do something about Funmi..."

The receptionist didn't catch the rest of Michael's sentence, but she saw Olabisi nod in agreement as they went into the office and closed the door behind them.

The receptionist shook her head slowly; Funmi was a fool, she thought.

Inside Olabisi's office, Michael surveyed the scene. He recognised the older man as the one he'd seen on television, and the corpulent lady draped in costume jewellery and sitting next to him, he surmised, must be his wife.

"Olabisi, isn't it time we ate?" Baba asked. Munira glared at her husband.

"Soon, Baba," Olabisi said soothingly. "Soon. In the meantime, I want you to meet my friend, Michael. He's one of the people I was telling you about that can help us with this thing we're doing."

"We want 50%. Everything must be split right down the

middle," Munira burst out.

"We can discuss all that later. Let's get some food for Baba first, eh?" Olabisi said.

Munira hissed. If Olabisi thought she could fob her off by talking to her like a child, she had another think coming. She turned her attention to the Chinese man, who was looking at her with a bemused look on his face. Did he think he was better than her? The Chinese should come with a health warning; everything they touched was scorched. Coming to Nigeria and flooding the market with their fake and dangerous goods. And if he was in this deal with Olabisi—whatever the deal was—Munira knew that she had to have her wits about her, even more so than before.

Now Michael spoke. "Olabisi is right. Let us eat first. You didn't tell me your name." He was speaking to Munira.

"It's Munira. I am Baba's wife, and nothing happens without my say-so," she said.

"Munira," Michael said the word as if he was tasting it on his lips. He smiled at her, with his bright white teeth. She wondered how he got them like that. In spite of herself, Munira felt a frisson of excitement course through her loins. She lowered her eyelids. Perhaps she was wrong. Maybe he would make her the first Nollywood star to live in China.

Olabisi looked at the two of them, and then at Baba, who seemed oblivious to what was happening between his wife and Michael. 'What kind of a man was this?' she wondered.

"I am very happy to meet you today, Munira. And I think you will be happy to hear the big plans my company has for you, your husband and Olabisi," he flashed her another smile. Munira felt white hot.

"Shall we go?" Olabisi snapped.

"I want *Mama Put*, street food, Olabisi," Baba said, standing up.

"No," his wife said. "We're going to Hamburger Inc. We're going to eat burgers and chips." She would show Michael that she had sophisticated taste. She loved Mama Put food as much as the next Nigerian, but she couldn't allow her husband to show them up in front of Michael. He would order pounded yam and egusi stew, stockpiled with as much as meat as whoever was paying could afford, and then proceed to annihilate the meal without any regard to his guests. With a hamburger, there was less chance of such embarrassment.

Baba wasn't worried. As far as he was concerned, he could have Mama Put food *and* burger and chips. He only wished that he had Dauda and Oladimeji with him; he missed those boys and even with Munira with him, he felt vulnerable.

# 7

The sweet seller smiled at Dauda as she rolled past. He pretended he didn't see her. Three days ago when he'd called to her, she'd cussed him to the high heavens. Since that day, she and countless others made it their business to roll past the auto-repair shop at least twice a day. Ever since the news broke out about Baba he'd rocketed up in the female attraction stakes from someone whose stock was so-so, to rock star status, and all in the space of three days.

The sweet seller stopped right in front of the gate, where they were still a few stragglers hoping to catch sight of Baba.

"Are you just going to stand there like a fool?" someone hissed at her. Dauda didn't need to look at her to feel her embarrassment.

"I'll stand where I want, ignoramus," the sweet seller hissed back. "Last I heard, your father didn't build this road." She kissed her teeth and started walking away, but not without looking back at Dauda to see if he'd overheard her exchange. Dauda felt her gaze on him, but still refused to look at her.

"Stupid girl. He's not looking at you. Who's the ignoramus now?" her nemesis cackled. The sweet seller ignored him and kept on walking.

Dauda smiled to himself and then stopped when he realised that he hadn't heard from Baba in just over 24 hours. He wasn't worried; he felt that he would know if something had happened to Baba. At the same time, this was possibly the longest he hadn't heard from Baba in all the years he'd known him. And in those years, he'd grown to love Baba, even if the man was a rascal and the antithesis of every cultural value or tradition that Nigerians held so dear. For starters, Baba was not religious. In all the years that Dauda had known Baba, he'd never seen him set foot in a church, mosque or even visit the jujuman, the local witchdoctor. In a country where even robbers prayed to all three deities before their thieving operations, this was an anomaly, and one which Dauda respected him for. Munira used to say that Baba was like a cockroach. In the unlikely event that Nigeria ever suffered a nuclear attack, Baba would be the last human standing, and knowing him, he would find a way to procreate and thus curse Nigerians with his extended bloodline, until the next nuclear blast. It was a harsh assessment, but Dauda knew Munira was right.

*Munira.* He wondered where she was. And why hadn't she called him, screeching down his ear and accusing him of hiding her husband? It was one thing for Baba to disappear, but it was another for Munira to disappear at the same time. He told himself that he was being silly. If they were AWOL, that meant that Munira was with Baba. Dauda wished them both well.

"Baba is in hiding for his own safety," he said in irritation to the stragglers hanging around the auto-repair shop.

"I don't know who you think you're fooling," one of them replied irritably. "You've probably kidnapped him yourself and will ask for ransom. Is this not Nigeria?"

*Is this not Nigeria?* This was a rhetorical question and as such did not require an answer. It was also the standard response to every catastrophe, scandal or event, from the micro (family) level to the national (political) level, in Nigeria.

*Is this not Nigeria?* Dauda was beginning to think the standard response was not good enough; that it was a catch-all phrase that meant nothing, explained nothing and did nothing for Nigeria. Even worse, it contributed to the country's rot. Idly, he wondered what the Mosquito Man would think of the phrase. Would he get it?

*Is this not Nigeria?* Dauda decided that he must kill that rumour immediately. Publicly accusing someone of kidnapping in public was a dangerous thing to do, even in anything-goes-Lagos. At the very worst, *he* would be in danger of being kidnapped by area boys and tortured until he told them where he stashed the supposed ransom money/Baba (whichever the kidnappers wanted). They wouldn't believe him if he told them the truth; which was that he didn't know where Baba was. And he didn't have any money.

No, he must kill the thought, the idea, before it took root in people's minds.

Pushing through the stragglers he admonished them with, "God will punish you! You think everyone thinks like you?" He kissed his teeth and flicked his arm, much like someone who was shooing away a pesky mosquito. He raised his voice. "Baba is not here. Please go!"

The crowd dispersed, but he saw a young man walk towards him. He recognised him as the BBC journalist who had interviewed Baba.

"Dauda?" Muyiwa called out to him.

"I said Baba isn't here. What more do you want?" Dauda's voice was sullen. He was tired. Dealing with people was exhausting. And why wasn't Dimeji out here with him, dealing with all these useless people?

"It's ok. It's you I want to see," Muyiwa said.

Dauda looked at Muyiwa for a few moments. "Oh, yeah?" He said, his voice inscrutable.

Muyiwa did not hesitate. "I think you and I can help each other. If you can get me, and me *only*, an interview with Baba and Bono together, I guarantee to make it worth your while," he said.

"How much?"

"US$50K."

Dauda did not blink. "Yes," he said.

At Hamburger Inc, the restaurant Munira had requested, Michael explained his offer to Baba. His partners were Chino-Centric and they wanted Baba to front their latest campaign. The only thing they asked from him was to ensure that Bono also featured in the campaign.

"My husband is not doing anything without me," Munira said. "Besides, I'm the actress in this family—"

"Of course," Michael said soothingly, he placed his hand on Munira's arm as he spoke. He even stroked the dimpled flesh the way one might caress a rare jewel. Olabisi looked away, but not before she caught Michael 'accidentally' brush his knuckles against Munira's side boob. She heard Munira's quick intake of breath.

Across the table, Baba had just finished demolishing the second of two burgers. His hands were a sticky mess of ketchup, mayonnaise and sodden bread buns. Even as Olabisi looked at him, he burped and scratched his stomach with his unwashed hands. She watched as the clothes she'd bought him earlier that day got marked with food stains. Is this how it was going to be from now? She wondered. Watching as her sometimes-lover tried to seduce a married, corpulent harridan in front of her, and also watching over said harridan's husband, who had the social graces of a wild animal.

Olabisi coughed. Munira appeared to gather herself. They were seated in a semi-circle. From the right was Baba, Michael, Munira (who had insisted on sitting next to him) and then, Olabisi.

"Baba, please mind yourself," Munira spoke sharply to her husband. "Imbecile," she muttered loudly. "Can't you eat like a normal human being?"

This time, Olabisi heard the frustration in her voice. For the first time, she found herself feeling a little sorry for Munira. What was her story? How did she even end up with Baba? But then, she gathered herself; it was none of her business. Everybody in Nigeria had a story, and hers was to make sure Water for Nigerians finally got the recognition and cash it deserved after many years of struggling.

Baba glared at Munira and burped again. Munira kissed her teeth and signalled to a waitress to bring soapy water to Baba. As the waitress arrived with the soapy water, Munira dipped her finger into the washbowl and declared that she wanted *warm* soapy water. Couldn't the stupid waitress see that her husband was elderly and could catch cold from the tepid water she brought him? Baba cautioned Munira to stop haranguing the poor waitress. Soon, they started arguing, while the waitress waited, unsure of what to do.

Michael turned to Olabisi and gave her a knowing smile. She ignored him. "Waitress, if you could bring the warm soapy water, that would be fine," Olabisi said.

She turned to Munira and spoke carefully, "Munira, I'm not sure what you mean by being in the advertisement for Chino-Centric..."

"I meant exactly what I said; I'm going to be in it. Baba and I are a team. And while we're at it, we're going to be paid as individuals, not as one unit, and I'm not accepting anything less than US$50K," she sat back, with a smirk on her face.

"Munira," Michael spoke mildly, "You will not feature in the ads and be paid US$50K each. It's not feasible. And your husband has yet to meet Bono. From what I recall from the BBC, Bono said he was interested in meeting him. But has anyone reached out to you from his office? No? I thought so. Perhaps when Bono is confirmed, we can negotiate, but not before."

Olabisi waded in smoothly. "Don't worry about Bono. WfN is used to dealing with celebrities, and projects such as ours are of a great interest to Bono, and with Baba's story, I am confident that we can attract Bono to our cause—"

"Which cause?" Munira interrupted. "I thought this was about Baba? Why are you two trying to cheat us?" Her voice, a slight screech at the best of times, now rose to dangerously high levels.

The waitress appeared with the fresh bowl of warmer water. There was silence while they watched Baba wash his hands and dry them on his clothes, ignoring the towel hanging on the waitress's arm.

Munira grabbed her husband's arm and propelled him out of the chair. "Baba, we're going. When these people are serious, they know where to find us," and with that, she stalked out of the restaurant with her husband in tow.

"She's not going anywhere. She wouldn't want to pay for cab fare," Michael said, watching her receding backside. He pulled his eyes away with difficulty and settled his eyes on Olabisi.

"She's got money. She made me give her N10K when she arrived at my office this morning. Said it was handshake money and that she wouldn't talk otherwise."

Michael laughed. He had underestimated Munira's business sense.

"I know what you're doing with her," Olabisi said. "You must stop it. I'm not having you sleep with her and ruining my chances to make this charity great."

"I'm not doing anything, Olabisi. And I think you should concentrate on wooing Baba and his wife back, before making idle threats. And fire your maid, she took money out of my briefcase this morning, in your office—I saw her. It's not the first time either."

"Leave Munira and Bono to me. And I've decided; Chino-Centric will 'contribute' US$500K to WfN as a thank you for bringing Baba and Bono to you."

"Deliver first," Michael said. Then, he gave her a look.

Olabisi gathered her belongings. "No. Not after watching you with Munira," and she left the restaurant.

Michael signalled to the waitress to bring their bill.

# 8

A fly buzzed in the oppressive heat. Munira fanned herself. She got off the bed, walked around for a few moments, then went to lie on the bed again. Baba sat on the lone chair in the room. He made as if to get up.

"Sit down," Munira commanded. Baba gave no indication that he heard her and stood up.

"Didn't you hear me?" Munira said irritably.

"I'm not listening to you. I'm going to the shop," Baba replied, walking to the door. Munira flung her feet to the side of the bed. "I'll come with you," she said.

"No, I don't want you to come with me. You spoil things. If it wasn't for you, we would still be with Olabisi in that air-conditioned room in her boy's quarters. But no, you had to spoil things. I've had enough," Baba said. "I'm going to the auto-repair shop, away from you. Away from this madness," and *hopefully I will find a way out of this madness*, he said to himself silently.

He did not know what Munira thought she would achieve by bringing them back to this hovel, but surely, even she must know that she was way out of her league with this Mosquito Man business?

Besides, he wasn't driven by money as much as she was. As long as he had food in his stomach and a roof over his head, he was happy. And that was one of the reasons that Munira got so mad with him; his lack of ambition. But the way he figured, lack of ambition had got him a relatively full stomach and a roof over his head every day of his 54 years, which as far as he was concerned, meant that he hadn't done too badly. Listening to Munira bargain to get more US dollars for this... whatever it was they were thinking of doing with him and the Mosquito Man, just made him realise just how ridiculous the whole thing was. Munira had never even seen a $20 bill, much less $50K. He found the whole thing, perplexing.

He didn't understand her greed. It was a particularly voracious kind that had infiltrated Nigerian society, infecting and corrupting everything in its wake. The need to have more and more and more. Ask a ten-year-old Nigerian child for directions anywhere and they would stretch out their hand for payment first. Also, he saw it on television; all the politicians and 'big people', flaunting their ill-gotten wealth. Was that really necessary?

As delightful as the day had been with Olabisi, save, of course, the embarrassing episode with the maid, he was glad to be in his home. But it was time to get out. He felt stifled. He needed to talk to Dauda about the direction this *wahala*, was going.

And now, there was an insistent knock on the door. Munira and Baba looked at each other.

"Baba, I was told you were back. Welcome," it was the

landlord.

"Mr Landlord, we're busy now. Please go away," Munira said.

"No problem. Some people are still outside waiting for you. But I will tell them that you have gone out via the back-yard. After all, we're friends and friends help each other," he laughed loudly at his own joke. A few moments later, they heard his receding steps.

Munira peeked through their curtains. "He's shooing them away," she said.

"Good," Baba said. "I'm still going to the auto-repair shop."

"And I've told you; you're not going anywhere without me," Munira said.

"Why do I need your permission to do anything?" Baba's voice had risen. "Why?"

"Because you owe me," she screamed.

In the silence that followed, the white elephant of her first night in Lagos stood between them.

Baba looked away. But he could feel her eyes on him, hating him and willing him to acknowledge what happened that night and make amends.

He sat back down. How could he make amends? Where would he start? And what about him? Had anyone asked him how he felt about her sleeping with all those men to further her Nollywood career?

He felt a strange tightening in his stomach when he thought of their lunch at Hamburger Inc. Munira insisting that she wanted to sit next to the Chinese man, him watching as the Chinese man caressed his wife's arm and 'accidentally', her side breast. Those breasts that gave him such great pleasure. He had also caught the contempt in Olabisi's eyes as she looked at him. Oh, he knew what she was thinking alright: what kind of man would allow another man to openly flirt with his wife and do *nothing*? The kind of man who knew his limitations, that's who, he told himself.

Munira deserved someone much better than him, he knew that. He knew also, that without her, he wouldn't survive. Because Lagos was a frightening place for people like him. It needed dragons, people like Munira, with the skills to survive its harsh environment. And despite the cavities in their relationship, it was easier for him to hitch his faded star to hers.

"We cannot stay in this room forever," he said.

"We're not. Olabisi will call. She needs us more than we need her," Munira spoke confidently. Her mobile vibrated with a text message. It was the landlord: *the director is back from London and would like to see you*, it said.

She decided that she wouldn't reply to the text message. Other directors and offers will come flooding in. Then, she would take her pick, and the world will see her star. Finally. She laid back on the bed. An hour later, when she opened her eyes, Baba was gone.

Baba dared not breathe until he was out of range of his building. He'd sat on the chair and watched Munira fan herself with an old-fashioned Chinese fan, until she fell asleep, her left hand clutching the mobile, as if for dear life.

Olabisi still hadn't called, and Baba concluded that it was a good thing. He had decided that he didn't like the Chinese man, and wanted nothing to do with him. He knew very well what the Chinese stood for and it was much like everything they stood for in Nigeria: they would take everything they could get their hands on and corrupt it with their fake version. It was simply the way they were. And having watched him with Munira today, he was sure that the Chinese man did not have good intentions towards his wife.

It was late afternoon. Finally, the sun was starting to lose some of its intensity. Baba walked quickly, with his head down, anxious not to draw attention to himself. As he approached the auto-repair shop, he saw a handful of people loitering outside. Across the road, Mama Seyi was still doing a brisk trade. He allowed himself a smile, he had never been so happy to see her. The events of the last few days had made him treasure the true constants in his life, like Mama Seyi's torment of him.

Mama Seyi looked up, and when she saw him, she pointed at him and opened her mouth. Before she could say or do anything to announce his presence, he turned into a side street on the left, semi-rundown, and cut into the auto-repair shop backyard. As he opened the backdoor that led into the auto-repair shop itself, he smiled to himself as he thought about the look on Oladimeji's and Dauda's faces when they saw him. His smile froze when he finally looked up from wiping his hands on his clothes to find the television reporter guy, sitting on *his* chair, watching television, and joking with Dauda and Dimeji as if they were lifelong friends.

Muyiwa saw him first. "Baba," he said, sauntering towards him with his hand outstretched. "It's so good to see you again," he said, with a deferential air and talking in Yoruba.

Dauda and Dimeji turned. Their smiles were exactly as Baba had envisioned it; welcoming. Baba laughed out loud.

"Come and sit down," Dauda said, gesturing to his seat. "What happened? One minute you were on television with this young man," he gestured to Muyiwa, "and the next, you disappeared. It's your wife, isn't it?"

"Of course, it's her," Dimeji said, as he slid under a car.

"You never know. Now that he's a star, maybe someone else is in the picture..."

Baba let their good-natured ribbing wash over him as he sat back on the chair.

"Food?" Dauda asked him, bringing him back to the present.

"Moi moi and akara, with a side of yams," Baba replied without thinking. It was a reflex. That was his favourite food.

Dimeji slid out from underneath the car. "I'll get it. I'm hungry myself. Besides, if Mama Seyi knows that it's for you, who knows what she'll do to the food?"

They all laughed. Dimeji winked and left the auto-repair shop.

Baba sat back on his chair. He was home, on familiar ground. This felt good.

"Just sit down and enjoy yourself. Nobody will trouble

you here," Dauda said.

The Mosquito Man appeared on the television screen. Muyiwa went to turn up the volume.

The newscaster, a black lady with hair extensions that probably cost the equivalent of his BBC salary, was talking.

"Bono says he can't wait to go to Nigeria for the All Africa Summit." The scene cut from the newscaster to a b-roll of the Mosquito Man talking to various African leaders. Then, the scenes changed. Slowly, they all realised that they were looking at the auto-repair shop gates on television. There was even a frame with Dauda telling everyone that "... Baba no longer comes to the auto-repair shop. He has been taken to a place of safety, the media interest is too much..."

The scenes cut back to the Mosquito Man talking at a press conference. He was answering a question posed by a journalist.

"Of course I will meet Baba when I get to Nigeria. He seems like the kind of man who gets things done," he said.

The scene was now filled with a picture of Baba, the one he took at the radio station.

Muyiwa turned off the television and looked at Baba, his body shaking with excitement.

"Baba, you're on CNN! Bono has publicly said that he wants to meet you. Baba, the sky is the limit," Muyiwa's eyes glittered as he translated and spoke to Baba. He seemed almost feverish. "Do you understand what this means?" he asked no one in particular.

Dauda knelt by Baba's chair. "Baba," he spoke gently.

"This thing is big *o*. You have become a big person now—"

Dimeji darted into the auto-repair shop, Baba's food in his hands. "Mama Seyi's told everyone you came in through the backyard."

"We need to get you somewhere you can be safe. Because if these area boys find you here—" Dauda was now speaking urgently.

"Not to mention your wife—" Dimeji cut in

"He should probably come with me," Muyiwa said. He exchanged a look with Dauda.

They all looked at Baba expectantly. "I'm not going anywhere until I finish eating," he said.

They all waited for Baba to finish his meal. He was just scooping up the last of the moi moi with his hands when they heard a commotion outside the auto-repair shop gates. Dauda peaked through the gates.

"It's Munira," he reported.

"Of course, it's her," Baba said. He did not seem perturbed, but carried on eating. Dauda gave Muyiwa a look and waved him over. They both peeked through the slit in the gate. In the fifteen minutes that Oladimeji had bought Baba's food and the Mosquito Man had appeared on television, news crews had arrived and were setting up shop. And right in front of their auto-repair shop was a perfectly made-up Munira, holding court to the media.

"As you can see, I do not have my husband with me, because the people in this auto-repair shop, who were meant to be his friends and take care of him, have decided to keep him away from me. What can I do? I'm just a woman," she held out her hands, like a helpless woman, not the witch she was, Dauda thought sourly. Even as he rained unspoken abuses on her head, he couldn't help but think what a great actress she was.

"Baba," he called out. "She's saying that we've kidnapped you."

Baba spoke quietly. "Dauda, all this wahala, is too much for me. Please, let's just go. I didn't ask for this. And I don't know why the Mosquito Man had to tell everyone on television that he wants to see me. If those area boys get hold of me..."

As he spoke, there was a loud banging on the gates.

It was the owner of the auto-repair shop, coming to enjoy his place in the spotlight.

"Muyiwa, take Baba. I'll join you," Dauda said.

Baba got up. As they opened up the backdoor that led to the backyard, they saw Munira bearing down on them with an army of news crews. Her smile said she had won. When she saw her husband, the smile turned into a hesitant one, but her gait never slacked.

Things got rather hazy after that. Baba (or was it Muyiwa?) started running, and so did the news crew. Munira attempted to give chase, but slipped and fell, causing several cameramen and their rigs to crash into her.

Behind him and Dimeji, Dauda could hear Mr Sowemimo, their boss asking "...why is Munira saying that you've kidnapped her husband?"

If he'd ever had any doubts about Baba's nimbleness, Dauda knew that he had no cause to doubt it now.

Somehow, in the midst of all the crashing, Muyiwa and Baba managed to bypass the media scrum, escape to his beat-up Volkswagen, and then, they were off.

"Would you like to come in?" Dauda spoke to Munira, aware that all the drama had been captured by the media and was probably being broadcast live on social media. Despite their sparring and contempt of each other, he didn't want her humiliated like this.

Munira gathered herself with some dignity, marched up to him and slapped him.

"This is the man who kidnapped my husband," she announced to the world.

# 9

In her office, Olabisi watched the media scuffle on television in dismay. Her mobile rang, it was Munira. She ignored it. She needed to think.

The phone rang again, this time it was Michael. She wanted to ignore it, but she knew Michael would just come over. In fact, knowing him, he probably was on his way over, she thought irritably.

"Yes?" She said, when she picked up the phone.

"Olabisi, this is not looking good," Michael said.

Olabisi sighed. "I know."

There was a short silence.

"I'm coming over," said Michael.

"Thank you," she said sourly.

When Michael arrived, he went straight into her office and leaned on her table, looking at her for a few moments.

"How's your mother?" He asked.

"Still hates you."

They both smiled at each other. There was a few minutes silence.

"Stop messing around with Munira. She deserves better," Olabisi said, after a while.

"I didn't know you cared."

Olabisi didn't think she did, but she felt that she could understand Munira's brashness. Her admission that she wanted to be an actress was surprising. If anything, she thought Munira would've wanted to go into fashion, given Nigerians' obsession with the industry. And as much as she hated to admit it, she saw something of herself in Munira: a fight, a desperation to be heard, to know that she mattered, in a society that fed on people's broken dreams.

Olabisi looked at Michael, "You should stop," she said.

Michael stood to his full height. He was bored of this conversation already. He walked to the other side of the table and sat down.

"If you don't get me those two clowns, the deal is off the table. At the very least, we'll need a photograph of the two of them with Bono AND the CEO of Chino-Centric, preferably against a huge background of Chino-Centric's logo. Get the latter and we'll add another US$250K to your fee—that's US$750K in total for your do-good charity. And while you're at it, I think it's time to start making it clear to the world at large that you're Munira's and Baba's go-to handler, because, from where I'm sitting, it doesn't look like anybody knows what's going on."

"I told you I was on it."

"Good," Michael said. He leaned across the table and indulged in one of his favourite past times; looking at her face. His parents knew of Olabisi, and like her parents, didn't much approve of their relationship. They wanted him to settle down with a "nice Chinese woman". But Michael didn't want a nice Chinese woman, he wanted Olabisi.

Olabisi met his gaze squarely.

"Your maid stole from me. Sort it out," he said, standing up. When he got to the door, he blew her a kiss and laughed to himself when she gave him the finger.

Munira tried Olabisi again. She squashed the sigh of relief that threatened to escape from her lips when Olabisi picked up the telephone.

"Olabisi?" She screeched down the phone as was her custom. On the other end, Olabisi wondered if Munira had ever talked in normal decibels.

"Why are you calling me now? I thought you said that the two of you could do this without me?" Olabisi demanded.

"I don't know why you're behaving as if I was the one that did something wrong. Somebody has kidnapped my husband and you're shouting at me. Can I just remind you that without Baba, we're both screwed? So you better get off your high horse quickly, and help me find him," Munira said.

"Fine," Olabisi said. "Don't talk to the media without me. Don't believe anyone who approaches about sponsorship deals without me. Don't talk, don't act, don't do anything, and for the love of God, stop your nonsense in front of the media. Do you think Bono, international superstar, would want to be associated with you if he sees your behaviour in front of the camera?"

Munira went quiet. She hadn't thought that far ahead.

Her one thought had been to generate interest in her acting work.

"Fine," she said, after a brief pause. "Where can we meet?"

"I'll come to the auto-repair shop and make a statement in front of the press. Don't say or do anything before I get there. Think you can manage that?"

Dauda eyed Munira sullenly when she hung up the telephone.

"I've told you that I don't know where your husband is," he said.

"I know you do. Baba is not a bright man. He willingly got into a car with a journalist and sped off, without me, to lord knows where. He would never think of such a thing himself," Munira fanned herself.

"And why did you have to announce to the world that I kidnapped your husband?" Dauda almost screamed at her, but restrained himself. He was glad that Baba got away with Muyiwa. Now, he just had to ensure that he was safe as well.

"If you tell me where he is, I'll tell the police that I was mistaken when they come and pick you up," she said. "This is Nigeria. You know kidnapping is a serious issue, and with this Bono man wanting to meet my husband, everybody is tense. Just tell me where he is and I'll make those accusations go away. You better talk to him," Munira nodded to Mr Sowemimo, the auto-repair shop owner, who had been listening to the conversation with interest. She leaned back on the chair and continued fanning herself, as if she had all the time in the world.

"Oga, boss, I've told you and her a million times: I don't know where Baba is," Dauda repeated.

"Good, then you can tell the police that when they come," Munira said.

Mr Sowemimo trusted no one, but he thought that Dauda might be telling the truth. He didn't like Munira, that much was true, and he liked her useless, old husband even less, but even he drew the line at Dauda being hauled off to Nigeria's notorious police station. He was a young lad, impetuous, rude and a thieving rascal, but he had a good heart. And in all honesty, sending Dauda to the police station, at the mercy of Nigeria's brutal rent-a-police, was a sure-fire way to destroy his young life.

"Munira," he now said, clearing his throat. "I believe Dauda. He doesn't know where Baba is."

"Then why was the reporter here with him this morning, then?" Munira shot back.

Mr Sowemimo looked at Dauda.

"Because I met him standing outside the gate when I opened up this morning. Because he'd already interviewed Baba and he was from the BBC, I knew he was a good person. So I invited him in. How was I to know that he would be telling your husband all kinds of things?"

"You can explain all that to the police," Munira said, looking at her mobile phone screen. There was a text message from the landlord: *The director wants to see you. We are coming to the auto-repair shop.*

Muyiwa had been on his mobile phone from the minute he got in his car. Baba didn't understand what was happening, because he spoke in English the whole time, but two words kept on coming up: BBC and Al-Jazeera.

For a few moments, he missed Olabisi's air-conditioned 4x4 and crisp leather seats. He remembered what Muyiwa said about the police not harassing them or being robber magnets if they were in a rusty, banged-up car and decided that Muyiwa didn't know what he was talking about. In the short while he'd been around Olabisi, they hadn't been harassed by the police. In fact, it would seem that her car and the perfume of wealthy righteousness that enveloped Olabisi, not to mention her attractiveness, cowered the notoriously corrupt Nigerian police into submission. It was a contrast to the way he'd seen the police operate all his life, which was tormenting and torturing people, harassing motorists for money, and even on one occasion murdering them.

Baba didn't want to remember that night, but sometimes, the memories would come. Munira had been in a good mood that week, so when she suggested a night stroll to get them both out of their stuffy hovel, he acquiesced. It was about 7.45pm, and the stars were out in full that night. Munira knew about his obsession with stars and was teasing him. All of a sudden, she had grabbed his arm, put her hand on his mouth, with a look of fear on her face. She pointed and he looked. A few hundred metres away were about five policemen. Palemo was a settlement that had sprung up by a mangrove, and there by a shrub, they could see three naked men. They heard the bullets, a few cries and then, the young men went down. The policemen got into a Black Maria, the car used to transport suspects, and drove off.

Munira and Baba didn't wait. They ran back to their settlement. For days after, they couldn't speak. Munira was bereft.

"Those young men had mothers, ambitions," she would say, and weep silently.

It was the nature of her grief that puzzled Baba. It wasn't the roaring grief that he expected. This was raw, insular. It was only later that he understood that Munira's grief was linked to her own life, to the desperation and frustration of Nigeria, a country with a vampiric appetite for crushing its people's dreams.

She still talked about those young men. "Their mothers will never know what happened to their children," she would say, and her tears would glitter her cheeks.

For all her brashness and abrasiveness, he knew that, fundamentally, Munira's fight was a fight to be seen, to be recognised, to be remembered, and to be heard. In her own way, she saw herself as a voice for the voiceless, for the down-trodden and the hopeless of Nigeria. She was unfaithful, because she saw her body as a means to an end, yet she was loyal to him. Truth was, if he had a choice between a life with or without Munira, he would always choose his life with her. Which brought him back to the present, to Muyiwa's car, and the fact that he'd run away and humiliated her again, in front of the world's media. Baba wasn't worried; he knew things would work out fine. But he had needed to get away. Sometimes, Munira didn't understand that she could only push him so far. Besides, this was the only way to make his displeasure known about her cavorting with the Chinese man. And, he decided, if she didn't stop, he would keep on humiliating her in front of the world.

"Muyiwa, what is all this nonsense? I thought we were going somewhere to help me clear my head?" Baba now asked Muyiwa belligerently. "And why are you using your mobile while you're driving? If the police catch us..."

Muyiwa made a sign to say he would be with Baba in a few moments and continued with his conversation. Baba grew irritated. That was the problem with young people—no respect. Well, he wasn't standing for it. Just as he felt indignation rise within him, he spotted WfN's 4x4 coming towards them, from the opposite direction. His eyes locked on the approaching vehicle, thoughts of its plush interiors and cooled air riveting him. As they passed each other, Olabisi's face coming into clear view, he registered the shock of recognition on Olabisi's face when she saw him in the car, and something akin to fury when she saw Muyiwa. Baba saw her tap Kayode, her driver's shoulder and her hands motioned for Kayode to turn around and follow them. Baba looked at Muyiwa. He was still talking on his mobile, oblivious to the events of the last few moments.

"Muyiwa," he began.

Muyiwa motioned to him to be quiet. Once again, Baba heard Al-Jazeera, which he recognised to be the news channel.

"Muyiwa..." Baba tried to get his attention again.

Muyiwa turned his car into a side street and was attempting to park so he could continue his phone call without threat of ambush by the bullying police, when he got blocked by WfN's 4x4. Baba and Muyiwa watched in stunned silence as Olabisi jumped out of the car, and banged on Muyiwa's bonnet screaming curses at him. Baba was surprised; he could not believe that Olabisi's Yoruba extended to the hardcore vernacular she was employing.

Baba looked at Muyiwa. "That's why it's good to listen to your elders. I'm tired of this nonsense. I just want some peace and quiet. After this, you will remember to treat your elders better," and with that, Baba got out of the car and walked towards Olabisi.

"Olabisi, it's enough," he spoke gently, as a father to a daughter. "Enough of this nonsense. Let's go to your office," he told her.

Turning Olabisi banged on Muyiwa's bonnet once again for impact, and stomped back to her 4x4, Baba in tow. By the time Muyiwa realised what was happening, Baba and Olabisi had driven off.

On his mobile phone, the Al-Jazeera contact that he'd been playing off against his BBC manager and editor, so that he could secure a promotion (or good defection, depending on what Al-Jazeera paid), waited for confirmation of their meeting place to interview Baba. Muyiwa could only look at his mobile phone, wondering how he'd lost his ticket to professional fame and fortune for the second time in as many days.

In the 4x4, Baba yawned. Kayode and Olabisi didn't even bother being discreet; they covered their noses.

"Baba, I'm going to call Munira and let her know that you're safe and that we'll be in my office. I'll send for another car to go and pick her up at the auto-repair shop. I'm sure that she wouldn't want to be seen hailing a cab, being that she's the wife of someone who's about to be famous," Olabisi said with a smile.

"Do what you want," Baba said. In a few moments, it seemed like he was asleep.

Munira hung up her mobile phone and announced to all that Baba was with Olabisi. "Although, I still believe that you knew something about this plan with Muyiwa, I'll leave it for now," she said.

Dauda sighed in relief. He had not wanted to spend the night in jail. As for how Baba managed to get out of Muyiwa's grasp and into Olabisi's claws, he wasn't even sure he wanted to know how. Whatever happened, he would ensure he got his money from Muyiwa. The deal had been to deliver Baba to Muyiwa, which he had done. Whatever happened after was Muyiwa's business, and problem as it turned out.

"I told you I didn't know anything," he said, looking at Mr Sowemimo, his boss.

"Munira, if the boy says he doesn't know anything, then, he doesn't. At least, we know where Baba is. Please tell the hordes outside that your husband is alive and well," Mr Sowemimo. He had thought that the publicity would bring in extraordinary business to the auto-repair shop, but so far, all he had were news people asking him the same questions and lots of people taking pictures outside his auto-repair shop. He couldn't help but wish they would be involved in a freakish mass car accident, and his auto-repair shop would be flooded with business.

"Anyway, I've had enough of this nonsense. I have other auto-repair shops to run." He looked at Dauda straight in the eye. "If I find out that you were involved in this whatever-you-want-to-call-it with Muyiwa, like Munira says, you will regret the day you set foot in this auto-repair shop. You hear me? And this goes for you, Dimeji, as well, looking as if butter won't melt in your stupid mouth." Mr Sowemimo gave them both a stern look. "Now, get back to work," he ordered. "And Munira, please, after today, you and your husband should find somewhere else to host your business, because you're hurting my own," and with that, Mr Sowemimo bid them all goodbye.

"If it wasn't for me, nobody would know about this rat's arse you call an auto-repair shop," Munira hissed.

"Actually, if it wasn't for me, all of this wouldn't have happened," Dauda corrected, to a blistering glare from Munira.

"Yes, yes. Can we just get back to work, now?" Dimeji said.

"What about her?" Dauda jerked his head towards Munira.

"Let it go, Dauda," Dimeji urged.

Munira ignored them both. The first thing she would

do when they got their money from Olabisi would be to buy out this auto-repair shop, if only for the satisfaction of seeing Dauda out on the street. She would keep Dimeji on, though. He was a nice lad. The landlord had said that the director would meet her at the auto-repair shop, which suited her fine. She didn't want any meetings in her home, because she was embarrassed, and she didn't want the director to have an idea about her, before she auditioned. If she met him at the auto-repair shop, he would see the world's media camped outside and immediately give her the respect she required. She only hoped that they would arrive before Olabisi's driver came to pick her up.

Thirty minutes later, there was a banging on the gate. Dimeji let in Munira's landlord, who was accompanied by a young girl.

Munira didn't bother getting up from her chair. "I thought you said the director was coming?" she asked coldly. She was in no mood for games.

The landlord walked across to where she was sitting and laughed. "Yes, she is," he said, pointing at the lady that had come with him.

Munira looked at the girl, then back to the landlord. Dauda and Dimeji didn't even pretend they were working. They both stood, arms akimbo waiting to see the drama that would inevitably follow.

"It's a woman," Munira said, as if talking to herself.

"Ma, I'm a film graduate," the girl said.

Munira flew out of her chair and lunged at the landlord.

## 10

Munira had been uncharacteristically quiet since she'd been dropped off by the driver. If Olabisi didn't know better, she would think she was wounded, only she knew Munira had rhinoceros skin, and technically, was incapable of sustaining any wounds.

She tapped the papers in her hands in an attempt to grab Munira and her husband's attention.

"So, I will call a press conference for an hour and announce that WfN is in partnership with you, and that we are handling all your media appearances. I just need you to sign this contract..."

"I'm not signing anything I haven't read," Munira said.

"Very well," Olabisi said, the two of them knowing full well that Munira had a reading age of a nine year old. "I suggest you get started now—"

"Maybe we should get Dauda to read it for us—" Baba began.

"I said I would read it," Munira snapped, snatching the papers from Olabisi's hands.

"Very well, then," Baba said. He sat back down, across the table from Olabisi.

"Are you just going to stand there while I read this thing?" Munira asked, jerking her head towards Olabisi. She was seated next to her husband.

"Munira, are you okay?" Olabisi asked. She made as if to reach out across the table, lay her hand on Munira's shoulder, thought better of it, and then withdrew her hand.

Baba looked at his wife. He hoped that black mood wasn't coming back again. Usually, he could detect the signs. Munira would behave erratically for a few days. She would be forgetful, leave tasks half-done or even, abandon them completely, before eventually, going to bed and staying there for days or weeks.

"Muni—" Baba took her hand.

Munira snatched her hand out of Baba's. "Don't 'Muni' me. You were the one who hatched a plan with Dauda to try and rob me of what's mine. But I won't let you, you hear me, I won't let you. Why are people always trying to steal from me?" She asked, looking at Baba and Olabisi. A tear trickled out of an eye and down her left cheek. She didn't even bother wiping it away.

Baba and Olabisi looked at each other, perplexed.

"Muni..." Baba tried to talk again.

"Just shut up and let me read this contract," Munira snapped again, knowing full well that she wasn't going to read anything. The only thing she would look out for on the contract were hers and Baba's names, and the figures cited next to their names. It was something she'd learned from one of her teachers in secondary school.

"We've booked a room in a nearby hotel for the press conference, so I suggest that we get going. I thought you would both want to freshen up at the hotel before the conference. Baba, there is a shower at the room we've booked for you and Munira," Olabisi pulled out a drawer under her table and pushed a toothpaste and toothbrush towards Baba, pointedly.

Munira attempted to read her way through the contract, but gave up the pretense. "Where should we sign? We need ink for Baba's thumbprint," she said.

Olabisi produced the ink, forcing herself to breathe evenly.

"So, where is the bit that says you will pay us US$50K, again?" Munira asked. She should've listened to Baba and got Dauda or Dimeji to look at this contract for them, but her pride would not allow it.

Olabisi came round the table and pointed to a few lines in the contract.

"And where are our names?" Munira asked. Olabisi pointed to another section of the contract.

"Hold on. What about our deposit?"

"There is no deposit. You get the full US$50K when Bono comes to Abuja and agrees to be photographed with you and Baba, at a Chino-Centric dinner. Chino-Centric has also agreed to back your next film, and if Baba wishes, they want to sponsor him to go to school," Olabisi said smoothly.

"And you, what do you get out of all this?" Munira asked.

"Don't worry too much about that. Just sign and let's go to the hotel. We just about have time for Baba to get ready. I hope you don't mind, but I've also asked for some clothes to be delivered to the hotel for you. I thought you would want to look your best in front of all those cameras."

Munira felt like she was missing something, she just wasn't sure what. But, at this point, she was tired, weary of it all. Of fighting. She'd spent her whole life fighting.

"Very well, then," she said, her voice low and sombre. "Let's go."

They bundled out of the office and into the car. As soon as they left, the receptionist turned off the air-conditioner and blasted Olabisi's office with air freshener.

The crowd outside the auto-repair shop had dispersed, for which Dauda was grateful. He saw on BBC World Service that Baba and Munira were with the rich lady and there was going to be a press conference.

As he sat on the bench, the sweet seller rolled past him again.

"Why don't you come and rest next to me?" he patted the empty space on the bench he was sitting on.

The girl stopped and smiled, which in itself startled Dauda; he was expecting her to cuss him as was her norm.

"Maybe, when I finish," she said, and started walking again, her tray of sweets on her head.

"What's your name?" Dauda called after her.

"Morenike."

Morenike. Dauda tasted the name on his lips and decided that he liked it. Across the road, Mama Seyi gave him a knowing smile.

Dimeji came out of the auto-repair shop, wiping his hands on a rag. He sat next to Dauda on the bench.

Dauda liked dusk. It was his favourite time of the day. The sun would've gone down somewhat, the Lagos traffic would be gearing up for its evening phase, and he and Dimeji, and until recently, Baba, would sit on the bench and offer a running commentary on the world outside.

"The radio station keeps on calling me about the plane ticket. They said that if Baba doesn't mention the station when he meets Mosquito Man, they'll sue us, because that's what's in the contract," Dauda said, when Dimeji sat down.

"Ignore them. This is Nigeria, who has money or time to sue people? And the airline donated the ticket, so technically, you're not beholden to the radio station anyway," Dimeji said.

The airline. Dauda had forgotten about them. They were supposed to take a picture of Bono and Baba in front of the plane.

"I swear, this whole thing is so silly. If I had known that it would come to this, I would never have called that radio station."

Dimeji yawned. "Yes, you would."

They were silent for a few moments. "How much do you think Mama Seyi has made in the last few days?" Dimeji asked.

"Enough to give us a free meal until the end of the month, at least," Dauda replied. Across the road, Mama Seyi dished out some food and motioned to her son, Fela, to take them to Dauda and Dimeji.

Fela was ten years old and his mother's only child. Dauda and Dimeji watched as Mama Seyi cautioned him to wait until the road was clear before giving him the signal to cross the road. They waved their hands in appreciation. Mama Seyi gave them a beatific smile in return.

"Do you think she thinks about her other son, Seyi?" Dauda asked as they dived into the *akara*, bean balls and *dundun*, fried yams.

"I'm sure she does," Dimeji replied. "Be careful with that BBC journalist, Muyiwa. I know you think I'm stupid, but whatever you're planning, be careful."

"I know what I'm doing," Dauda said.

They continued eating.

The room was packed. It seemed as if every media agency in the world had sent their reporters to the press conference. Michael still didn't understand how Olabisi had retrieved Baba from the BBC journalist and he didn't much care, either. His people were happy, and their happiness brought him one step closer to his dream of building a casino in Nigeria.

The casino was a chance to do something different. He wanted something like Macau in China and Vegas in the States. Every visionary was once thought of as insane, and in time, they proved their detractors wrong.

He wasn't concerned about security issues or what he referred to as the so-called terrorist threat in northern Nigeria, because he knew what the so-called terrorists got up in their private time. They were no different from the Taliban in

Afghanistan or Isis in Syria, quoting the Koran in one hand, while with the other they were trading and raping young children. They were foul. They were also good people to do business with. Nigeria might be the most religious country on earth—every third building was either a mosque or a church—but the people were also the most enterprising. What they professed and what they did were two different things, and as long as they themselves did not see a contradiction in their actions, they didn't see why anybody else should have a problem with it.

As for him, he wasn't religiously minded. His parents were atheist. They had no allegiance to any deity, except the present, and were too busy amassing wealth to bother about the next life. They'd been to Nigeria a few times and benefited immensely from Michael's connections to the business world, there. Last Michael heard, his father was making inroads in Madagascar. Something to do with spices, he wasn't sure. He wondered if Olabisi had fired her maid yet.

Thinking about the maid made him think about Munira. She wasn't his type, but she also exuded a crass confidence that somehow made him want her. What drew her to someone like Baba, he could only guess. From Munira, his thoughts went to Bono, the Mosquito Man. He liked his music, but disliked his do-good preaching about saving the world. Still, it would be interesting to find out what the man was like in real life, which brought him back to the present; the crammed meeting room of the hotel that Olabisi had ambitiously called 'the Bono conference'. He hoped that everything would go smoothly.

Earlier he had heard the shrill screech of the microphone as Olabisi's staff did sound checks. Now as he waited, the roar of about one hundred eager journalists quietened down to a lull when Olabisi entered, striding purposefully at the head of the group, followed by Munira, proudly thrusting forward with her immaculate breasts on display and Baba, who looked miserable like a deer caught in headlights.

Michael had chosen to stand at the back of the hall. He didn't want undue attention on himself, certainly not from Munira. All eyes were on her as Olabisi leaned into the microphone. She paused, triumphantly surveying the room, then opened her mouth to talk, when simultaneously from beside her came the ruptured sounds of an emancipated fart. A second passed, and the entire front row of journalists covered their noses as a noxious fume permeated the air. Olabisi gagged and shut her mouth quickly. Two seats away from her, Munira pinched Baba so hard he squealed, emitting an even more riotous and pungent fart.

Behind her on the dais, Olabisi's enterprising receptionist dug into her tote bag and retrieved a mini body spray with which she discreetly perfumed the air. As the sweet floral scent took precedence over the recent rancid odour that still faintly lingered in the air, it seemed to revitalise Olabisi who drew near to the microphone once again and began speaking.

"As you can see, Bono, whom our intrepid adventurer has called the Mosquito Man, has quite a colourful character to acquaint himself with," she began.

The room erupted in laughter. There was even a minute

of clapping. Michael breathed in a bit easier. They just might get away with this after all.

Watching Olabisi, Munira caught a glimpse of what her life could be like if she was famous and loved. Earlier they had agreed that Olabisi would speak for them. Knowing what Baba was like in stressful situations like this, she had slipped a tablet into his soft drink, at the hotel. The chemist had said that it would just make him less of himself. He hadn't mentioned the farting bit. Not that she minded. This way, Baba was manageable.

Surreptitiously, she watched Olabisi as she answered the journalists' questions. She didn't seem flustered, instead she was taking in the scene before her, as if it was her due. Munira wished she was like Olabisi. If she had been born with the same opportunities, maybe she would've gone to London, studied and come back to Nigeria to live life on her own terms, instead of continually chaffing against society's expectations and limitations of her. She heard her name being called and wondered if she should get up. She looked at Olabisi for guidance and Olabisi nodded slightly. As Munira got up, she heard a thud, looked to her left and saw that Baba's head had hit the table. A few seconds later, she heard him snoring. Anger rose within her. It was typical of him to ruin her moment in the limelight with his thoughtlessness. She let out an 'argh' of frustration and gave him a few angry shoves on his back. The room came alive with cameras flashing, as her actions were captured and broadcast live to the world.

## 11

In the audience, Muyiwa watched the events unfolding before him. Somehow, he wasn't surprised that Baba had chosen to sleep during the conference. He was learning that, with him, one just had to expect the unexpected. In a way, he was glad that it happened. Baba, Munira and all the rest of the people who colluded against him were now reaping the rewards of their evil. He cast a particularly baleful eye at Olabisi, who, at that moment, chose to look directly at him. When she caught his eye, she gave a cold stare and in the same gaze, dismissed him, as an empress would dismiss an eunuch.

*Witch!* He screamed inside. They exchanged a cordial smile, well-removed from the shouting session they'd descended into a few hours earlier.

Muyiwa was undeterred. He still had a lot riding on Baba. His Al-Jazeera contact was also at the press conference. Their deal had been simple. Muyiwa would bring Baba to a secret location and record an exclusive interview with him, which would be broadcasted on Al-Jazeera. In return, he would be made their West Africa correspondent, essentially, the same job he had with the BBC, but with much better perks and infinitely more dollars in his pocket.

He loved and respected the BBC, but Al-Jazeera loved and respected his right to earn a decent salary and an equally respectable standard of living.

As he almost subconsciously scanned the room, always on the lookout for a developing story, he spotted Michael Li hovering in the background. Somehow, he wasn't surprised to see him at there. On paper, he was described as a 'consultant', but Muyiwa knew that he was involved in at least three of the biggest building contracts ever awarded to foreign investors, on Nigerian soil. He also knew that he was Olabisi's consort, the NGO worker who continued to scandalise traditional Nigerian society with her independent lifestyle. Muwiya sighed hard, his eyes on Olabisi. She didn't give a damn. And being rich, she wasn't required to give a damn. Her father was one of Nigeria's 'godfathers', shadowy figures who controlled the country's economy and political stage. She needed the legitimacy of Baba's dream the most.

Muyiwa folded his arms in frustration. He hated his country. Idly, he wondered about Michael Li's investment in Baba's story and filed it away as something to investigate. As Olabisi and her guests got up to leave a glass of water toppled spilling its content all over the conference table. Baba was being carried away by two men. As they reached the room's exit, Munira turned around and spoke in pidgin, broken English, "I am actress. Come back again."

Muyiwa saw Olabisi hasten her along and they exited the room. The room emptied of journalists shortly after. Muyiwa hung around, not even sure why himself. As he started packing up his rucksack, he saw Michael slip into the room that Olabisi and her disastrous entourage had entered, about ten minutes earlier. He didn't think twice, he followed. As he entered the room, he saw Michael Li propped up against the wall, as if he was waiting for someone.

"I suggest you turn back," Li said conversationally, as if he and Muyiwa were talking about the weather. Muyiwa stopped, looked around and then back to Michael.

"Yes, you. I said, 'Turn back'." Michael's tone was conversational, but there was no denying the threat in his voice.

Muyiwa hesitated for a few moments, then turned back. If he didn't know before, he now knew that there was a story between Munira, Olabisi and Michael Li that needed investigating. He just had to find it.

In their hotel room, which Olabisi had designated 'campaign HQ', Baba was laid out on the bed, snoring heavily, a thin drool seeping out of his mouth. Michael looked at him distastefully, with dull eyes, that when settled upon Munira, resplendent in a kaftan that skimmed over her corpulent body and showed off her abundant breasts, lit up.

His thoughts tumbled around in his head.

He preferred his women to be skinny, like Olabisi.

He didn't know why he was so attracted to Munira.

He wanted to sleep with her and sink his mouth into her magnificent breasts. But he knew that if he did, he would lose Olabisi. And there was no one like Olabisi.

Munira was shouting at someone on her mobile. "Dauda,

I told him he's fine. And stop calling me, otherwise I'll call the police on you, again," she was breathing heavily as she spoke. She listened for a few moments, then spoke coldly. "You can tell the radio station and airline to stick their ticket where the sun doesn't shine. And I don't know why you're going on about Baba signing a contract. He's illiterate: how do I know that you and the radio station did not coerce him into putting his thumb print on something he couldn't even read anyway?" Munira shook her head and continued. "Goodbye, Dauda. And I'm telling you again: if you call me, I'll call the police on you. Go deal with the radio station yourself. You brought this on yourself," she said, and she hung up.

She looked up from her mobile and a wide smile came on her face when she saw Michael in the room. Olabisi gave Michael a warning look. Michael crossed the room, and knelt down by her, taking Munira's hands in his.

"Munira!" he exclaimed, as if they were old friends. "How are you?" He gestured towards Baba's softly snoring body, "and this your husband..."

"He'll come round soon. I think I overdid it, this time," she spoke offhandedly.

Watching and listening to the two of them, Olabisi wondered if she'd been transported to an alternate universe. She had expected Michael to come charging into the hotel room, with eviscerating words about what happened at the press conference and a few threats about withdrawing his financial support from the deal. Failing that, she also thought that he might leave the hotel and call from his car or home, so he could give full rein to his anger.

She had pictured different scenarios, but not this. Him fawning over Munira. There was something off, but she didn't know what.

"Michael!" she snapped him to attention. Turning to Munira she asked, "Can we talk about what happened at the conference?"

Munira eyed her, gathered her clothes and deigned to give Olabisi her full attention.

"Very well, then," Munira said.

Olabisi reined in her temper with difficulty. "Munira, what did you do to your husband?"

"Don't worry, it's nothing. He'll be awake soon and then, we'll call another conference," she said.

*Are you stupid?* Olabisi wanted to scream at her. *Do you know what it takes to summon a conference of that magnitude?*

She took a deep breath.

"Actually, it's everything. Because of what you did, I would be surprised if the Mosquito Man was still interested in meeting you and Baba," and before she could stop herself, the words spewed out. "What kind of a marriage is this, that a woman drugs her own husband and talks as if it's normal? And don't deny it. I know you did something. I *know*."

Munira stood drawing herself up to her full height. Michael put a restraining hand on her shoulder. "It's okay, Munira. We don't have to do this, now. Let's just find a way to deal with this," he said soothingly.

Olabisi looked at him. What was going on with Michael?

171

Her mobile rang. There were a few 'yes' and 'hmmm' and then she hung up.

"That was Bono's people. They said they're not interested in meeting Baba and that if we continue using his name in association with our shenanigans, they'll take us to court," she said. She drew up a table and sat down, breathing heavily. Then, she stood up and started shoving papers into her bag. Michael and Munira watched her silently. Olabisi finished packing her bags and left the room. As she left, she heard Munira say, "Just to be clear: my husband and I are not paying for this room and you guys still owe us for our 'performance' today!"

Dauda found Morenike outside the auto-repair shop, waiting for him.

"What time do you finish?" he asked her.

"Whenever I finish selling whatever is on my tray," she told him.

"Maybe you should come by when you're done," he said.

"I'm not sleeping with you," Morenike said.

Dauda made as if she had struck a dagger at his chest. "Maybe, me too, I don't want to sleep with you," he said.

They both laughed. A silence fell between them. Morenike shifted her feet and then, hauled her tray of sweets to her head.

As she walked away, she called out to him. "I'll come back," she said.

Dauda grinned and went back to the auto-repair shop.

Immediately, he went to a car and wrenched out a part, which he pocketed. That would cover the meal he was taking Morenike out to tonight. He tried not to think about Baba. He was certain that he was okay. For all their fractious relationship, he knew that Munira would never harm her husband. She was fond of him. Nonetheless, he was concerned about Baba. The man did not react well to stress. He didn't like being in enclosed spaces, in crowds or unfamiliar surroundings. Under such situations, most people took on a fight or flight stance, whereas Baba's was to have a meltdown.

As usual, thinking about Munira increased his stress levels. She had the plane tickets to Abuja, and the radio station and airline had been calling him nonstop, asking for their goods back. And if he knew Munira, she would sell those tickets, pocket the money and pretend she'd either lost them or that she never had them in the first place.

No, he wouldn't think about Munira and Baba. Instead, he would think about Morenike, the sweet seller. He had been surprised when she stopped and asked for his name. A part of him knew she was only interested in him, because of Baba, while the other part reasoned that even if that was the case, by the time she realised the truth, which is that he was a good, decent, human being, she would like him for himself.

She lived locally, which suited Dauda just fine. He hoped she had a sister or cousin of some sort that she could introduce Dimeji to. The guy was great, but he was much too serious. For a few moments, he allowed himself to daydream about he and Dimeji going on double dates with Morenike's sister/cousin/friend. The daydream turned sour, when out of nowhere a white man wearing mosquito sunglasses appeared on his fantasy double date and started flirting with Morenike.

Dauda opened his eyes and cursed the Mosquito Man with impotence, wherever he was.

He wished he'd never called the radio station. Yes, he wanted clean water supply for Palemo, but the cost was proving too much to bear. He took out his mobile and punched in a number. "Muyiwa, we need to talk. You owe me money," he barked into the phone. As he hung up, he looked up to see Dimeji shake his head at him.

"One day, if you're not careful, you'll shake your head so hard it'll fall off. And where will you be?" Dauda asked irritably.

## 12

The next day, Muyiwa went back to the auto-repair shop. He arrived just as Dauda was opening up and could be heard-telling a few stragglers with annoyance, "I've told you that Baba is not here and I don't know what is happening with the Mosquito Man, either. But let me know if you find out."

His face hardened briefly when he turned around to see Muyiwa. The stragglers, a few boys, still hung around.

"Maybe you were the one that did something to him," one of them said. "The way he passed out in that press conference was not normal. Somebody did something to him."

"Just you wait," Dauda said, running inside. When he came out with an iron rod in his hand, the stragglers were gone.

"Maybe you should carry that with you everywhere you go, now," Muyiwa offered.

Dauda ignored him. Across the road, Mama Seyi called out to him. "Dauda! Fela is bringing your breakfast."

Dauda had wanted to go back inside, but waited for Fela to bring his breakfast of steaming akara with ogi, a traditional porridge made from fermented maize. As Fela handed him his breakfast, Dauda rubbed the boy's head in affection and cautioned him to wait for the road to clear, before telling him to cross the road back to his mother. His older brother, Seyi, had died on this very road a few years before, in a horrific car accident.

"You can't ignore me forever," Muyiwa said when Dauda went back in with his steaming breakfast.

Dauda stopped walking and turned around. "Have you got my money?"

"Have I interviewed Baba?" Muyiwa shot back.

Dauda ignored him. He fired up the television using the car battery, and proceeded to eat his breakfast.

Dimeji came in and took in the situation at a glance.

"Good morning," Muyiwa greeted him.

"Morning," Dimeji replied. He changed into his overalls and went outside. A few moments later, they heard him call out to Mama Seyi to bring him breakfast.

"Where is my money?" Dauda spoke quietly.

"You know as well as I do that I don't have it," Muyiwa answered. "But the deal is still on. I think there's something more to this matter. I saw that Chinese—"

Dauda got up and marched to Muyiwa. "Chinese man, uh? Chinese man? My end of the deal was to deliver Baba to you, which I did. Now you sit here, talking to me about Chinese men," Dauda breathed in slowly, to steady his breathing. "Do you know what you have done?"

Muyiwa stood up. "That's what I'm trying to tell you: all is not lost. All you need to do is try and get Baba again..."

"Get out," Dauda spoke through clenched teeth.

Dimeji peered through the gates. "Morenike is here," he announced.

Dauda pulled himself together and left Muyiwa inside the shop. At the sight of Morenike, his mood lifted considerably. She looked even better than she did yesterday.

They'd had such a nice time. After finishing her round, she'd been true to her word and had come back to the shop. They'd sat on the bench, bought some suya and spoke. He couldn't even remember what they talked about, but he knew that it made him feel good every time he made her laugh. At about 8pm, she'd stood up and said that she had to go home, otherwise her father would worry. She'd held up her phone and counted the missed calls: "Ten!" she said.

"Is your father over-protective?" Dauda had asked.

"Yes," she had said, smiling. "We pray together every morning, and then, before leaving the house, he lays hands on our heads and prays for our protection."

Great, Dauda had thought, a religious nutter.

And now, seeing her first thing in the morning, before she started pounding the streets of Lagos, hawking her sweets, somehow he felt better.

He leaned on the gates and scuffed his rubber slippers on the ground. "Morning," he said. He was aware that he was smiling like an idiot, but somehow, he couldn't stop himself.

"Morning," Morenike replied, giving him a shy smile.

Muyiwa appeared. He gave her an assessing look, and Dauda saw something flicker across his face.

"Dauda, we'll talk later," Muyiwa told him, and walked to his car. He gave Morenike one last look as he got in and drove away.

"I have to go," Morenike said. "But, I'll come back."

"I'll be here," Dauda said. He gave her one big smile and watched her walk down the street. He turned to go back to the auto-repair shop, while across the street Mama Seyi gave him a coy, knowing look.

He waved at her and went inside the auto-repair shop.

Munira couldn't sleep. At dawn, she slipped out of the hotel bed and took up position by the window, watching as Lagos woke up. She liked this time of the morning. The air was relatively clean, the traffic was just starting to build up. On the bed, Baba still slept on, apparently comatose.

Munira sighed. She'd over-drugged him on purpose. The press conference was so important that she felt that she couldn't possibly take any chances with Baba. She took a sip of her Lipton tea. It wasn't as hot as she liked it, but it would do for now. It was strong, sweet and thickly laced with condensed milk.

She pondered on yesterday's events, the landlord who had come with the young film graduate. He had promised her another director, the one everyone was talking about, who had even won a FESPACO award. Instead, he'd come with some girl he was sleeping with.

Munira hissed. On the bed, finally, Baba yawned. Munira went back to her tea. A film graduate! The landlord was fortunate she hadn't brained him. When he said the girl was a film graduate, a red mist had descended upon Munira. In truth, she barely remembered lunging at the landlord, but she did remember being pulled away from him, and a voice someone saying that someone called Kayode was there to pick her up and take her to Baba. She had fixed herself, reapplied her make-up and walked out of the auto-repair shop to face the cameras smiling.

Now, she looked at her mobile screen. There were several missed calls from the landlord.

Baba yawned again. "Munira..." he called out softly.

Munira put down her tea and went over to him. Baba looked terrible. She hoped the chemist hadn't given her fake pills. Baba opened one eye and yawned without closing his mouth. Munira covered her nose and turned away. His breath was foul. Michael Li had said they could stay in the hotel for another night, that she need not worry about Olabisi, because he would handle her.

"Munira," Baba called out again.

Munira took one of his hands in hers, still covering her mouth with her other hand.

"Baba, what happened?! One minute we were talking and you were about to tell the world what you would say to the Mosquito Man, and the next pfffft! God will punish your enemies and those who try to scupper our work!" she exclaimed.

Baba disengaged his hand from hers. "I know what you did; you're a witch," he said.

Munira got off the bed and went to sit by the window again. There was no point in talking to Baba when he got ideas in his head.

Baba rolled out of the bed, yawned and went to the bathroom. "I need to eat," he said to nobody in particular. Munira ignored him. Outside, the city was was moving. She heard Baba pee noisily in the toilet and burp at the same time. He was foul. He came out of the bathroom scratching his balls, complaining about how hungry he was, and how Munira had drugged him because she wanted to steal from him.

When Munira couldn't take it any longer, she marched to his face and screamed. "Yes, I drugged you, you useless old man! Because, I'm tired of you, of this life. Because you fail to live up to your responsibilities as a man. Because, thanks to you, I live like an animal and if I'm not careful, I'm in danger of dying like one. In Ibadan my life was hard, but never did I imagine that it would turn out like this. And it's because of men like you. Men like my school teachers. Men like the landlord. It's always you men. Everything you touch, you corrupt!"

When she finished, she was breathing heavily with tears coming down her cheeks. She wiped them off angrily and went back to her position by the window. The tears kept on falling. This time, she didn't make any attempt to wipe them off.

Baba stood there, undecided. He feared another episode of her darkness on the way. The Mosquito Man had been a bad idea from the beginning. If it all went to pots, he was genuinely afraid of what it would do to Munira's mental state. His stomach growled. He sat on the bed. "I still need to eat," he said, hating himself. But truth was, he didn't know what to do. Left to him, he would happily go back to his simple life of being verbally abused by Mama Seyi and made fun of by Dauda and Dimeji. Those people knew him, and even then, his life had a routine. This new life had way too many variables and people with hidden intentions that he had no way of deciphering. Take this hotel for instance. Given a choice, he would've liked to have gone back to Palemo to sleep in his own room. He knew his way around the room. Here, he was tiptoeing, afraid to touch one thing, terrified of breaking another. Munira had been helping herself to drinks from the fridge, and had even stored some of the chocolate in their bags. She said that it was fine, because they weren't paying for it. Yet, it filled Baba with unease.

Munira wiped the tears off her face and blew her nose noisily into a handkerchief.

"Maybe we should call Olabisi," Baba said.

Munira looked at him as if he was stupid. "And do what? What makes you think that she would want to have anything to do with us after what happened at the conference? The farting was one thing, but you passing out... How do you think she felt?" She asked him, speaking slowly, as if to a fool.

"You tell me. You're the one that drugged me," he shot back at her. "In any case, we can't stay here. Who's going to pay for all this?"

"Michael Li has paid for us to stay until tomorrow,"

Munira said. Her mobile phone bleeped and she picked it up.

"What?" she said to the caller. Baba thought he heard the landlord's voice on the other end of the line. Whatever he was saying displeased Munira so much she hung up on him.

"Was that the landlord?" Baba asked her.

"What's it to you?" Munira shot back. "Go shower and brush your teeth. And don't even think of looking for that wretched chewing stick, because I threw it away when you were sleeping. We are high class people now. How many rich people do you know use chewing stick? And I hope you left the bathroom in a reasonable state after dumping your innards in the toilet. In fact, just wait for me and let me show you how to use the shower before you disgrace me further."

Munira went into the bathroom. "Baba! What happened in here?!" she yelled.

At the WfN headquarters, Olabisi sat, staring into space. She had to deploy a new tactic with Munira and her husband, she just didn't know what. Her office door opened and Michael Li came in.

"Who let you in?" she asked him irritably.

Michael smiled. "And good morning to you, too," he said. "Sleep well?"

He came round her desk, put his hand under her chin and assessed her face. He made as if to kiss her and she batted him away.

"Did you sleep with her?"

Michael kissed her. "No, and I won't. I really want to,

though," he said. He kissed her again, then tapped her desk.

"Enough of the self-pity. There's work to do," he told her. "Call Kayode. We're going to the hotel. You'll call Bono's people again and then, you'll call another conference. And this time, you will nail it."

"Those two—" Olabisi began.

"Those two nothing," Michael said firmly. He stood up and helped her up as well. "Here's something to make you laugh. I called the hotel this morning and they said that Munira and her husband had been ordering room service and partying like mad."

Olabisi picked up her bag and laughed. Poor Munira, she really didn't know Michael. She linked her elbow through Michael's.

"I still don't like it when you start flirting with her," she said.

"Let's not belabour the point. I've already told you that I'm not going to sleep with her. About your maid, have you sacked her yet? Just remember that I'm the person she stole from."

"Why does it matter so much to you if I sack her? And I'm sure she didn't 'steal' that much anyway. Let it go," Olabisi said, still smiling.

Michael would not let it go, but he also knew that this was not the time to argue with Olabisi. He shuddered to think what would happen if she found out that he had been sleeping with her maid. To the world, Olabisi might present a front of liberalism and defender of the downtrodden, but she would

183

draw the line at sharing her lover with a lowly maid from the backwaters of Nigeria. Her pride would not allow it.

He opened her office door and they both stepped out into the wider WfN office.

"We're off to a meeting. We'll be back soon," Olabisi called.

"Yes, madam," the receptionist said. Michael smiled at her. She had been a good lay. Discreet, unlike Olabisi's maid. Only thing was that he'd gotten bored with her. He still gave her money though, for services well performed, so to speak.

As they settled in the car, Olabisi wondered what she would find at the hotel. Sometimes, she was frightened by her own desperation and ambition. She wanted so badly for her charity to succeed, she could almost taste it. She knew what people thought of her, but she didn't care. Or, at least she pretended that she didn't. And it had been that way all her life.

Her mother had been her father's favourite mistress and to her father's credit, he had provided well for her education. He made sure she went to the best schools, just like his other children. She and her mother lived a few streets away from him and his family, which she understood, as she grew older, was because it was convenient. She went to all her father's birthday and office parties, without her mother who, as the mistress, was uninvited. When the driver dropped her off home, to her mother's, she always knew that her father would come by later that night to see them.

She endured those parties. Standing at the edges, not sure

where she belonged, and watching as her father, his wife and three children would pose for photos. Then, her father would signal for her to join them. If anyone ever wondered or thought that it was strange that she was joining the photos, they didn't say anything. As for her father's wife, she approached Olabisi as one whose presence was to be endured. She was cordial to her, never said an unkind word to her, and on numerous occasions Olabisi overhead her admonishing her children to treat her kindly, "because, no matter what happens, you're still siblings."

Her father owned mining and oil blocks. She knew what Nigerian society said about him being a gangster and a so-called godfather, but as far as she was concerned, that was their perception. Her father, the man she knew, was a good man. Someone who had sponsored thousands of people into education. Someone who told her heroic stories about his childhood poverty and his fortuitous big break. Someone who told her, a long time ago, that she was and always would be, the apple of his eye.

He did not approve of her lifestyle choices, which was why she stayed away from him. And since her mother's death, all he did was lecture her.

Her mother had passed away from cancer and Olabisi had been there when she died. As she listened to her mother's laboured breathing, Olabisi determined that nobody, especially not a man, would have mastery over her life. In her lucid moments, her mother would talk about her early days of courtship with her father.

"He was so handsome," she would say.

"He was married, mother. Did you ever think about that?" Olabisi told her once, rather tartly.

Her mother had given her a pitying smile. "One day, when you're older, you'll understand that sometimes, you make life choices and live out the results..."

"Like you did. You talk about Jesus all the time and by the same token, you've been a mistress to the same man for practically all your life."

Her mother had looked away. "God will forgive me," she said. "I did what I had to do to get out of my situation."

Olabisi had felt bad, then. "I'm sorry," she whispered.

Her mother had met Michael. And the only thing she said to Olabisi was, "Don't make the same mistake I did. You deserve someone of your own."

Maybe her mother had seen something of herself in her daughter.

In the car, Michael reached out and patted her hand. "Thinking of your mother?" he asked.

He knew so well. She nodded.

"She was nice to me. Probably the only mother in Nigeria who didn't hate Chinese people," Michael said, smiling.

Olabisi gave him a grateful smile. Kayode, the driver swung the car up the hotel driveway. Olabisi took in a deep breath. Unlike her mother, she wasn't religious, but she did pray that she wouldn't find a mess at the hotel.

Kayode parked the car. Olabisi breathed in deeply again and got out. She and Michael headed for the hotel reception.

Technically, a buka was a roadside food stall. They're also reputed to serve the best no-nonsense type food. The kind one's great-great-grandparents would make. There were also rumours that buka owners laced their food with juju, witch-craft potions, to ensure their patrons came back again and again. Then, there were the other extreme rumours of bukas using dogs and other types of unquantifiable meats in their food.

Muyiwa was at such a place. This particular buka was one of the most well-known in Palemo. Today's special was his favourite; thick-cut goat meat, lean, with just that hint of toughness that he liked, swimming in a coating of vegetable oil, and a rich, fried pepper and tomato stew, and a small dollop of okra, all ready to be consumed with his favourite: pounded yam. He rolled up his sleeves and dived in with his hands. He ate noisily and gustily. Although he considered himself a cosmopolitan, there were times, such as this, when he relished the opportunity to just be: to eat with his hands, abandon all social graces and enjoy the moment, in a way that he couldn't really do with his peers at the BBC.

Sweat dripped from his forehead as he ate. He motioned to the waitress to bring him a napkin. As he wiped his brow, he heard a street seller call out: "Sweets! Come buy your sweets and biscuits!"

He looked up from his meal and watched as the street seller continued walking down the street, clicking her tongue and calling out to people. After a few moments, he returned to his food. When he finished, he stretched. He had a couple of leads to pursue with a story, but it was nothing that he couldn't delay. He motioned for the waitress to bring him an ice-cold drink. While he waited, he pondered his next move. He had to figure out what he should do with Michael Li. His gut feeling told him that there was something to the story, he just didn't know what. While it was possible that he was over-reacting, after all, it wasn't that unusual for Michael Li to be involved in anything that Olabisi was doing—they were lovers, everyone in high-society Nigeria knew that— Muyiwa knew there was something else to this. Everything Michael touched, he corrupted, and something like his lover having connections to Bono was an opportunity too good for someone like him to pass up.

Muyiwa had also heard rumours about plans for a mega casino being built in Kaduna. Nigeria might be a secretive society, but the rumour mills were never wrong. They might be wildly inaccurate, but they also always had more than a whiff of rumour about them. As the saying goes, "There's no smoke without fire," and in Michael's case, those rumours were true. There were already casinos in Lagos, but knowing Michael, whatever he was proposing would be on the same level as his ego.

Muyiwa took a slug of his cold drink and immediately got brain freeze. The waitress had stacked the soft drink with ice. Nigerians loved ice. It was one of their antidotes to the unrelenting heat. As his brain unfroze, he decided that Michael would be worth investigating. If anything, if his journalist hunch proved to be right, he would still have a job with the

BBC.

He finished his drink, paid up and took a leisurely stroll to the auto-repair shop. It didn't matter what Dauda felt or thought, there was still life in the Mosquito Man story.

As he approached shop, he noted the difference between the crowds that had been just a few days before, to the deserted street before him now. There was Mama Seyi, getting ready for the lunch time rush, with her son, Fela, beside her. He wondered why the boy was not in school.

Mama Seyi saw him and pointed towards the auto-repair shop, indicating that Dauda was in there. That was the thing with Lagos. Everybody knew each other's business. He mouthed his thanks and banged on the auto-repair shop gate.

"Baba is not here!" he heard someone, most likely, Dauda, shout.

"Dauda, it's me," he said.

There was a silence on the other end and then, he heard footsteps. The gates swung open, and he found himself looking into Dauda's hostile eyes.

"Have you got my money?" he asked, not bothering with pleasantries.

"Have I interviewed Baba?" Muyiwa replied.

Dauda made as if to close the gates, but Muyiwa used his foot to block him. Dauda wasn't deterred, he continued trying to close the gates. Muyiwa removed his foot just as the gates slammed shut in his face.

Olabisi knocked on the hotel room door. It was opened by a

flamboyantly dressed and made-up Munira.

"Olabisi!" Baba called out from his seat by the window. "It's good you're here—"

"We're not going to Palemo today, Baba, so you can just be quiet," Munira interrupted him.

"That's what you think. I'm tired of this place. I'll call Dauda…"

"You don't even have a mobile phone, much less know how to use one!" Munira shouted at him.

Michael stepped in the middle of the room and held out his hands, like one defusing a bomb.

"Baba, it's okay. If you don't want to stay here, you don't have to," he spoke soothingly.

Baba looked at him. "Where did you learn Yoruba?" he asked him.

"I had a lot of Nigerian friends in school in England. And I also spent a lot of time in Nigeria as a student," Michael replied.

"Thanks for the history lesson, Michael, but let's talk about the Mosquito Man. As you know, yesterday's meeting didn't go well, so we have to reschedule. I'm also trying to get hold of the Mosquito Man's people, so that we can apologise fully and let them know how serious we are," Olabisi said. "In the meantime, I think Baba is right. You guys should lay low for a while. I suggest you move into our compound for your own protection, until we have everything sorted out."

Very clever, Olabisi, Munira thought. She wanted them where she could see them and track their movements. All her talk of doing this for their safety was just nonsense. But, Munira decided, she didn't mind. Better to have an address on the Island, which would make her more attractive to directors and other show business people, than to have a Palemo address.

"I'm not leaving Palemo," Baba said.

Michael signalled to Olabisi to meet him in the bathroom.

"It may not be a bad idea for him to go to Palemo," he said, as he closed the door behind him. "It's good for optics."

"I know that. But I need to keep an eye on him, and I can't do that in Palemo," Olabisi said.

"What if you called the conference in Palemo?" Michael suggested.

Olabisi thought for a minute. Michael's idea was a good one. She could convene the press conference right in front of Baba's house. Before that, she would do a guerilla style mini-documentary with Baba as their unreliable narrator and Dauda—she shuddered at even using him—as the voice of the youth. Baba would show them round Palemo, the world would see the community through his eyes and, through that, they would be able to re-engage Bono. They would start filming immediately and aim to upload to all their social media channels within the week. The day after final uploading, they would convene the press conference.

Naturally, in the midst of the media attention, it would become clear, even to Baba, that it would be unwise for him to stay in Palemo. Between the area boys, the media scrum that would inevitably descend on his home, the best thing for him to do would be to stay somewhere safe—out of sight where he could do the most good: Olabisi's house.

"I've got an even better idea," Olabisi told him.

# 13

On the bed where he sat, Baba concentrated on what Michael and Olabisi were telling him. He liked what they were saying, because finally, it sounded like they understood that he wasn't into this Mosquito Man business for the money. People were dying in Palemo, because they lacked access to water. And even though Olabisi had kept on saying that she helped communities like Palemo get water, he wasn't sure what that meant. His few forays into her office had shown people with computers and fancy clothing looking busy. If they were supposedly giving poor people water, where were all their equipment: the drilling machines, the water tankers that should be parked outside their office?

"It doesn't quite work like that," Olabisi said, when he raised it with her. She hadn't even been annoyed. Rather, she was happy that he was taking interest in the work. "We partner with companies who do that stuff for us for free, because it makes them look good."

"Is that why you guys have never come to Palemo?" Munira asked.

They'd never had a project in Palemo, because the partners weren't interested in Palemo, she wanted to say. It was too big, too messy, the inhabitants "too thieving", one corporate social responsibility executive had actually said to her.

"These things take a long time," Olabisi answered.

Baba didn't understand why. They needed water, and all they had to do was bring their tanks and do some drilling. What was so hard about that?

He couldn't wait to go back to their one-room home in Palemo and also spend some time with Dauda and Dimeji. He missed those boys, the two of them, so different, yet fundamentally, good human beings who challenged and infuriated him in equal measure.

His time with rich people and all these television people with their cameras had convinced him that rich people weren't to be trusted. They were out for themselves, even the ones like Olabisi that purported to help people like him.

Still he liked the idea of showing the world Palemo. And Olabisi was right that Dauda was just the right person to do this thing with him. Olabisi had said that the end of the documentary would also feature Munira pretending to go to an audition, which would help her attract some directors. She would also feature in some scenes. "...playing the role of devoted wife," Olabisi had said. To which Munira had snapped, "I am a devoted wife."

Olabisi believed her. She just thought that they had very different ideas of what being a devoted wife meant.

Baba was bored. "So, can we go now? I'm tired and hungry," he said.

They all stood up. Michael came away from the window.

As he made his way out the door he told them offhandedly, "By the way, all the money you've spent in this hotel will be taken from your final payment."

Munira gave him a murderous look.

As they approached Palemo, Baba's spirits lifted. Even though they had only been away for two days, it had felt like a lifetime. The 4x4 rolled past the auto-repair shop. Baba saw Dauda closing up and talking to a girl with a tray of sweets on her head. He saw Dauda brighten up in recognition as the 4x4 went past, yet he never took his eyes off the girl. As Baba raised his hand to wave at Dauda, Munira hissed "Put your hand down, you fool. You're in a shaded car. They can't see you!"

He put his hand down. In the driving seat, Kayode smiled. "You're happy to be back, no?" he said.

Baba grinned. Next to him, Munira thought about how best to face their landlord, and determined that she would face that music when that time came. Pulling up outside their building, she saw that the cobbler had packed up for the day and was walking away carrying a clear plastic bag filled with exercise books. It was 7pm, so it seemed that he was going to night school. He was one of the first people she would help once she got her big break as a celebrity, she decided.

As for the other people in their community, she wished them nothing but harm. They'd done nothing but made her feel like she didn't belong. Shame on them! Her time in Lagos had been nothing but pain and humiliation, but things were moving up. Whatever had happened in the past with Baba, the press conference and even that Chinese snake, she was determined to leave it all in the past and concentrate on her future. A future where she would be in control of her own destiny. Maybe even, a future with a child. As soon as this thought came into her head, she killed it. Hope was dangerous.

A few neighbours poured out of their houses and watched silently as they disembarked from the 4x4. Olabisi had told them to lie low and not do anything to bring attention to themselves.

"We're back to square one and I need to know that you trust me. The Mosquito Man is no longer interested in you, because of what happened at the press conference yesterday. It will take a while to get his trust again. In the meantime, I need to know that you guys are trustworthy. That you won't just decide to go behind my back and start making deals with anyone who shows you just a little of money. As a sign of good faith and despite Michael's advice, here's N50K. This is not small money for a charity, especially in this economic climate."

She gave both long looks before continuing.

"I've also spoken to Michael and asked him to double your fee if you both play ball. We are at a very critical stage and we all need to remain focussed on what we're doing. If I hear even a whiff that one of you is doing a deal with someone else, your deal with WfN and Chino-Centric is off, immediately. Do you understand?"

"We're not children. Just give me the cash," Munira had

said. It was enough to buy them a new mattress and also buy the cobbler some textbooks. She also needed new shoes.

Kayode helped them unload their belongings from the car. In the space of two days, seemingly, they had acquired a few belongings. Baba's new wardrobe, the ones he hadn't stained with food. Her new make-up kits. Colourful flowing kaftans. Shiny, gauzy costume jewellery, from earrings to bangles, all intended to draw attention to herself. Because, there was nothing she hated more than being ignored, treated as if she didn't matter. Her parents might not have understood her, but she understood herself. She mattered. No, she corrected herself. She and Baba mattered.

"Kayode, don't put these things on the ground," she commanded. "Take them inside the building. Baba, I don't know why you're standing there like an idiot. Direct him to our home."

Across the road, the cobbler smiled at her and she smiled back. They both knew that they would talk, probably first thing in the morning. He liked his tea just the way she liked hers, too: in a massive cup, scalding hot, drowning in condensed milk and three cubes of sugar. She realised that she had missed him. The hotel had been great, but lonely.

She followed Baba and Kayode as they headed into the building. Mama Jide's door swung open. "So you decided to come back?" She said.

Munira ignored her. She turned the key and gestured to Baba and Kayode to dump their belongings inside. Sweat poured down her back. "Baba, get a candle," she said.

"Forget candle, here's a solar torch," she heard the land-lord's voice. And just like that, he was in her home.

"We don't want anything from you," she said, her voice curt.

Kayode looked around. "I think that's everything from the car. I'll be on my way now," he said.

"Thank you," Baba said.

Munira didn't respond. She found a candle, struck a match and soon the room was alight in the faint glow. After placing the candle in a candle holder, she raised the candle to her face. She turned around, walked to the door, opened it and spoke softly. "Get out," she said to the landlord.

He didn't argue. He left their room. Baba took the candle from her, sat on their bed and patted the empty space next to him. Munira obeyed. She put her head on his shoulder. She didn't know why, but she felt afraid all of a sudden.

"Baba, I hate this room," she said, in a small voice.

Baba didn't say anything. He didn't know why she hated the room so much. It provided a roof over their heads. Sure, it was humid, they had rats, but they weren't like those people sleeping under the flyovers, at the mercy of cultists and robbers.

"Do you remember my first night here?" Munira asked.

Baba patted her head. There was no point in revisiting the past. "Munira, we have a lot of work to do. How about you go bathe and try and get some sleep, uh?"

In the dark, Munira smiled sadly. She wished they could talk about that night. What those men did to her. What she had to endure. And Baba outside, patiently waiting for the whole thing to be over, so they could start their "new life".

What life? She now thought. It'd been five years and she still battled with nightmares.

What had that night been for? She sometimes wondered to herself. She was still here, in this fetid room. And she still hadn't made it in Nollywood.

"There's not enough water to bathe. I'll just wash my face," she said.

Baba patted her head again affectionately. He knew Munira was thinking about that night. But there wasn't nothing he could've done. If she hadn't slept with those men, they both would have been killed, he told himself. In any case, that was the past. It was best to leave things there.

The next morning, Baba was up and showered by the time Munira opened her eyes. "Where are you going?" she asked him suspiciously.

"To the shop," Baba replied, putting on his sandals. "I want to tell Dauda and Dimeji about the documentary."

Munira fell back on the bed. In truth, she wasn't even sure she should leave Baba by himself, but he was a grown man; she couldn't chaperone him forever. Every time she'd done that, it had resulted in disaster.

"Just remember what Olabisi said about not telling anybody anything," she said, turning over. She sat up. "Come back for lunch," she said.

Baba looked at her in surprise, then shook his head. "Give me some money for Mama Seyi," he said.

"No," Munira said. "I'll call her and tell her I'll settle your outstanding credit myself," Munira said. If she gave Baba the money, there was no guarantee he would have any of it left in the time he left their building and the time he would get to the auto-repair shop. Money leaked out of his pockets. Baba was prone to reckless acts of kindness, which made him an easy prey for beggars. Even if he survived that onslaught by the hordes of beggars, she was sure the area boys would get him. She saw that he was wearing one of his old agbada, traditional outerwear and nodded her head in approval. Anyone who saw him wearing those rags wouldn't think to harass him for money.

Baba finished messing around with his slippers and stood. Munira saw that he was smiling. Maybe he felt it too, that things would change between them. She wasn't sure but she felt it was a good thing. A memory of her first night in Lagos and the visit to the clinic a few months later threatened to overshadow her thoughts, but she shook her head violently. No, she promised herself. From this time onwards, she would look to the future only. No more going back.

She smiled her approval. Baba, startled, decided not to say anything. He stopped when he got to their door to turn the lock. "Munira, you'll see that we have done a good thing," he said.

"Just lock up after you." She yawned and turned over.

She heard him wish the cobbler a good morning and smiled to herself in anticipation of the look of surprise on the cobbler's face when she would give him the money for his textbooks.

Then she heard a key turn in the lock from outside and the door quietly pushed open. She stiffened. She would recognise that measly walk anywhere. She looked up, suddenly face to face with their landlord.

"Munira, is this the way to treat someone who has been so nice to let you live in his house rent-free and even gave you a brand new director, like you've been asking?" he asked, a strange smile on his face.

Munira sat up. "I'm not talking to you," she said. She saw his gaze travel to her chest and pulled the bed covering all the way up to her neck.

"It's not a choice," the landlord replied. "I think I've been tolerant enough," he said. "The young girl might be a film graduate, but she was top of her class, and you are going to help her get her film made," he said, looking at her keenly. "It's not a choice," he repeated.

He also had a look on his face she recognised too well. "Can I at least brush my teeth?" she asked.

"I'll wait by the door and watch you go and come back to the room," the landlord said. "You're not escaping me this morning," he added, face hard.

Munira sighed and gathered her toiletries. She had money, but it still wasn't enough. Yet.

Baba wasn't sure what it was, but he felt there was something different about him, Munira and his neighbourhood today. He felt that people really saw him. Sidestepping the potholes on the road, he felt himself walk taller the further along he got to the auto-repair shop.

At the bus station, he stood for a few moments remembering his ride from Ibadan to Palemo about thirty years earlier. It was the early 1980s. He had about N200 on him. He'd never heard of Palemo. The day he left his village in Ibadan, he didn't tell his parents. His parents were fishermen and although he fished as well, he was tired of smelling like fish. They didn't bother sending him to school, because it was a costly investment with future benefits, whereas fishing had immediate financial benefits.

Initially, Baba didn't mind. However, as he grew older, he noticed that the older the men in the village got, the more maudlin they became. They would spend all day under the shade of the *iroko* tree, drinking palm wine in bouts of sullen silence or raucous exchanges, while the women went to the farm. And then, one day, he had the realisation that things never changed in their village. Everything remained the same and *he* would be the same as well if he stayed. He didn't discuss his plan with his parents, but had simply packed his bags and made his way to the bus station. He remembered that on the bus, people had complained about his fish smell all the way from Ibadan to Lagos.

Disembarking from the bus, he'd looked around at the busy streets. It was so noisy he had actually felt that his ears would explode. Someone pushed him into the main road and he narrowly avoided being mowed down by a taxi. The taxi driver had rained curses on his head. Even the Yoruba spoken in Lagos has sounded different. He made his way to the road-side and asked a young boy where he was.

"Palemo," the boy said, giving him a strange look. Before he could say anything else, the boy had scurried away.

Palemo. Baba had looked around in wonder. He liked it.

And today, as he stood looking at the bus station, he couldn't help but wonder—again—where time had gone. If he had thought the bus station was busy then, now it was positively heaving with humanity. Each day brought thousands of people into Palemo. People much like him, who'd come from all over Nigeria to partake of the Lagos dream. People like him and Munira. People who would probably die like animals, unknown, in the pursuit of those dreams.

His first few years in Lagos, he had tried. He had done every job going. A human mule, carrying heavy goods for market shoppers. He had slept anywhere he could find succour: by the roadside, on the beach, even on trees. And every year, he'd found his spirit becoming more crushed. And then, one day, he knew that the key to his happiness was not caring. He'd worry so much about not having enough to eat, wear or, even, where to live that, after one particularly bruising day, he swore to himself that he would stop worrying about things that he couldn't control, and spend his life living for the day. By that time, he was twenty-five and had spent five years in Palemo.

It was lonely for a while. He liked women, they just didn't like him. One day, he left his room and decided to walk around Palemo. It was late afternoon. He went down a narrow street that he rarely frequented and saw two young boys, about four-teen or fifteen years old, he guessed, being beaten by an older man. Across the road, to his left, was a woman who had two boys with her. She was frying akara and dun dun. To this day, he didn't know why he decided to walk down that narrow street. Maybe it was the sight of the older man knocking the two boys about. Or maybe it was the smell of the akara and dun dun, his favourite meal, that confused his faculties. Either way, he found himself walking down the street and before he knew it, he had gone in castigating the older man and yelling for him to stop beating the children.

The man had turned round and discounted him immedi-ately, and Baba knew why. His teeth were copper-coloured from chewing kola nut. His agbada was faded, and he was barefoot. Everything about him screamed, *I am poor. I am invisible. I do not matter*.

The two boys had looked at him with gratitude. Across the road, the lady with the children shouted. "Mr Sowemimo, it's true. Leave those boys. You're always beating them."

The woman then smiled at Baba. The man she called Mr Sowemimo, turned back to the boys and said: "God is obviously smiling on you today. Now go and clean those cars again and if I see a single speck on them when I come back, I won't be held accountable for my actions. Nobody, not even Mama Seyi, will save you from me," he warned.

"Because you're God," one of the boys muttered.

Mr Sowemimo made as if to turn back, but changed his mind. He got in the car and drove off, but not before giving

Baba a cool look.

"Mister, you sit on that bench and I'll bring you some food," the woman called Mama Seyi said. "And don't worry, you don't need to pay this time. You've saved those boys." She gestured to one of her boys to take the dish to him. "Seyi, go give this to that man," she told him.

The boy couldn't have been more than eight years old. As he crossed, a water tanker came careening down the street. The next thing Baba remembered was Mama Seyi screaming and Seyi's severed head right by his knee.

He didn't like thinking of that day. The memories were hard and cruel. He didn't blame Mama Seyi for her anger towards him. Sometimes, even he thought that Seyi would still be alive if it wasn't for him.

He had arrived at the auto-repair shop. Dimeji was opening up this time. A wide smile appeared on his face when he saw Baba.

"Baba!" he cried out. "You remembered us!" He looked puzzled. "What are you doing, here?" he asked. "They got tired of you, already?" He added, laughing at his own joke.

"Mama Seyi," he called out to her, who was just arriving at her stall. "Baba is here. Can he have akara and dun dun, please?"

She nodded and got to work. Baba was surprised. He had expected a few bloodcurdling curses. Even Dimeji was surprised. He looked at him in askance. "Things are really looking up for you, Baba," he said.

Dimeji swung open the auto-repair shop gate to let Baba in. Once inside, he changed into his overalls and powered up the television with the car battery. The television flickered to life and BBC World Service beamed into the shop. As he settled back in his chair, Dimeji brought him a steaming cup of Lipton tea. Baba took a sip and felt ludicrously, stupidly happy. He watched in silence as the anchor woman reeled off the day's news. Usually, he would comment on the news, as Dimeji or Dauda would translate whatever was happening onscreen for him, but for now, he was content just to be.

Dimeji left them and came back with a steaming plate of food for his breakfast. Baba attacked the meal with his usual gusto. When he finished, he looked around. Dimeji saw and asked him what he was looking for.

"I need something to wipe my hands on," Baba said.

Dimeji burst out laughing. He was still laughing when Dauda came inside the auto-repair shop a few moments later. When he saw Baba, he broke into a smile and went to hug him. As he changed into his overalls, Dimeji explained why he had laughed.

"Baba asked for a rag to clean his hand after eating," he said, to which Dauda burst out laughing too.

"I don't see why that's so funny," Baba said, irritably.

Dauda wiped his eyes. "Baba, you never wipe your hands on a rag. You lick them clean and wipe them on your clothes. And after spending two days with rich people, you come back here asking for a rag, like some prince," he said.

Baba ignored them and decided to watch the television

instead. He would share the news of the documentary later.

\*\*\*

She wouldn't fret. Kayode had told her that Munira and Baba had seemed subdued yesterday. "It looked like they were ready to be serious about this thing," he had told her when he came back to report.

Olabisi wished she could believe him. It was 7am, the morning after. She called Kayode and asked if his younger brother was still looking for work. The boy was the bane of his brother's life. Kayode responded affirmatively and Olabisi got to work. Next, she called Munira and didn't receive an answer. Nigerians were early risers, so calling someone at 7am wasn't that unusual. She scrolled through her mobile phone. She had a few hundred emails, 80% of which were from organisations who wanted to partner with WfN. The same organisations that she had sent multiple proposals to and requested upteenth meetings with their chief executives. The Bono effect was well and truly at work.

There was a knock on her bedroom door and Funmi her maid came in.

"Good morning, ma," she said. "I was thinking yams and eggs this morning."

Olabisi shook her head. "Just bring me some tea," she said, flinging her bedroom covers away. She had to send her packing, but she just didn't have the strength. Good maids were hard to find. At the same time, she needed Michael and if he had taken exception to her maid, then Funmi needed to go: WfN was worth more to her than a replaceable maid.

Olabisi fell back on the bed. She had to respond to those emails, arrange for Kayode's brother to keep watch on Munira and Baba's house for a few days, visit her father, pull together the project team for the documentary, because she wanted them to start filming straight away, which meant that she had to get out of bed, and probably go to Palemo to speak to Munira and Baba in person, as Munira wasn't answering her mobile.

Olabisi suddenly felt exhausted. She decided that she would tick off her list one by one. She would brush her teeth, enjoy her coffee and then start with the emails.

Ten minutes later, one email stopped her in her tracks. It was anonymous. The subject header was: Nigerian socialite partners with murderous Chinese conglomerate for profit. She shouldn't have clicked it open. For all she knew, it was a virus, but she couldn't help it.

She clicked the email open. There were a few links to news stories in Kenya and Zimbabwe. Not really sure why she couldn't seem to stop herself, she clicked the links and read. When she finished, she put her mobile phone aside and called out for Funmi saying that she would need her breakfast after all.

He humped, collapsed on top of her and rolled to the side of the bed with a self-satisfied smile. Munira got off the bed and started getting dressed. She heard a shuffle on the other side of the door. She sighed deciding that she didn't care. What was the point?

She took a *wrapa*, a long piece of fabric and tied it around herself. Then, she sat on the lone chair in the room and faced her landlord.

"This is the last time this will happen," she said, and she meant it.

The landlord sat up on the bed, then stood up and started walking towards her. He stopped when she raised her hand. He sat back down on the bed. Munira looked at his limp penis and looked away. On the other side of the door, she heard quiet shuffling receding. Mama Jide was going back to her cavern, she deduced.

"Munira, we've been through this before. This will stop when I get my rent. And stop pretending that you don't enjoy it," he said, getting off the bed. As he came towards her, Munira pushed him away and went outside. She sat on the bench and gestured to the cobbler to come sit with her. When he sat down, she asked him if he'd missed her.

"Well, the street has only just returned to normal, so I expect the madness will start again," he told her.

She slapped him playfully. She could hear her room door opening and closing, and the landlord's steps as he went back to his own room.

The cobbler gave her a pitying smile. "He is a snake," he said.

"Don't worry, it's not for long," Munira reassured him. "Wait here. I brought you something," she said. She went back inside the building and came back with the bag she'd bought him and some money.

The cobbler took them gratefully. "You always take such good care of me," he said.

"You're a good man," she told him. "Do well in night school and who knows what the future will bring."

They chatted for a few more minutes then the cobbler went back across the road. Munira hung around for a while, enjoying the scene. Several people walked past and pointed at her. But she didn't care. Before, she would've rather died than be seen outside of their room without a full face of makeup, much less wearing an old wrapper, but this time, she didn't mind.

She went back in the room, played around with her jewellery and went to stand in front of her mirror, to indulge in her favourite pastime: worshipping herself. Even that failed to distract her. The phone rang for the umpteenth time and she ignored it, knowing that it was Olabisi.

She ought to have a shower, but she couldn't summon up the energy. She felt she knew what the issue was, but didn't want to name it, for fear of calling it into being.

It was the black dog, and it had come to taunt her again, and at a crucial time in her life.

Munira went back into the bed and laying down pulled the covers over her head.

# 14

Olabisi bit her lip in frustration. Munira wasn't answering her mobile. There was nothing to do, but head down there herself. But first, she had to deal with the information that had arrived in her inbox that morning.

The email had links to news reports citing several cases against Chino-Centric for malpractice and manslaughter, accordingly. There were images of poorly-designed buildings that had fallen down and caused many deaths. In Zimbabwe, they were accused of poisoning a community with contaminated water. The news items had also helpfully supplied images of the falling buildings and corpses of those that had been maimed or killed. Olabisi saw a few images and decided that she didn't want to read any further.

Now, in her office, she clasped her hands on the table. WfN needed Baba. It also desperately needed Chino-Centric to provide the funds for the expansion of WfN's services. She punched in Michael's number on her mobile. When he picked up, she didn't even bother with preliminaries.

"Are the rumours true?" she asked.

"Chino-Centric is a global company. There are many rumours attached to it."

"I've just seen the pictures of the building in Nairobi and that town in Zim—"

"Is that it?" Michael snorted. "The infrastructure was built by Kenyans and Zimbabweans, so if they were sub-par, it's nothing to do with Chino-Centric and everything to do with the people who worked on the project."

"Michael—" Olabisi started, but Michael cut her off again.

"You have to make a decision on what's more important: what's supposedly happening in Nairobi and Zim, that's beyond your control and what is happening in your own backyard, that you can do something about."

And then, he hung up. Of course he was right, Olabisi said. Like he said, those projects had been headed by Kenyans and Zimbabweans, so in theory, they were at fault, not Chino-Centric. And why worry about something that was far away from her doorstep? Wouldn't her energies be better focused on the good she could do in Nigeria, right now?

Olabisi chided herself for being silly. She called her receptionist and started making arrangements for her film crew. Whatever happened, the Bono show must go on.

"Didn't you see how he disgraced himself on television?" Dauda said, and shook his head at people's stupidity. He slammed the gate shut and came inside. This time, he flicked the television to Al-Jazeera. "This one is much better than BBC," he said.

"I wonder why you say that," Dimeji said wryly. Dauda

shot him a filthy look, grabbed a chair and went to sit by Baba, who had been uncharacteristically quiet.

"I can't believe Munira let you out," he said. "Where is she?" he pretended to look around.

"At home," Baba said, curtly. He paused and said, "I think the darkness is coming back," he whispered to Dauda.

Dauda didn't understand Munira's 'darkness', but he knew that it made her lie in bed for days sometimes weeks at a time. And if it was coming back now, it did not bode well. But, it did give him an idea.

"So, you're saying that the Mosquito Man is no longer interested in you and Munira?" he said.

"No," Baba gathered his belongings. He was beginning to feel hungry again. He wondered if Munira had called Mama Seyi as she'd promised.

Dauda watched him fidget. "Baba, calm down. I'll ask Mama Seyi to bring you some food," he said.

Baba smiled gratefully. The kid had a good heart. "I'm doing a film!" he burst out, "and the two of you are going to be in it!" And he told them both about Olabisi's idea to do a run of Palemo, with Baba (and Dauda translating). Of course, Munira would also have a role to play in this as well, he said. They would film her pretending to go for auditions, or even, have a fake audition, so they could stimulate interest in her acting career.

"Can you imagine if she got a role!" Baba said.

Dimeji slid under a car. "Just make sure you go by this auto-repair shop and get Mama Seyi in the shot, otherwise the two of them would never believe you," he called out from under the car.

Dauda was silent. "But, Baba," he said. "Why do you need Olabisi to film Palemo for you?"

"Because she said it's the only way to get Mosquito Man to take an interest in our cause again," she said.

"Isn't it better for someone who knows Palemo to do this?" he asked Baba, looking at him without guile. "Listen, I can video the whole thing on my mobile," Dauda punched a few buttons and started recording their faces. After a while, he played back the recording to Baba.

"See?" he said. "You don't need Olabisi and other rich people to do this. Remember, the Mosquito Man idea came from you. Because of you, the whole world now knows about Palemo, so it makes sense that if you want to do a film, then it should be done by the people of Palemo. People like you and I," he said.

Baba began shaking his head, then stopped when he realised that what Dauda said was making sense.

Dauda pressed on. "Look, this whole thing just got terribly complicated. All we meant to do was tell the Mosquito Man to help us tell the president to bring water to Palemo, not so? Next thing we know, all kinds of stupidity happened. You swanned off with your rich friends and then fell asleep in front of the whole world on global television. That's not who you are."

Dauda held up his mobile phone. "Tell you what: why don't we go round Palemo now and start videoing all these things. You'll just talk and I'll hold the mobile phone and translate into English what you're saying. And when we're finished, we'll put it on the internet—that thing I'm always telling you about—and maybe ask Muyiwa—remember the BBC guy—to help us get it to the attention of the Mosquito Man."

Baba's head began shaking again. He wasn't sure what Dauda was saying, but he was pretty certain that Munira and Olabisi, not to mention, Michael, wouldn't like it.

"Dauda, I don't know—"

"Baba, what are you afraid of? We're just walking round Palemo and showing it to the world through our eyes. Besides, it was your idea. And you should also know that I'm the one who has borne the brunt of the abuse from the airline and the radio station when Munira disappeared with the tickets. But, did I mention anything about it to you? No! Because I knew how stressful your life was already with all these news people on your tail. But if you don't want to stick to the original, simple plan of getting water to Palemo, and would instead prefer to wait for some godfather's daughter, who doesn't know anything about suffering or lacking water, to 'help', then that is fine," Dauda said.

There was a gentle knock on the gate. A young sweet seller stepped inside the auto-repair shop. Dauda beamed and went to meet the girl, who smiled back shyly at him.

# 15

Munira heard someone knocking on the door. Their room was stifling hot. She threw the covers off her body and opened the door. The landlord stood in front of her smiling sheepishly. Munira glanced to his side and saw that he had the girl director with him. She sighed and let them in the room. She sat on the bed and motioned for the girl to sit on the only chair in the room. The landlord leaned against her makeup table.

If he broke it, he'll buy a more expensive model, Munira thought to herself, fiercely.

The girl gave Munira an uncertain smile. "Good morning, Ma," she said.

"There's no need for all that. Say what you have to say and you and your pimp should leave," Munira replied coldly.

"Munira, that's not a nice thing to say to someone who can make you a star," the landlord said.

The girl looked from the landlord to Munira, giving them both an uncertain look. She drew in a deep breath, as if drawing strength, and like someone being led to the guillotine, plunged straight in. She had seen Munira being interviewed on television, so she knew she had very little time to convince her of her suitability for the film.

"My name is Dorcas—" she began.

"That's very nice, Dorcas, but I'm not interested in your name. Like I said, just say what you want and you and your pimp should leave," Munira eyed the landlord again.

She looked down on her mobile phone screen and saw that she'd had ten missed calls from Olabisi. She wanted to crawl into bed. She wanted to defeat the black dog that she knew was surely coming, provoked, by the events of the past few days. This time, you will not win, she told herself, half-fearful, half-defiant.

"Munira, listen to the girl," the landlord pleaded. "Just listen, and if you don't like what she says, we'll leave and you'll figure out another way to pay back what you owe me in rent."

Baba watched Dauda caress the girl's cheek, while she smiled shyly.

"How old are you?" he asked her, from across the room.

The girl hastily backed away, and went out through the semi-open door.

"Why did you do that?" Dauda said irritably. They had been discussing when the girl would finally come and see him in his home, which he shared with about five other people. They each had their own mattress. He'd even negotiated a two-hour slot that the room would be empty, so that he and Morenike would be alone. He didn't even know what they would talk about when they were alone together—he just knew that he wanted some time alone with her.

He hoped that she wouldn't start quoting the Bible or some sort of religious stuff to him. It wasn't that he wasn't religious, he just thought that God had much more interesting things to do than to listen to prayers from someone like him.

He went back to sit with Baba. They watched some more television, with Baba commenting on everything he saw. Once in a while, some people would straggle into the auto-repair shop and Dauda would scream at them that the show was over, that Baba didn't have any money and the Mosquito Man was no more.

After about an hour, Baba cleared his throat.

"Dauda," he announced, like a man who had made an important decision and was now ready to unleash it to the world. "I have been thinking about what you said and you're right. I think it is better for me to do this film with you," he said.

"Good," Dauda said, patting Baba's shoulder. "Should we celebrate with some Coke and more akara?" he said.

"No, not today," Baba said.

Dauda looked at him in surprise. In all the years that he'd known Baba, he'd never known him to turn down food, and if it was free, then all the better. He would accept and then make the person wish that they'd never offered, particularly after seeing him eat.

Dimeji slid out from under the car and wiped his greasy hands on his overalls.

"Baba, are you sure?" he asked him, ignoring Dauda's glare. "I don't know Olabisi, but I think she means well. And what about Munira? If you and Dauda go round doing this thing today, where would that leave her? Aren't you supposed to be doing this thing together?"

"Who asked for your counsel?" Dauda said in frustration. One of these days, he swore to himself that he would kill Dimeji. His self-righteousness was endearing at the best of times, but frustrating at the most.

Baba paused. "I don't think Munira will be able to do this thing..." he said. He wanted to tell them about his fear of the blackness back to haunt her, but decided to keep it to himself. And maybe, it was best that she wasn't involved in the film at all. Her behaviour, since the news broke about the Mosquito Man, was concerning. She was erratic, prone to emotional highs and there was a desperation about her, that if Baba was honest, was frightening to him. The stakes were too high, all her dreams and hopes were on everything working out for the Mosquito Man deal, he didn't know what would happen if things didn't go according to plan.

Dimeji was right, Baba considered. Olabisi and Munira might have wanted to be involved with this film about Palemo, but his and Dauda's way was better, because it was the way that he'd originally envisioned it to happen. All the madness about sleeping in hotel rooms, buying clothes, press conferences... they weren't him. He just wanted water for Palemo, and till this day, he wasn't even sure what Olabisi and Michael Li's role in doing that was. Besides, what had the Chinese ever done for Nigeria, except to flood the market with fake goods and medicine? They had blood on their hands, he decided.

Baba took in a deep breath. "Dauda is right." He stood up and gathered his agbada. "Dauda, you said you didn't need much, except your phone? Then, let's go. Let's show the world Palemo!"

Dauda began slipping out of his overalls.

"And what about work? If Mr Sowemimo comes, I wouldn't come to your defence!" Dimeji said to Dauda's receding back, as he and Baba left the auto-repair shop.

Outside, Dauda adjusted his mobile phone. He swung it in the direction of Mama Seyi.

"Baba, all you have to do is talk," he said. "Tell the camera about Mama Seyi's akara and dun dun," he told him and Baba started talking.

Mama Seyi ignored them. Next to her, Fela smiled and then burst into laughter when Dauda started making faces at him from behind the camera.

Baba cleared his throat heavily. After being around people who spoke eloquently, he suddenly felt self-conscious, then decided that he didn't care. He wasn't doing this for some rich girl. He was doing it for Palemo.

"Mama Seyi makes the best dundun and akara in Palemo, but she's not a nice person," he started. Dauda laughed and encouraged him to continue. He hoped his mobile phone battery would hold out. He thought that they would go to several places that he knew held special significance for Baba. Like the bus station, for example, he often talked about his first time arriving in Palemo and seeing all the cars weaving past him and wondering if he'd landed in some far away city.

"Keep talking," he encouraged Baba.

Mama Seyi hissed at them both.

On the main street, Baba pointed to a winding queue of people waiting to fill their jerry cans with water.

"These people will have been queuing for hours, and they will be back in this queue a few days from now. You see these children," he pointed at some primary schoolchildren in their school uniform, clutching child-sized buckets. "They should be at home, doing their homework or playing football. But instead, they're here, queuing up to get water."

Dauda swooped the mobile, so that it captured the schoolchildren. He was surprised no one had harassed himself or Baba yet. Anybody who walked around carrying a camera and filming used to be viewed with suspicion, but he guessed that it was now the norm. In fact, some of his friends even videoed themselves having sex with women, and asked him to view it and rate their performance, which to his surprise, he found thoroughly distasteful.

He brought his mind back to the present as Baba motioned for him to follow. By now, it was dusk. Dauda didn't want to stay out too late. However much people ignored video filming during the day, he wasn't sure he wanted to be around doing it at night.

He realised that Baba was heading towards the mangrove swamp which wasn't a good idea. Occultists spent a lot of the time at the swamp and he'd also heard that the police conducted a fair amount of extra-judicial killings at the swamp as well.

"Baba, I don't think..."

"Dauda, don't worry. We won't be long," Baba said. Standing in front of a mangrove tree Baba swung his arm behind him. "This is a mangrove swamp," he said speaking in Yoruba, and looking straight into the camera. "Terrible things have happened here, still happen here. Maybe the Mosquito Man can get our president to drain the swamp of its secrets and find a way to use the swamp to provide us with clean water."

Dauda shut off his camera hastily. "Okay, Baba, that will do for now," he said. He will delete the footage about the swamp. They were not making a political video. They were making a video that would make him famous, that Palemo would also benefit from. Any mention of the swamp and he knew that he and Baba would be corpses by the end of the day the video was released.

Baba started speaking, thought better of it and started walking.

"You got all that?" he said.

"Yes," Dauda said. He would call Muyiwa as soon as they got back to the auto-repair shop. He wasn't a wordy person, but even he knew that he had quality footage from their excursion. He'd seen another side to Baba. At the bus station, he'd pointed to the exact spot where he'd disembarked after leaving Ibadan. A few hundred metres away, he pointed to a roadside spot he'd bedded down for the night. Then, they'd gone to the communal shower, where he said he'd had to stop washing himself, because lesions appeared on his body, due to the contaminated water he'd been using. He'd even shown Dauda the school he thought he would study in, "But, after a while, I knew I was wasting my time. Besides, can you imagine all those schoolchildren laughing at me?"

Now, as they approached the auto-repair shop gates, Dauda turned to face him. "I'm surprised that Munira hasn't been to the auto-repair shop or bombarded me with phone calls," he said.

Baba wasn't. If she hadn't come to the auto-repair shop or called Dauda to rain abuses down on him, it could only mean that the blackness had come, and that Munira had been rendered captive.

The young girl cleared her throat again. "I know you have concerns, but I promise that I know what I am doing. I entered an international film competition..."

At the word "international", Munira couldn't help it, she was intrigued. She looked more closely at the girl. She was tiny, in truth, and hardly looked as if she was out of secondary school much less university. Her face was bare, which was surprising in itself, as Nigerian women rarely left their houses without at least two layers of make-up.

Munira wondered how long the girl had been sleeping with the landlord. "... The BBC judge said I was good..." the girl was saying. She dug into her bag and drawing her hand out, thrust a sheath of papers into Munira's hands. It was the screenplay.

Munira glanced at it, placing the papers on the bed. She

would look at it later. It took her a while to read things. But she knew herself: she would work hard to memorise her lines and ensure she did justice to her character and the story.

"I'll read it later," Munira told her. "But right now, I need to go out," she looked at the girl, pointedly. The girl got the hint and packed up her things.

"I'll wait for you outside," she told the landlord. She left the room, nimble on her feet, closing the door gently behind her.

When she left, the landlord took her place on the chair.

"Munira, she's really good," the landlord said.

Munira sighed. Whoever the landlord slept with wasn't her business. Indeed, the more the better for him, because it meant that she was left alone, which suited her fine.

Her mobile phone rang. She glanced at the screen and saw that it was Olabisi.

"I assume that those are your new rich friends," the landlord said.

"And I'm telling you that it's none of your business," Munira replied. "Okay, assuming I'm interested in this," Munira sneered, "what is the next step?" she asked.

He leaned in and on reflex, Munira pulled back. His foul breath was scorching. "I'm saying that if you back this film, then you don't owe me anything. No rent. No nothing. Of course we can still have sex, but if you put your support behind the film, it will wipe the slate clean," he said.

"Fine," Munira snapped. "I'll do it."

"There's more," the landlord said. "It's not just about you

doing the film. We need money to back it, so you will help us promote the film to the Mosquito Man, and most importantly, get the money to help us film..."

"And if I don't?"

"Oh, you will," the landlord said. He stood up. "The script is good. And I know that you're a good actress. This is not just about me. It's also about you," he said.

Munira was quiet. "How old is she?" she asked him.

He smiled and left the room. Munira peeked out of the window and watched him get into his car with the girl. She went back to bed, reached out for the screenplay and started reading. As she read, she knew the landlord was right. The screenplay was good. She didn't know where or how she could get support for the film, but she knew that there were ways. She wondered if she could even get credit on the film as a producer. Her phone rang again. She didn't pick it up.

"We've done a good thing, here," Dauda said, as he and Baba made their way back to the auto-repair shop. Calling Muyiwa to make him an offer, he'd deliberately kept the details to himself, only to say, somewhat cryptically, that he was with Baba and he had something he knew Muyiwa would be interested in.

Mama Seyi had packed up, so they had bought some *suya*, on their way. A car sidled close to them. As they arrived at the shop the driver wound down his window and made as if to ask them for directions. Dauda put his phone in his front pocket and lowered his head to hear what the driver had to say. Behind him, Baba was sat down on the bench, attacking the food with his usual gusto.

The driver started talking and as Dauda leaned closer to hear what he was saying, the driver shot his hand out through the window, reached into Dauda's front pocket, took his phone and drove off. It was over in seconds. Dauda stood there for a few confused moments wondering what had just happened. He patted his front pocket in disbelief and found that it was indeed empty. Behind him, Baba called out, "Dauda, you should have bought some more suya." Then, as if it was nothing to do with him he shouted, "There's none left for you!"

Just then, Muyiwa's rickety car pulled up outside the auto-repair shop. The journalist got out of the car and came round the corner to where Dauda was. "You said you wanted to see me," he said.

Dauda looked from Muyiwa to the car that had just sped off and back to Muyiwa again. He gave a strangled cry and lunged at Muyiwa's throat.

Baba looked up to determine where the all the sudden noise had come from. When he saw Dauda lunge at Muyiwa, he made sure to finish off all the suya, before attempting to separate them both.

He planted himself between the two of them, and slapped Dauda round the head a few times, before asking what the problem was.

Dauda wiped his face. He looked like he was about to cry, then he pointed at Muyiwa. "It was him!" he said, his voice shaking with fury. "He arranged for someone to steal my phone!"

"Baba, I have no idea what he's talking about. He told me to come, so I came. The next thing I knew, he threw himself at me," Muyiwa said.

Dauda made as if to grab Muyiwa's throat again and found himself restrained by Baba. The old man was surprisingly nimble.

Baba looked at them both. "Dauda, what are you talking about?" he asked.

Dauda pointed at Muyiwa again and repeated what he said. "The phone was right there. In my pocket. And why of all things would they want to steal that from me? Why not my wallet?" he gnarled at Muyiwa.

Baba admitted that he still had no idea what Dauda was talking about.

"Baba, they stole my phone." Dauda started to explain, again.

"Who stole what? You're not making sense!"

Dauda pointed at Muyiwa. "Baba, the car that just sped off. The driver pretended that he was going to ask me for directions, and when I leaned in to hear what he was saying, he stole my mobile and sped off," he said. "A few moments later, this one," Dauda scoffed in derision when he said this and kept on pointing at Muyiwa, "This one came."

It took a while for Baba to understand what Dauda was saying. "You mean that everything we just did on film is gone?" he asked him.

"Yes!" Dauda said. He took another look at Muyiwa and went to sit on the bench, his shoulders dejected. No matter what he did, he just couldn't catch a break.

It would've been so easy. All he had to do was offer Muyiwa the film AND an interview with Baba for an increased fee, and everyone would be happy. Mosquito Man and his people would get to see Palemo from Baba's perspective. He would be impressed, so would approach Baba. He, Dauda would act as Baba's middle man. Unlike that Olabisi woman, he actually cared about Palemo. The end result from all this was that Palemo would get water. He would be able to take Morenike, the street seller to nice places and, maybe, even Baba would get some respect in his old age. He shot poisonous darts towards Muyiwa his frustration rising, but realised that he shouldn't leave the journalist with Baba, because who knows what he was telling him. He walked back to where they were both standing.

"Baba, I promise you that I don't know what he's talking about," he heard Muyiwa's earnest plea.

"Baba, it was him," Dauda insisted.

Baba had heard enough. "It doesn't matter who said what and where. It's gone," he patted Muyiwa's shoulders. "Dauda, I'll head home now," he said.

"Let me come with you," Dauda offered. "You don't know if the people that stole my phone are still around," he said.

"If they are, they would've done whatever they wanted to do by now," Baba said. He wiped his hands on his agbada and held them up when Dauda started protesting again.

Dauda and Muyiwa watched him as he walked down the street, seemingly oblivious to the activity around him. Muyiwa turned to Dauda.

"You're the one that wasted my time by coming here," he said.

Dauda ignored him. He ran after Baba. He had to be sure that Baba made it home safely. The alternative—being skewered by Munira if Baba didn't—didn't bear thinking about.

Muyiwa looked at their receding backs. Shattered, he decided to spend some time on the bench, before going back home. He tried to understand what had just happened.

The stars were out in full force tonight. A young lady stood in front of the auto-repair shop. She gave a hesitant smile. He recognised her as the sweet seller.

"I was looking for Dauda," she said. "He's not answering his phone." She peered closer at him. "You're the BBC guy that interviewed Baba!" she said.

Muyiwa stood up. "Yes, I am," he said.

## 16

Baba and Dauda walked in silence. After about ten minutes, Baba said tilting his head skyward, "It's been a while since the stars shone this bright," he said.

Dauda, looking up, agreed. "Baba, I'm sorry about the video," he said.

Baba stopped walking to stare up at the sky. For a while Dauda thought he'd lost him.

"If there was a way to go to school and study the stars, I would do it," Baba ruminated.

Dauda doubted it, but wisely, kept his mouth shut. They continued walking.

"Munira hasn't called you today," he said.

Baba nodded absent-mindedly. He had been thinking that himself. Before the Mosquito Man madness, Munira wouldn't have called him anyway to find out what he was doing. But the way she threw herself into this whole thing was something else. Before he had thought that she was being usual, brash, self. Then, her erratic behaviour; cavorting with Michael Li, jumping from one disastrous situation to another. The whole thing was a calamitous mistake.

"The rich woman, Olabisi, gave us small money, today,"

Baba offered.

"That's good. But imagine how much we would have made for Palemo if that thieving journalist hadn't stolen our video," Dauda said bitterly. He would crush his balls, grind them and force him to eat, when he got his hands on him. Or even better, get one of the area boys to do the deed. At least they would leave *him*, Dauda, alone. He kicked at an empty fruit juice packet in frustration.

"Dauda, sometimes you focus too much on the wrong things. Maybe that film wasn't meant to be. But tomorrow, Olabisi will come and we'll do it with her," Baba shrugged. "Anyway, with this rich people, it's probably better to do something like this with one of them. They don't like people like us, you know that," Baba shrugged again.

By now, they were in front of his building. Their building was dark, only punctuated by the low orange glow of candles and blue light from mobile phone screens. Baba could pinpoint exactly what everybody in his neighbourhood was doing to the second. As he turned into his street, he knew that the humid air would be filled with the stale smell of marijuana, sweat and cooking as people got on with the evening business of life.

It was six o'clock, which meant that the cobbler would have packed up his wares to go to night school. On weekends, in the evening, if he wasn't eating outside his stall, he would be talking to Munira on the bench outside their building. He had entertained such aspirations for himself a long time ago, but knew that he lacked the capacity for such intellectual endeavours. His place was with the mass of humanity. He gestured to the cobbler's bench across the road from his building. A local area boy came up to the two of them and they both froze, expecting trouble. But the boy did not do anything. Instead he laughed.

"Baba, don't worry. We know you don't have anything, otherwise, we would've come for you," he looked at Dauda. "As for you, you're a rascal. We're watching you," the area boy said, before walking away.

That was the way they operated, lawless gangs of boys terrorising and extorting people for money. Sometimes, Dauda wished that he could move away from Palemo and live in the Island, where all the rich people lived. But then, the rich weren't secure either. They rode in bulletproof cars and locked themselves in houses behind eleven-foot, gated walls.

What was the point of having all that money if they couldn't even enjoy it freely? He wondered.

Baba pointed towards the swamp. "Munira and I saw the police kill some young people, here once," he said.

They weren't the only ones. Everyone in Palemo had, at some point, or the other, either witnessed such killings or prayed they never found themselves on the receiving end.

They sat down on the bench. Baba patted Dauda's knee. "You will find another mobile telephone. I don't even know why you spend so much time on that thing anyway," he said. "Maybe this will force you to look up and see what is happening around you, instead of looking at your screen all the time. I'll tell Munira to buy you another phone."

"Thank you," he said. As capricious as Munira was, he had also been the recipient of her generosity.

They were an unlikely pair, Baba and Munira. She was a loud, abrasive and annoying, and he, Baba was just... Baba. That was all. Yet, they stayed together, defying every cultural convention of what a normal Nigerian marriage should be.

"Baba, why do you put up with her?" he asked, hesitantly.

"Because I made her like that," Baba said, simply. "She's had to make some sacrifices, the kind that you will probably never have to make or experience."

Dauda didn't understand what Baba was saying, and he decided to let it slide. It was nighttime and it was at least a thirty-minute walk to his house. He also hoped to see Morenike.

Morenike! Dauda jumped to his feet. They were supposed to meet tonight.

"Baba, well, you're home and you're safe now. I need to go. I'm meeting someone tonight," he said. He yawned and started walking away.

Baba watched his receding back then started across the road to where Munira was. He could see a light burning in their room. He took in a deep breath, stood up and headed for his home.

Their room was open as the night was humid, so Baba just walked in. Munira lay on the bed fanning herself with a battery-charged mobile fan. He went over and lay down beside her on the bed turning his face towards her. They watched each other in silence for a few moments.

"I hope you didn't get up to any stupidity with that rascal, Dauda," she said.

"He's not a rascal," Baba said. "And you need to buy him a new phone."

"Why?"

"Because somebody stole his phone because of us," Baba said. He wasn't going to tell Munira that the phone was stolen while they were filming behind her back, something Olabisi had warned them not to do. "He was just minding his own business when one of those useless area boys snatched it from his hands. If it wasn't for him, you and I wouldn't even be in this Mosquito Man business, in the first place," he reminded her.

"Which area boy?" Munira asked, her voice rising. She knew them all and feared none.

Baba thought fast. If he gave her a name, she would march to the boy's house and beat him senseless until he shat out Dauda's phone from whatever orifice he'd hidden it.

Except there was no area boy.

"I don't know," he said. He got off the bed and began taking off his agbada. Munira stood up and peered into his eyes.

"Baba, what's going on?" she asked him.

"Nothing. I'm just trying to help someone who has been very good to us. That's all," Baba replied. He got into the bed.

Munira peered into his eyes. There was something shifty about Baba's story, but she didn't know what. But she did know that she would get to the bottom of it the next day, when she would march to the auto-repair shop and smack Dauda's head senseless. Then, she would give him the new phone.

Munira got into bed with Baba. She reached out for his underpants. A few moments later, Baba's soft moaning filled the dark, warm, night.

There was still no answer from Munira. Olabisi debated whether to go to Palemo, but knew that she had to give them some space. She had asked her driver's brother to set up camp outside their building. The boy was a loose cannon, but he was a broke loose cannon, which suited Olabisi perfectly.

"If you do well, you will get double," she had told him.

He had smiled and shunted off. Not for the first time, Olabisi wondered how two siblings could be so different. Kayode, her driver, was hardworking. He never complained about her long hours. He was expecting his first child and saving up for his wedding. His brother, on the other hand, spent his time smoking weed, getting into trouble with just about anyone and hassling Kayode for money.

Just then, her mobile phone rang. It was Kayode's brother's number.

"Ma," he started. "I don't know if this is something you want to know, but Baba and that young man have been filming something in Palemo on the boy's mobile phone. What should I do?" he asked.

Olabisi was calm. "Steal the young man's phone," she said and hung up the phone. Just over an hour later, he came over and dropped the phone at her house. He was so proud of himself. Munira took the mobile phone and placed it on her dining table. She stared at it for a while.

She wondered, why would Baba do this? She had really thought that they were getting to the place where they understood and trusted each other. Her driver's brother did not mention seeing Munira, so she had no way of knowing if she knew of Baba's latest shenanigans with Dauda, much less if she was a part of it.

It wasn't Baba's fault, she concluded. The man was like the wind. He went any way that he wanted, motivated only according to how opportunities presented themselves. But still, she couldn't help but feel a little hurt.

She didn't know Dauda, and from all intents and purposes, Baba and Munira, albeit grudgingly, it would seem, were fond of him. But she could not and would not allow him to destroy everything that she had worked for.

She called for her new maid to bring her a hammer. When it was brought to her, she went outside the house and took pleasure in smashing the mobile into obliterated pieces. When she finished, she swept up the debris herself and dumped it in her bedroom trash.

# 17

Munira yawned and reached out for her mobile phone.

"Morning, Munira." It was Olabisi. "I've got the camera crew," she said. "We'll be with you and Baba, traffic permitting, in just over an hour." She hung up abruptly.

Munira yawned, her mind going directly to what outfit she would wear. She decided on her gold-embroidered kaftan. Everybody complimented her when she wore it. And if this video was going to be seen by white people, then she wanted them to see her in all her 'African magical glory'.

She prodded Baba. He made a noise and shifted away from her. She kicked him in the shins. "Wake up, you fool," she said. "Olabisi is coming to pick us up."

Baba shifted even further away from her and made as if he was going to sleep. Under the covers, Munira lifted her feet and pushed him off the bed.

"Munira! Are you crazy?" Baba yelled, scrambling to his feet. "If I didn't know better, I would think you were trying to kill me!"

Munira ignored him. "Olabisi is coming here in an hour. Go and shower and make sure you brush your teeth with toothpaste," she said. "Nobody wants to smell your chewing stick breath. And you better scrub yourself well as well," she continued. "We are going to be walking around Palemo. No need for you to stink out the group when we're filming in your hometown."

Munira turned her back. "Baba, we haven't got all day. Get moving," she said. She stretched and closed her eyes.

Muyiwa wasn't sure about anywhere else in Lagos, but he knew that Mama Seyi had the best akara and dundun in the whole of the city. The akara weren't too greasy, like they tended to be in some places. Instead, they were light and crisp. Biting into them was like a taste of bean heaven. And when paired with dundun, the fried yams, Muyiwa knew for sure that he had reached second heaven.

He was on his second helping when he saw Dauda approaching the auto-repair shop. The boy ignored him and proceeded to unlock the gate. Muyiwa made sure he finished his meal and told himself to take a third helping with him when he was ready to leave the auto-repair shop. He wondered if he should do a web series on street stalls of Lagos. That was the kind of stuff that would do well on YouTube and basically destroy his journalistic integrity. Still, it would be a fun side project. He decided that he would do it; set up his own YouTube channel, 'Street Food Stalls of Lagos'. It was the kind of stuff Westerners liked. Maybe he could even be a YouTube star. Maybe he was being stupid. Muyiwa forced his over-active imagination back to the present.

He wiped his hands on a napkin and followed Dauda

inside the auto-repair shop.

"You're either brave or stupid," Dauda said without turning around. He was changing into his overalls. "I know you stole my mobile. But don't worry, I know people who will ensure that you do not get away with this thievery."

Dauda turned around to face Muyiwa. "You stole from me," he said.

"For the last time, I haven't got any idea what you're talking about," Muyiwa said. "Why would I steal your phone when you said you were going to meet me?"

"Because you know that Baba does not have a mobile phone. You didn't have a way of contacting him, and somehow you knew that we were doing—" Dauda stopped himself. There was no need for Muyiwa to know what they were doing. He had been counting on the element of surprise and there was nothing to say that after he got his new mobile from Munira, he and Baba couldn't do the same again, but he doubted it. Olabisi and her film crew would probably start filming today.

Dauda drew in a deep breath. There was no point in going over the past. He made himself think of Morenike and felt calm. He could hear her voice telling him he took things too seriously, and should relax more. Which was strange for him, because all his life, he'd been told the exact opposite.

"Muyiwa, what do you want?"

Muyiwa took a few steps towards him. "To talk. That's all," he said. He sat himself on Baba's chair and watched as Dauda set up the television. He fumbled with the switches and settled on Al-Jazeera.

"Get off Baba's chair," Dauda said mildly. Muyiwa stood up.

"Look," his voice was earnest. "I know that things haven't exactly worked out between us. I don't even know where you got this idea that I'm trying to cheat you or something. But, let's say that we leave all that in the past and concentrate on what's important: Baba and getting water for Palemo residents. That's the most important thing. Is it not?"

The auto-repair shop gates swung open and Dimeji came in. He didn't seem surprised to see Dauda and Muyiwa inside. He greeted them good morning and proceeded to change into his overalls. When he finished, he went outside. Muyiwa and Dauda heard him call out to Mama Seyi for breakfast. There was a thud as he sat down on the auto-repair shop bench in front of the gate.

Muyiwa stood. He felt rather silly, standing there, waiting for Dauda to bestow upon him his talkative presence.

"Muyiwa, did you steal my mobile phone?" Dauda asked him again.

Muyiwa threw up his hands in frustration. "I honestly don't know what you're talking about," he said.

Dauda didn't believe him, but he still had something to gain from partnering with Muyiwa, so he decided to let it go. Just then they heard a commotion at the gate and a familiar shriek. Dauda looked at Muyiwa for a few seconds before stepping outside. Munira was there with a WfN 4x4 and the lady Olabisi whom Dauda had seen on television a few times.

She was even more stunning in close range, he thought to himself. For a few minutes, he fantasised about how Morenike would look if she had the same money as Olabisi, concluding that she would look better.

Baba was wearing an agbada that he had never seen before. Munira a rainbow-coloured kaftan that commanded respect. As usual, her face was caked in her expertly drawn make-up.

Munira was shouting at the driver to mind her clothes. "I don't know where you learned to drive," Dauda heard her say. Dauda wasn't sure, but he thought that he heard the driver retort under his breath, "At least I can drive."

Baba's eyes brightened when he saw Dauda. "See, Dauda, I told you that we would come for you," he said, a little too brightly Dauda thought. If he wasn't careful, he would rumble their secret to Munira.

There was three people carrying what seemed like film equipment in black padded, leather cases. I had fewer than that and I still made a great video, Dauda thought bitterly.

Olabisi came round to meet Dauda and held out her hands. "I'm Olabisi. I've heard so much about you," she said.

Her gaze was cool, equally assessing and arresting at the same time. Dauda took her hands in his. He didn't know what to say, so he just nodded.

Muyiwa came out of the auto-repair shop. As soon as Olabisi saw him, her face hardened.

"What is he doing here?" she asked Dauda coldly.

"I can go wherever and do whatever I want," Muyiwa

replied.

"Why are we waiting?" Munira looked around. She looked so happy, it was almost childlike. "We have a film to do!" she clapped her hands delightfully.

"Dauda, see how much I care for you, after all the insults and abuses you give. I bought you a new phone when Baba mentioned that you lost your own," Munira reached out into her voluminous handbag and handed a new phone to Dauda. He took it from her. It was a good model, and most importantly, not made in China, so it would last long. He turned the phone over in his hand. The whole thing was so stupid. He didn't even know anybody's number, which meant that he had to start adding numbers manually. In her own way, Munira did care. She was just a pain in the ass.

"Thank you," he smiled at her. "I know you care, but you didn't have to bribe me with a phone to help you with this film. After all, we're doing it for Palemo, aren't we?"

Munira smiled magnanimously. She turned to the cameraman. "Are you sure you're capturing this on camera?" she asked him. The man gave her a restrained smile. "Yes, ma," he replied.

Olabisi was still shooting daggers at Muyiwa. All this time, Dimeji was eating. "Dauda, who will look after the auto-repair shop while you're going round becoming a film star?" he asked him.

"Enough of this waiting around. Let's go," Munira said.

Olabisi pulled herself away from Muyiwa. "This is not finished," she warned him.

She turned to face her film crew. "Baba and Munira, I want you both to go and stand over there and walk towards the auto-repair shop, as if you were just coming to it for the first time this morning. Dauda and Dimeji, you get back inside and come out when Baba and Munira knock on the auto-repair shop door. Then, just talk as you normally would. The next shot will be of Baba getting food from Mama Seyi. Baba, you will face the camera and talk about how much Mama Seyi's food means to you—"

"Yes, and be sure to film the bit when I give her money," Munira jumped in. She knew white people liked generous people, so if the film showed her kindness, the Mosquito Man would be more favourably inclined towards her.

Olabisi knew better than to argue with Munira. Best to feed her delusions and then edit out everything they didn't want, in the final cut. She didn't need to be in the filming, but she wasn't willing for any more things to go wrong.

"Yes, Munira," she said.

Baba beamed. Everything was coming together, just like he wanted. Dauda had a new phone. Mama Seyi would get her money. The Mosquito Man would see their film and he would be reassured of their commitment to getting water for Palemo.

"Muyiwa, you're not needed here, so please disappear," Olabisi said.

"And I told you that it was a free country," he shot back.

"If you don't leave this auto-repair shop, I will personally kill you myself," Munira threatened.

Muyiwa looked around him and decided that it was best to leave. "It's not over, Olabisi," he said.

"If I hear my name on your lips again, I will cut them off!" Olabisi called to his receding back. "Right, Baba and Munira, start walking!"

Baba and Munira walked to the end of the street. Munira talked animatedly. As she gesticulated, her red-painted nails and bangles made clinking noises. Beside her, Baba remained quiet.

"Baba, if you ruin this for me, it would not be funny," Munira spoke from the side of her mouth.

The cameraman and the sound engineer both approached them. Munira looked at the huge microphone and she beamed. Looking at her, Baba wondered how it was that she came to be with him. She was made for the camera.

"You're the one ruining it for me," Baba replied. "I don't even know why you're here. You were only supposed to be filmed pretending to go to an audition."

"Shut up," Munira hissed.

It was 8am. A small crowd was beginning to gather around them. For a few seconds Olabisi wondered if they would have been better filming a guerrilla-style documentary on her smartphone. She summoned one of the crew members. Really, the man was nothing more than a thug, but he came in useful for situations like this.

"People are gathering, so make sure they don't mess up my film," she told him. As he hurried to marshal the gathering crowd, she was tempted to stop filming and ask Munira again to confirm that she wouldn't be troubled by the area boys.

She didn't care what the do-gooders called them. They were gangsters, who spent their days and nights terrorising hardworking citizens. For all the talk about the rising Nollywood industry, she knew its greatest danger was the area boys who terrorised the film crew at every shoot; demanding protection money.

They were the scum of the earth, she thought to herself.

Her thug corralled the crowd. She moved in closer to watch Munira and Baba. She noticed how animated Munira appeared in front of the camera. It was like she morphed into another character, another being. She was thriving and the camera loved her. Glancing at Munira's co-star, Olabisi found it was impossible to judge what Baba was thinking.

As they approached the auto-repair shop Baba knocked on the gate. Dauda came out with a bemused smile on his face. Olabisi bit her lip. The whole point was that it would look natural. She held up her hands to motion for them to stop.

"Dauda, try and make it look natural," she told him. "Does Baba knock on the gate when he comes in the morning?" she asked him.

"Of course not," Baba said. "If there's no one here, I wait. Then, when they come, they open up, and we both walk in."

"Then, let's do that, then," Olabisi said.

They started filming again. Olabisi looked around and saw that the crowd was getting bigger. She drifted away and

called her band of rent-a-police. It was only a matter of time
before the media found out about the filming and descended
on the auto-repair shop.

## 18

Baba turned back with Munira and walked up to the top of the street, again. Dauda's filming had not taken this long or been this stressful. He motioned to Olabisi.

"Baba, what are you doing?" Munira hissed at him. She was sweating heavily. This was the third time they'd walked to the beginning of the street, because Olabisi wasn't happy with the way they were doing it. Apparently, the two of them were 'acting'. She'd also asked Munira to "tone it down." To which Munira told her to shut up, and said accusingly, what did she know about acting? An argument ensued, which ended only when Baba walked off, and was reluctantly cajoled back to continue, by Dauda.

In the meantime, the crowd had swelled. They were now being filmed by a Nigerian News crew. He wasn't sure but he thought he could see Muyiwa lurking behind a cameraman.

Baba gritted his teeth. This was getting too much—again.

"What does it look like?" he replied. "I've had enough, so I'm leaving," he replied. He made as if to wipe the sweat off Munira's face and she batted away his hands in irritation.

The crowd twittered. The film crew hung back in deference.

Baba made as if to walk off again, but Munira jerked him by his agbada. She turned to face the camera with a sweet smile and spoke in Yoruba. "This is how we argue. Like most men, he doesn't like stress, so he just walks off."

The cameramen just kept on watching. Olabisi made motions with her hand for the film to keep on rolling. Baba sighed. Then, he thought that he was being selfish. So what if Dauda's mobile had been stolen. This was not about him. This was about getting water for Palemo. To a certain extent, it was even about getting back on track with Munira. To being a normal couple, maybe even have children.

He began walking and talking to the camera in Yoruba. "So, in the morning, I come here. I look to see if Mama Seyi has set up her stall and ask her to give me breakfast." They approached Mama Seyi who gave them a self-conscious smile. Munira positioned herself in front of the camera, reached into her bag and brought out some cash, which she handed to Mama Seyi, in the manner of a benevolent benefactor. Mama Seyi held out her hands, and looked at the camera. For a while, Baba thought she would complain about how the money wasn't enough, but she didn't. Instead she pocketed the money and gave Munira a meaningful nod. The kind of nod that said, *You owe me for not disgracing you in public.*

"Mama Seyi makes the best dundun and akara in the whole of Lagos," Baba said. He pointed and crossed the road to the auto-repair shop. "And here is where I spend most days. It was in this auto-repair shop that I saw the Mosquito Man and I got the idea that perhaps he could help us get water for

Palemo—"

"And while he's here, I spend my time going to auditions, because I'm an actress," Munira interrupted.

"No one asked you," Baba said.

They started squabbling. Olabisi sighed. It was going to be a really long day.

They were at Palemo bus stop. Olabisi had decided that they didn't need her film crew. This time, they were going to go organic and use her mobile phone. The crowd of people had swelled. Munira refused to leave Baba's side, so Olabisi conceded and let her appear in every scene. She was persistent, that one, Olabisi thought and had cleverly pretended to go along with the idea that she would appear in the audition scene only, all the while knowing that she intended to insert herself in every single scene, so she couldn't be edited out. Oh yes, Munira was as sly as she was abrasive. Inwardly, Olabisi applauded her conniving, enterprising spirit. She just wished that she wasn't the recipient of her cunning.

When they reached the bus stop, Baba grew solemn.

"Baba, what are you thinking?" Dauda asked him in Yoruba. As if he didn't know. As if they hadn't been through this yesterday.

Baba wasn't listening. In his mind's eye, he saw himself arriving in Palemo. All he had was a shirt and drawstring trousers. He was so full of hope, then. The bus stop had been busy, and he'd thought that he'd found himself in some foreign country. Even the women were different; they were more forthright, which scared him, because he'd had no idea how to approach them.

Baba didn't answer Dauda. He went to a spot by the crowded road and pointed to it. "There, right here, is where I got off the bus," he said.

"Baba, tell them what you did after," Munira said, her voice gentle.

The sudden pain flitting across Baba's face and lodged in his eyes, mirrored her own emotions and she stifled the desire to weep for the two of them. She patted him on the shoulder.

Watching them, Dauda sensed that they were united with something that was powerful, yet, invisible to those who were watching them. Even Olabisi cautioned everyone that was around them to be silent.

Baba looked at Munira remembering the look of awe on her face when she alighted the bus after their marriage in Ibadan.

"Baba, thank you for bringing me here," she had said excitedly. He hadn't said anything, because he was content to just watch her. At the back of his mind was the thought and concern that the loan sharks would come calling for their money soon, and he had no idea how to pay them.

"Remember what you said when you got off the bus?" Baba said to Munira, looking at her with a strange look on his face.

Munira didn't want to remember. Baba had taken her to their room in Palemo and a few hours later, the loan sharks had come. She refused to dwell on the terrible hours she endured after, at the hands of those men.

"We will not speak of such things, Baba" Munira said. By now, she was sweating heavily. Baba reached out to wipe her face, and she let him.

Everybody continued watching them, because it was clear that they were in their own world.

"Baba, how did you know there was a problem with water, in Palemo?" Dauda interrupted. He wasn't sure how long he could continue doing this. Already he'd been away from the auto-repair shop for a few hours. If Mr Sowemimo knew, he, Dauda, was dead meat.

"My first night. It occurred to me that we were surrounded by water. The swamp, the canals, and yet, clean drinking water was a serious problem. So I didn't bathe," Baba said. "Or, I did. But only every couple of days, to preserve water. And when I did find water to bathe, I developed lesions all over my body," he finished.

So that was where he got his hygiene habit from, Olabisi thought.

They continued walking. Baba pointed out a building. "This is the only school in Palemo. I thought about going there for a while, but can you imagine a twenty-year-old man in a class full of six-year-olds?" He said. "When I was there, they just had a few tables and chairs. Now, I'm told that they don't even have that. Just mats that children sit on and a blackboard."

"I went to this school," Dauda said.

"And look where it got you," Munira said. All three of

them laughed.

They moved on from the bus stop to the swamp. Munira and Baba grew quiet.

"Terrible things happened here," Baba said. He stretched out his hand towards the water. It was rank and packed with people in canoes going about their business. "We have water and yet, we do not. What is stopping the government from draining this swamp and using technology to give us water? I may not be an educated man, but I watch television. I know that it can be done."

There was a scuffle. They all turned to see a rotund man surrounded by what can only be described as henchmen.

"I command you to stop this right now! You do not have filming permission," he said.

"And you are?" Olabisi asked him, with a lift of her eyebrows.

"I am the councillor," he said. He tried to snatch the phone from Olabisi's hands. Everyone stood by silently. Nobody liked crossing politicians.

"If you touch my phone, I will make sure you lose your job by this time tomorrow," Olabisi said.

The councillor took a menacing step towards her. Olabisi didn't flinch.

"Do you know who I am?" he asked. He raised his hands as if to strike her. Kayode ran in and put himself in the middle. Olabisi pushed Kayode away and stood in front of the councillor.

"I do not need permission from you to film here, because

it is not a commercial film. I'm a civilian documenting what's going on in this community. Remember my name; Olabisi Thomas and I'm telling you that by this time tomorrow, you will not have a job," she said.

The councillor's henchman rushed towards her, but the councillor held up his hand to stop them. "You too should remember my name," he said, before walking off.

Olabisi wiped her eyebrows. "I think we've done enough for today. Well done, Baba and Munira. Let's say we pack up and go and eat," she said.

She swiped her mobile phone and walking away for some privacy spoke into it. The words "has just threatened me," hung in the air. She listened for a few moments and then hung up the telephone, satisfied.

"Everybody, let's pack out," she said.

Dauda looked at her. He had no doubt that by tomorrow morning, their local councillor would be out of a job. And it was entirely the councillor's fault. He was so stupid, Dauda thought. Instead of threatening them, all the councillor had to do was congratulate Olabisi publicly for bringing the world's attention to Palemo. Now, he was out of a job, probably for life.

Most people knew Olabisi's father was a well-known mogul and one of the people who pulled Nigeria's economic and political strings. He was known for being merciless. He would ensure the councillor lost his job and make sure that he never worked anywhere, that's even if he would ever walk again by the time Olabisi's father's thugs finished with him.

No one raised their hands to a rich man's kid in Nigeria, even if that rich man's kid was openly sleeping with a Chinese man and in her 30s and unmarried.

Stupid councillor, Munira and Baba thought. He really should've let it go. They wondered when his body would be fished out of the swamp. Really, it was a matter of time.

# 19

Baba gave a satisfied belch and patted his stomach.

"Didn't I tell you to use toothpaste this morning, instead of chewing stick?" Munira asked him, covering her mouth with her lacquered hands.

Baba ignored her. He summoned the waitress.

"Bring me ice cream," he commanded.

"He's not having ice cream or anything else," Munira said. She shooed the waitress away. "And shut up," she warned Baba. "With everything else I have to put up with, I don't need your ice cream induced wretched farts poisoning me as I sleep."

Olabisi coughed. On the table, her phone vibrated. She looked at the screen and smiled.

"Baba, you see. I told you it would work. We put up the video on the internet and already it's got ten thousand views," she said.

"He doesn't know what the internet is," Munira said.

"I don't care either," Baba said. He raised his hand again.

"If you raise your hand again, I will break it," Munira threatened.

Baba put his hand down. It wasn't even that the restaurant

was nice. Mama Seyi's food was so much better. But the food was there and he had been told that he could eat anything he wanted, so naturally, he availed himself of the opportunity.

"So, what do we do now?" Munira asked.

"We continue as usual," Olabisi said. "And we remain honest towards each other. If anybody asks to do a deal with them, you tell me. Not because I want your money, but because any deal you make automatically negates the one you made with Michael's company. And remember, the more you stick to the deal, the more your final pay-out will be. You know his company already; Chino-Centric. They made $100bn in Nigeria alone last year, so money is not their problem. And they're not patient people. So if they hear that you're going behind their backs, they will not be happy," she said, looking at them both clearly and for a full minute each, before turning her face.

Munira didn't blink. She hated being spoken to, like she was stupid. Also, it reminded her of her time in Ibadan.

"I've told you not to talk to me like I'm stupid," she said. "If that's all, Baba and I will be on our way," she said, getting up.

Olabisi's mobile vibrated again. She picked. There were a few "hmms". When she hung up, she clasped her hands and put them on the table.

"That is the Mosquito Man's people. They've seen the video. They said they want to meet you in Abuja next week when he comes for that conference. They also said the only people they would work with is WfN," she said. "They've seen our work and they know we're genuine. They're worried that there are so many scammers in Nigeria, working with one person only is their way of keeping things neat."

Munira beamed. That's it. She was going to be a famous producer and Nollywood actress.

Baba looked down on the table, with a deeply troubled expression.

Back in the auto-repair shop, the crowd had assembled again. Mr Sowemimo was strutting up and down and playing to his audience.

"So you see. It's because of me, because I gave Dauda time off to go and do his filming, that you all could see that video on social media. Because I'm a local businessman, a member of this community, and I understand that the film is important..."

On his favourite chair in the auto-repair shop, Baba shook his head. The man had done nothing for Dimeji and Dauda since they started working for him as apprentices. He barely paid them a salary, knowing that they had nowhere else to go. Was it any wonder that Dauda stole from him?

"Baba, should we get you some dundun and akara?" Dimeji now asked him.

He shook his head. Dauda and Dimeji looked at each other in surprise. Baba never turned down food.

"I don't know why you're both looking at me like that," Baba grumbled. "But seeing as you ask, please tell Mama Seyi to pack plenty of meat with the akara and dundun. I've brought her so much business today and she hasn't even thanked me," he complained.

Mr Sowemimo came inside the auto-repair shop looking pleased with himself. "See how I support you, Baba," he said.

He glanced around and his face hardened momentarily. "Dauda, if you dare leave my auto-repair shop again to go gallivanting with Baba, you'll see your Maker," he threatened.

"I've seen him already and he tells me I'm doing well so far," Dauda quipped.

Dimeji shook his head. Dauda and Mr Sowemimo were heading for a showdown and he knew that he would be caught in the middle. Even he had to concede that Dauda had grown more insolent. Perhaps Baba's fame was going to *his* head. Dimeji headed towards the door that led to the backyard. Let the two of them fight it out between them.

Mr Sowemimo started talking, then stopped. "I won't let you spoil my joy today. I can see ten new cars in the auto-repair shop and my mobile has been ringing all day." He turned to Baba. "They're waiting for you outside," he said. "Why don't you go out and greet them?"

"They'll wait there forever," Dauda said.

Mr Sowemimo shot Dauda a filthy glance, yawned and stretched his limbs. "I'm going home. But I warn you, if I hear of you disappearing again without my permission—"

Dauda didn't let him finish. He slid under a car and started pounding something in its underparts.

Baba motioned to Mr Sowemimo to leave him alone. He's young and foolish, he mouthed.

Mr Sowemimo nodded to agree with Baba. Dauda was a rascal, but he was also a good mechanic, which was why he kept him on. Everytime he thought about kicking him to the streets, he would think about how much he paid for him. Dauda and Dimeji were his, because he'd bought them, but the truth was that they could walk out and leave the auto-repair shop any time they wanted and what could he do? They were adults. And even if he summoned a few area boys to rough them up and back into submission, he knew it wouldn't work. Dauda was potty-mouthed, but he was still popular with the area boys, so they wouldn't dispense the kind of justice that he wanted.

"Baba," Mr Sowemimo now said. "I'm going out. Should I ask Mama Seyi to bring you some food?"

"Dundun and akara with plenty of meat. And tell her to add ice cold Coke to it as well," Baba replied.

"It's not your fault," Mr Sowemimo said. He left the auto-repair shop.

Dauda slid out from under the car. "Baba, you should be celebrating your achievement. The Mosquito Man wants to meet you again," he said.

Baba looked woeful. Dauda wiped his greasy hands on a rag and came to sit beside him.

"I hate that man," he spat out. "He's always telling me that he bought me, so can do whatever he wants, but one day, I will show him." He looked at Baba.

"Baba, what's wrong? Are you afraid that Munira will come and mess things up again?" he teased him.

Dimeji came back inside and positioned himself in front of the television. He turned up the volume slightly and turned his back to them. Dauda and Baba resumed their conversation.

"Dauda, is this the right thing?" Baba asked him quietly.

Dauda got up and went outside. Baba heard a roar from the crowd and a flurry of questions from the media.

"Baba, where is your wife?"

"Baba, come out and talk to us!"

"Baba, when is the Mosquito Man coming?!"

Dauda came back inside the auto-repair shop with some steaming dishes, which he gave to Baba.

Baba opened them up.

"She's only given me five pieces of meat," he said. "After all I've done for her." He hissed and started eating.

"Shouldn't you even wash your hands first?" Dauda asked.

Baba spoke with his mouth full. "Have I ever?"

Dauda showed Baba his mobile screen. There was a picture of the auto-repair shop. There was a bulging crowd of people and film crew waiting in the scorching heat.

"Baba," Dauda flicked through several images. "These people are screaming and waiting for you."

"But why?" Baba asked. What did they want? His sense of unease and foreboding grew even stronger.

"Because this thing is bigger than you," Dimeji said. "It's about Palemo and our water problem."

Baba and Dauda looked at him in surprise. He rarely, if ever engaged in their conversations. And when he did, usually, it was to admonish Dauda about one thing or another.

Baba shook his head and continued attacking his food. Dauda let him eat. When he finished, before he could start wiping his hands on his agbada, Dauda hastily produced a napkin for him to wipe his hands with. Baba used it, finished and threw it on the floor, then sat back and watched the television for a few moments. The late afternoon bulletin came on. As if in slow motion, Baba saw himself on the screen with Munira and their adventure by the swamp being replayed. The scene cut and suddenly, they were showing outside the auto-repair shop. There was a reporter talking. Dauda, Dimeji and Baba leaned in to hear what she was saying.

"We're outside the auto-repair shop where Baba normally hangs out with some mechanic friends of his. Some people say the young boys are really his sons, but it's hard to say. We interviewed the auto-repair shop owner, Mr Sowemimo and this is what he had to say about Baba and the Mosquito Man."

Again, the scene cut again and swung to Mr Sowemimo. Dimeji muted the television and went back to work.

Baba's sense of unease deepened. He wished there was somewhere he could go and just disappear. When he started this thing, it was a mad idea. And now, it was going places that he never thought possible.

He wished Munira was with him. She might be cruel, but at least she understood him. She would know what to say to get rid of his fears. He decided that he was going home.

He stood up and sat back down again. There was no way he could leave the auto-repair shop in one piece. He wondered how Munira was faring. She had preferred to go home after their meeting with Olabisi.

All those people outside, waiting and clamouring for him. He wondered where they had been in the past thirty years he'd been living in Palemo. Some of those people he saw every day on his way to the auto-repair shop. They laughed at him, especially when he and Munira would fight publicly and start calling each other names. And now, when they thought they could get something from him, they suddenly started treating him well and giving him respect. The only people who remained constant in their relationship to him were his wife, Dauda and Dimeji, and even the area boys, who were gangsters through and through. Before all the palaver with the Mosquito Man, they would sometimes harass him for money, for a joke, because they knew he didn't have anything. And in any case, they knew, feared and respected Munira in equal measure. They still were the same now.

And there was the issue of the radio station and the plane tickets they'd given him and Dauda. He didn't know what Munira intended to do with those tickets. Knowing her, she would probably sell the tickets and pocket the money, doling it out to him in portions, as if he was a child. And that was the thing about Munira. She was crass and cruel, but she was honest. Take the money they received from Olabisi for instance. He knew that she would have secreted it away in a bank account somewhere and in several nooks in their home. Most Nigerian balked at the thought of giving their wife control over their finances, but Baba was happy for Munira to do it for them.

Truth was that, he found money unpleasant. In his 54-odd years on earth, he had learned that he didn't need much to survive. As long as he had a roof over his and enough to line his stomach, he didn't need much.

Life was stressful and terrible in Nigeria, especially Lagos, a city that wrought havoc on people's lives. But he'd learned not to worry too much about what he would eat, because somehow he always got by. Yes, there were times when, before he married Munira, he wouldn't eat for days. And when he did, he learned to consume as much as he could, as fast he could, to last him until the next meal. But he felt, money did strange things to people. Nigerians worshipped money. They talked about it incessantly; where to get it and what to do with it once they got it. It was made worse by the thieving politicians who used the country's money as their own. They and the godfathers who ruled the country with an iron fist.

His own tribes people, Yorubas, were even the worst when it came to the worship of money. They were the flashiest of all Nigerian tribes. Any excuse to throw a party and parade their wealth, they did it. There is a well-known Nigerian saying: 'Yorubas don't need an excuse to have a party'. Which was true. Even in his tiny hometown in Ibadan, they threw parties for the stupidest reasons.

Money corrupted people. He was beginning to think that Olabisi was different from her father, but hearing her on the phone as she sought to destroy that councillor's life, without so much as a heartbeat, convinced him that rich people really only thought of themselves.

But he needed her. His and Dauda's plot had been hare-brained to say the least. People like him, Munira and Dauda did not know how to speak to white people like the Mosquito Man and even that Chinese guy.

They needed her. Palemo needed Olabisi.

He returned his gaze to the television. He would wait until after the auto-repair shop closed and make his way home through the backdoor.

He wondered if Munira was with the landlord and decided that he didn't want to know. He breathed in heavily.

"Dimeji, you can put the volume back on. Maybe you should change the channel to that music that you useless young people like," he said.

Dimeji complied. Dauda went back to work.

Munira and Baba were behaving, her spy said. As far as he could see, nobody had spoken directly to Baba in the auto-repair shop. He didn't have a mobile, so Olabisi knew that he couldn't contact anybody.

Munira was holed up in their one-room home. She refuses to come out of her room. Her second spy said that the crowd had thinned out.

So far, so good. It was a master stroke lying to them about the Mosquito Man saying that they would only deal with Munira and Baba if they worked through Water for Nigerians, but it was necessary. She had to keep WfN in the picture. Besides, she meant what she said about increasing their payout for good behaviour. She was sure she could wrangle the extra funds from Michael. With the exposure they would get from Munira and Baba, and the money they would also get from Chino-Centric, life was looking very good indeed. Her father had also called her back to let her know that the councillor was 'taken care of'. She didn't ask what he meant nor did she want to know. She smiled to herself. She'd sent a lesson to anyone who would try and bully any woman in public again. When the councillor had raised his hand to strike her and also strip her naked, Nigeria's favourite way of humiliating 'troublesome women', she'd been so angry, she hadn't thought twice about calling her father.

She turned on her laptop and started going through her emails. There was another one from her anonymous sender. She clicked it open. This time, the images were of collapsing buildings in Cairo. She closed the email and stared into space.

Like a queen, Munira waved, as she stepped out of the WfN's jeep, first to the cobbler across the street and then, to the crowd. Her feet had barely touched the floor before Kayode the driver drove away with a squeal. Munira opened her mouth to rain abuses on his ignorant head, but decided against it. She was a big star now. It wouldn't look good for her to be seen on camera behaving like an uneducated woman.

The crowd roared. The media surged towards her. Munira stood and said, just as Olabisi had taught her, "I have no more statements to make. Thank you and have a good evening," and because she wanted them to come back tomorrow, just because she could, she added. "Come back tomorrow for some special news!"

She waved again and entered her building. Inside her room, she took off her kaftan. Absentmindedly, she thought that she should update her wardrobe again and made a note to ask Olabisi to fund the expense. If she wanted Munira and Baba exclusively, then it was only fair that she should pay for the privilege.

It was hot. What she wanted to do was have a cold bath, but she couldn't do that, not with the media and useless money grabbers camped outside her home. One of the curses of living in a settlement was the fact that they had to bathe in the open. She thought of the hotel's bathroom and sighed. Even though she had made a big deal about staying at the hotel, the truth was that she was happy to be back in Palemo. This was a community of people who respected her. She knew some of them couldn't stand her, but at least they knew her. Nobody turned down their nose at her, because they were all busy trying to survive. And whatever they think she does, she knew, just as much as they knew, that they were all just trying to survive.

At the hotel, she'd felt the disdain of the staff, and had been unable to shift the feeling that she wasn't meant to be there. It wasn't that anybody said anything directly; indeed they went out of their way to be courteous, but she knew that they made fun of her and Baba behind their backs. She wasn't sure, but she thought she'd even heard the maid who came to clean their room titter, because she'd overheard Baba ask if they had enough space to pack the hotel towels. He had thought that they were free, as had Munira as well.

When the maid had said, condescendingly, "The towels are for use at the hotel and not to be taken, that would be stealing, sir," Munira hadn't stopped to think. Before Baba could do anything she'd dealt the maid two quick slaps for her insolence.

It had been over in a few seconds.

She wasn't sorry for slapping the maid. She would do it all over again, and this time, give her even more slaps. She hated being patronised and condescended to. But she hated Baba being patronised and condescended to even more.

He was a good man. Useless, but worth more than all of those thieving rich people, she thought to herself, fiercely.

Sweat poured down her chest. She took a battery powered fan from her handbag and turned it on. The gentle whirring calmed her for a while.

After a few minutes, she got off the bed and peeked through the curtains. The media companies had gone and the crowds had thinned. The knocking on her door had gone down as well.

She spotted the cobbler across the road and smiled to herself. She couldn't wait for him to finish night school. She would throw him the biggest party ever, Yoruba style, a proper *faaji*, enjoyment, as Yorubas would call it.

She heard footsteps and a tentative knock on the door. At first, she ignored it, but then decided to open it. It wasn't the landlord, he was a wily one. He had his own keys to every room in the house, and with her, a special code.

Munira went to the door and opened it slightly. It was the little-girl-film-director.

"I thought it best for us to talk," she said.

Munira opened the door wider and let her inside. She waited to be told where to sit. Munira gestured to the only chair in the room. She sat down, while Munira sat on the bed.

"Does he know you're here?" Munira asked her.

"Of course not," the girl said. "But I'm sure you were expecting me anyway," she added.

Munira let her speak. She had been thinking of a way to get hold of the director, as the landlord refused to give her mobile number, but she didn't want the director to know that.

"I think you know why I'm here," the girl said.

"Why don't you tell me, so that I can make up my mind myself," Munira said.

The girl started speaking and as she spoke, Munira could see that she had underestimated her indeed. Her small frame and youthful face belied someone that wise and canny beyond her years.

"I'm tired of having men rule over my life," she said. "From my father, to my brothers, and now this man, this landlord, a sugar daddy, that thinks he owns me. I know what I'm capable of, and I think that you and I, we can do great things for this movie—without him," she sneered when she said his name.

"Do you know what he will do if he finds out?" Munira asked. She could take care of herself. She just didn't want to take care of someone else.

"Aunty—" Munira found herself bristling when the girl called her aunty, then calmed down. Coming from the girl, it was a sign of respect, not a term of ridicule that casting agents would use to mock her at auditions.

*Aunty, should you be here? The casting call said women aged between 18-24.*

*Aunty, the role is for slim young girls. At your age, shouldn't you be...?*

But not this young director. Munira considered herself a good judge of character. She peered closely into the girl's eyes and saw her life mirrored in them. The girl looked away.

"I just want to be secure and to be free," she said. Tears fell down her cheeks.

It was then that Munira knew, just like every person who had ever been abused, knew.

"You can stop crying now. It's okay. We will do the film together, without the landlord. Just act normal and when I get the money from this Mosquito Man's deal, we'll make our film. By then, it will be too late for the landlord to do anything, because I will have the Mosquito Man and his people on my side. Also, I will be even more rich and famous than I am now, and there will be nothing that he can do about it."

The girl sniffed and wiped her eyes. "Thank you," she whispered.

Dauda loved this time of his day. It was early evening. The crowds and the media people had left. Mama Seyi was packing up her wares. She asked if he wanted her leftovers. Dauda asked for meat and crossed the road to get it.

"Mama Seyi, you've had a good week, not so?" he asked her, as he sank his teeth into the meat. It was perfect, just the way he liked it. Spiced with *ata rodo*, chilli, garlic and ginger, and fried to perfection.

"We thank God," she said. "I saw your girlfriend with that boy from the television, the one who put Baba on television first," she added.

Dauda spoke automatically. "She's not—", then decided against it. Yes, she was his girlfriend, and what's more, he liked her being called his girlfriend. He didn't have much in this world, so this was something. "You did what?" he asked, when what she said dawned on him.

Mama Seyi locked up her stall. "Yes, I saw her. I forgot to pack something when I was going home, so I had to come back. And that's when I saw the two of them together, outside, on the bench," she pointed across the road to the bench outside the auto-repair shop. The bench only came out at lunchtime or in the evening, after they'd finished packing up. Sometimes, Dauda sat with Dimeji and they went over the details of the day. But most times, they sat in silence, watching the world go by.

"Come," Mama Seyi signalled to Fela. "Think before you act," she said, speaking over her shoulder, to Dauda, as she started walking down the street with her son.

# 20

Michael Li watched the images of the falling building. His face was impassive. When the clip finished, he turned to Olabisi.

"I fail to see where you're going with this," he said.

Olabisi opened her mouth to talk, then closed it.

"The buildings were constructed by local staff, and by a Chino-Centric subsidiary, a company registered in Egypt as an Egyptian entity, so I really don't see what this has got to do with Chino-Centric, or you," he added pointedly.

"We're a charity. We save lives by giving people access to water—" Olabisi started saying.

"Don't be stupid," Michael's voice was harsh. "If you're so concerned about helping people and saving lives, you would've spared that local councillor's life yesterday."

"That was different," Olabisi protested. "People like him threaten and intimidate women all the time..."

"You are your father's daughter," Michael said.

There was a tense silence. "You will never speak of my father again," Olabisi said.

Michael shrugged. Her father was a thug. She knew it, she just chose to ignore it.

"Anyway, this conversation is pointless. Just make sure

you get a picture of Bono right in front of a Chino-Centric logo or stand. It shouldn't be hard. We'll throw a party on behalf of Baba and Munira, right after the summit. The picture will also have our CEO in it, so it sends a clear message to the world that we are not monsters. Bono, Africa's saviour, is hanging out with us, so we can't be bad!"

"Chino-Centric is facing a class action for manslaughter in five African countries."

"No," Michael corrected her. "Chino-Centric's subsidiaries, independent entities separate from Chino-Centric, the global brand that provides water to billions of people from all over the world, are the ones facing the class action. These subsidiaries are wholly run and managed by local African staff, so in reality, it's the African companies that are facing a class suit, not Chino-Centric itself."

Michael changed the subject abruptly. "How are our two superstars?" he asked.

"They're well. We're calling another press conference this evening. Bono's spokesperson is going to talk via video link and then, we're off to Abuja in the next few days, to prepare for the summit. I even got a session," Olabisi added.

The invitation to host a session had come unexpectedly and no doubt, as a result of her sudden notoriety and association with Baba. They'd even made a specific request for Baba to be at the session. "Of course," Olabisi had said, knowing full well that she had no intention of honouring the request. If they actually thought that she would unleash Baba in a room filled with international guests of esteem, they had another think coming.

"Good," Michael said. "For the record, we will not have this conversation again. Deliver the goods and there's some solid cash in there for WfN and those crazy two. As a bonus, I'm not even going to sleep with Munira, although I really want to," he flashed Olabisi a sexy smile and left her office.

On paper, Chinese firms in Africa might concede strategic oversight to Africans, but Olabisi knew that, as a matter of policy, their operations and strategic implementations were overseen by Chinese people. Inherently racist Chinese people. And she also knew that they used inferior quality building materials.

*If their buildings were falling down due to bad construction quality, what makes you think they'll do differently in Nigeria?* The little voice inside her head reasoned.

But through WfN, she reasoned, she could use Chino-Centric as a force for good. Besides, $750K could really do a lot for thousands of communities in Nigeria. Communities like Palemo. It would be silly of her to turn down Chino-Centric's offer. And in any case, as Michael had pointed out, these were African companies, run by African people. The blame should go towards the African governments for not having a system of checks and balances. So *their* people's blood was on *their* hands.

She returned to her laptop.

Dauda sat on the bench. At first he was angry. Then, he thought he couldn't breathe. Then he felt like seeing Morenike and hurting her the way she'd hurt him. He stood, then sat back down on the bench.

The night was humid and still. The kind that ushered in the rainy season and blanketed Lagos in a pelting rain that, at times, seemed murderous. Ordinarily, he liked this kind of pre-rain night. He would sit on the bench for a few minutes, or an hour, depending on his mood and just watch the world go by. Tonight the air was so still he could catch people's voices. Turning his head to the side, he caught snippets of family life from all around; radio music, soft murmurings about mundane things; close the door, open the window. And then he heard them; Morenike's light laughter rising up and around Muyiwa's deep voice.

The blood rushed to his head. He stood up as if drunk. He walked the few metres from the bench to the street.

When Morenike saw him, she gave him what he used to think was his special smile. Meant for him and him alone, and now tainted by idea that Muyiwa too had been a recipient of it.

He ran over, ignoring Muyiwa and angrily grabbed her arm. "What is this nonsense?" he shouted. "Are you just one of those girls, stringing men along for money?" he shouted, shaking her arm.

Morenike howled in pain. "Dauda, what's wrong with you? Stop this," she tried to wriggle free.

Then Muyiwa reached out to stop him and fell back with a shout as Dauda landed him a blow on his cheek. He railed back lashing out in retaliation, but Morenike threw herself between them and the blow landed on the side of her head instead. She reeled from the impact. They both reached out to grab her before she fell to the ground.

Dauda pushed Muyiwa away. "Get your hands off her. If you touch her, I'll kill you, I swear I will. You've done nothing but bring stress to my life ever since we met," he said.

Muyiwa stepped back. He felt his face. There was going to be a nasty bruise and terrible swelling there in the morning. He spat out a mouthful of blood and saliva.

"Dauda, you're losing it," he started saying.

"And I'll lose it even more if you don't step away," Dauda replied.

Morenike groaned. Dauda picked her up and attempted to sit her upright on the bench. He felt her head gently. There didn't seem to be any swelling.

"Go and buy ice from the night market," he commanded Muyiwa.

Muyiwa looked as if he wanted to argue, but thought better of it. Morenike groaned again.

"We just met at the entrance of your street," Morenike spat out from the side of her mouth.

"Hush. You shouldn't talk," Dauda said. He wondered how he would get her home and what he would tell her father when he did get her home. He conceded that she would probably never leave her house again.

"You're too hot-blooded," Morenike said, her voice slurry. She passed out.

Dauda shook her. She came to and tried to get up. "I

sneaked out of the house. I have to go home. Otherwise my father will kill me," she swayed.

At this rate, he will kill us both, Dauda thought. He caught her as she swayed and helped her back to the bench. She rested her head on his shoulder and groaned.

"What were you doing with him?" Dauda asked, hating himself for asking, for doubting her.

"I told you; we met at the street entrance. I just wanted to check you were okay. First, you said some people stole your phone and then, I see on the news with Baba," she held her hand to her face and felt it gingerly. "I shouldn't be talking," she said.

Why did he doubt her?

"After tonight, if I'm still alive after my father's beating, I'm sure this is the last time we'll see each other. You were always so hot-headed..." her voice had started to slur again.

He shook gently. "Shh, don't talk. Muyiwa will be here shortly," he said. He pulled her closely to him and they both waited in silence.

Muyiwa returned with some ice cubes in a plastic bag, which they both applied to Morenike's head. Dauda, grudgingly, conceding that he needed help.

Morenike groaned. Suddenly, Dauda had an idea.

"We'll take her home and tell her father that we saw her being attacked by some area boys. We stepped in to help. And if he asks how we knew her home, we simply say that she showed us the way."

"You're willing to help me do this?" Muyiwa said.

"Two men helping her to get home is better than one. The story will sound more credible."

"You should know, you've been doing it for a while," Muyiwa said.

Dauda decided to let it pass. He would beat him to a pulp later. First, he stole his mobile phone, and then, somehow, managed to assault his girlfriend.

"I'm coming for you," Dauda told him. "And when I do, you will never forget me."

"Whatever," Muyiwa said. He stood up. "Are we going to talk all night or are we going to get this girl home?" he asked.

They both grabbed one of Morenike's arm each and loped it around their shoulder.

Moreniked winced and groaned. "I said to be gentle, you ignoramus!" Dauda said.

Muyiwa ignored him as they started walking with her barely conscious between them.

## 21

This time, the press conference was even more packed than usual. On the high table Baba looked at Olabisi. She looked exquisite. Munira looked like her beautiful self. She had forsaken her elaborate kaftan for an even more elaborate iro and buba, the traditional Yoruba attire. He shuddered to think how much Olabisi had paid for it.

As for him, he was in his simple traditional agbada. Unlike his fellow Yorubas, he didn't like being ostentatious and calling attention to himself. The only thing that Munira insisted on was that the agbada not be white.

"You eat like an animal, but that doesn't mean the whole world should know about it. Black. That way, any food stains or sweat patches would be hidden," she had said.

As if he cared what he wore anyway.

To his right was Olabisi and to his left was Munira. The more he looked at her the more he noticed, something about her looked different, but he didn't know what it was. As always she sparkled under the camera. If there was one thing he wished he could do for her, it was this, bring her under the camera lights, where she truly belonged.

Under the table, Munira patted his hand and gave him a

reassuring smile. He didn't smile back, because that wasn't really his way.

Olabisi tapped the microphone and the hall grew silent. "Thank you everybody for being here today," she started. She stretched her hand towards Munira and Baba. "Ladies and gentlemen, I give you Munira and Baba."

The room erupted into wild applause. Baba felt Munira urge him to stand up, which he did.

He wasn't sure why they were clapping, but he was beginning to find out that people applauded the silliest things. Munira pulled his agbada and they both sat down again. Baba spotted the young man from the BBC in the audience, only this time he was sporting a large bruise on his cheek. He didn't know how or why he thought this, but he knew that Dauda had something to do with it. He tried to focus his attention on what Olabisi was saying, but it was difficult. His new agbada itched and he was starting to feel claustrophobic.

Olabisi was talking in her oyinbo, white accent. He liked it when she spoke like that. Even when she spoke in Yoruba to him, most of the time, he could only make out eighty per cent of what she was saying. Baba shifted sideways. He wondered what Dauda and Dimeji were up to at the auto-repair shop. He hoped Dauda was behaving himself with the sweet seller. She seemed like a nice girl, quite unlike the streetwise girls who he was used to seeing with Dauda. He wondered what the girl saw in a useless boy like Dauda.

*Much like how people wonder what Munira is doing with you*, a voice inside his head said.

Once again, he tried to focus on what Olabisi was saying. It seemed that she was now talking about Water for Nigerians and why it is good for Palemo. He followed her hand as she pressed a button and the video they made appeared on the screen.

It was so strange seeing himself on the screen like that. His face looked old, weak and battered. On the other hand, Dauda seemed confident and full of life. He spoke to the camera like someone who was born to do it. Maybe it was because his generation were used to being on camera all their lives. He could see them sometimes, their eyes down and focused on the mobile screens, instead of the road they were crossing. He'd seen so many instances of where someone almost got killed by a speeding car or *okada*, motorcycle cab, because they weren't looking at where they were going.

Dauda would ask him a question in Yoruba, wait for Baba to speak and then, turn to the camera to interpret for the viewer in English.

Baba sneaked a look at the room and wondered what they were thinking. Did they see Palemo through his eyes, or was all they saw a settlement built on canals, reeking of shit and decomposing rubbish?

When they saw the school, did they see half-empty classrooms with mats and blackboards, and grime-coloured walls, or did they see that the children who couldn't afford to be there, even though their education was meant to be free, and had to go out hawking food and bring in money for their families? These same children who would grow up to be area boys, gangsters and prostitutes?

Did they see all that?

He continued looking at the video. There was Munira, her make-up way overboard as usual. The video had captured a scene in which they were bickering about his eating manners. The audience chortled. The last scene was the mangrove swamp. The room faded out to Baba's haunting words, as he and Munira looked straight at the swamp. They had pulled closely together, as they both remembered that terrible night when they had witnessed the police killing those young men.

"Terrible things have happened here. Who knows what secrets the earth will give up when they drain this swamp to get water for our community?"

The screen faded to black. The video itself was ten minutes long. There were a few moments of silence. Then, someone started clapping. Very soon, the room erupted into rapturous applause for the second time that evening. Everyone stood up. There were cries of "Baba!"

This time, Baba didn't need to be told what to do. He gathered himself and pulled Munira along with him. He smiled at her. She looked startled for a moment and then, she smiled right back.

Olabisi saw the applause and felt the adulation in her pores. She'd done it. The idea itself was so simple. As far as videos went, it wasn't slick. Her decision to ditch the film camera and have them film on her mobile had been a good move.

Editing had been quick as well. She had explained to her

film editor that she wanted something simple. Something that told Palemo's story and Baba's link to the place. She'd also decided that they wouldn't clean up Baba and Munira's character, and instead let them be. That last scene, in which they had leaned into each other and looked ahead at the swamp, united by a private event they'd clearly witnessed, but couldn't share with the world, was powerful. Baba's haunting words to the camera and to the world: "Who knows what secrets the swamp will unearth when it's finally drained and used to give the community water?"

She tapped the microphone and the room fell silent. "Thank you. Thank you. We will take questions shortly. But for now, I believe we have Bono's spokesperson on a live link."

The energy level in the room went up. They looked towards the video screen again. A man came on the screen.

"Hello, Baba," he said.

Olabisi saw Baba look around. "Baba, he's just greeting you," she said. "Just wave," she advised him.

Baba waved. Munira followed suit, her mouth set. Olabisi wondered what had set her off. Only a few minutes ago, she was glowing from the reception she got from the video, and now, this.

"Thomas, it's good to see you," Olabisi said.

"Good to talk to you live via video link. Baba, Bono, or should I call him the Mosquito Man, couldn't be here with us today. But he sends his regards and says he can't wait to see you in Abuja next week."

Munira spoke into Baba's ear to translate. Baba nodded,

because he wasn't sure if he was meant to answer the white man or not.

"Thank you," Olabisi said. "We can't wait to meet you too."

The man waved and the screen cut off. Olabisi turned to the press.

"We will now take questions. Just to let you know how this will work. You will direct your questions to me and I will direct to Munira and Baba, if needed."

The cameras exploded. A few dozen hands went up. Olabisi could see reporters from CNN, Bloomberg and Sky. There was Muyiwa with an unsightly bruise on his face. She couldn't help but wish that whoever had given the bruise had given him some more.

She spotted Michael at the back of the room, his hands folded into one, behind his back. Olabisi knew he was pleased. As he should be, she had worked her ass off to ensure that this press conference went without a hitch.

Munira's set mouth had become a grimace by the end of the conference. As soon as they finished and were alone, she rounded on Olabisi.

"I thought you said the Mosquito Man was going to appear on the video?"

"I said that he might. And even if he had, what would you have done?" Olabisi shot back.

Munira didn't know, but that didn't matter, she thought.

"Anyway," Olabisi continued. "I think that after today, it

283

would be safer for you to move into my compound. At least until when we get back from Abuja," she said.

"I'm not moving anywhere. Palemo is my home," Baba started saying.

Munira put her hand on his shoulder. "Baba, calm down. Olabisi is right. I'm surprised that nobody has burgled our home yet." She turned to Olabisi. "It wouldn't look good for us to move into your compound after everyone has seen this video with Baba saying how much he loved Palemo. Maybe you should assign a security person to look out for us," she said.

She would rather stay in Olabisi's compound, as it was more benefitting a woman of her growing fame. But being in such proximity with Olabisi meant that their every move would be monitored, which meant that their money-making opportunities would be limited.

She knew what she and Baba had agreed about not doing any deals with other people. But who was Olabisi and that Chinese man to dictate how they lived and make money? If Olabisi agreed to assign them some bodyguards, they would still be protected, but nobody would know what she or their visitors discussed in their one-room home. Whereas in Olabisi's compound there was the constant threat of being eavesdropped.

She saw Olabisi scrutinise her face, as if trying to figure out what Munira was up to. Finally, she sighed.

"Very well. I'll give you guys some security," she said.

Munira tried not to scream in relief.

"Can I go to the auto-repair shop now?" Baba said.

Dauda tried to watch the video of himself and Baba when it came up on television, but found it hard to concentrate. All he could think of was Morenike. He had to find a way of getting to her and checking that she was fine.

That was last night. And now today, he was on television with Baba and all he could think of was how Morenike was doing. If she'd seen the video, she would've teased him mercilessly about his arrogant 'swagger' and potty mouth. She was always telling him to slow down and not be so hot-headed all the time.

To top it off, Mr Sowemimo was back in the auto-repair shop, poking his ugly, fat nose where it wasn't wanted.

"I suppose now, you think you're a superstar," he sneered to Dauda.

Dauda didn't answer. He continued working on his car.

"If you think this means anything, it doesn't. Just remember that nobody wants anything to do with a useless twenty-year-old with no qualifications," Mr Sowemimo continued.

"The same twenty-year-old who is now on television, with millions of people watching him around the world?" Dauda said. He didn't wait for Mr Sowemimo to respond, choosing instead to slide underneath the car he was fixing.

Mr Sowemimo walked to the car, and peered down at Dauda. "I'm staying here to monitor everything you're doing. You're a nobody, you hear me? Nobody!"

Dauda ignored him. He knew Mr Sowemimo was fearful that he would leave the auto-repair shop for good and sitting here all day was his way of guaranteeing that he wouldn't leave.

As if he could hold him hostage, he thought to himself. He paused and reached for his mobile. He dialled a number.

"Hello? Who's this?" It was a male voice.

Dauda hung up. It was Morenike's father, which meant that he'd commandeered her phone. He told himself that he would damn the consequences and just go over to Morenike's after work. He had to see her and make sure that she was doing well.

"Mr Sowemimo, I don't know why you want to give your-self a heart attack over Dauda. Who would want to employ a useless boy like him?"

Typical Dimeji. Trying to soothe Mr Sowemimo's ruffled feathers. In another life, he should've been a diplomat, not a mechanic in a mangrove swamp, Dauda thought.

There was a loud banging on the auto-repair shop door. "Baba is not here!" Mr Sowemimo said. "He's in London!" he laughed at his own joke.

"We're here to see Dauda, not Baba. We're from the radio station. Remember us? We helped to start this whole thing."

Dauda slid out from under the car. He wiped his hands on his overalls and ignored Mr Sowemimo who was watching him with arms akimbo. Dauda knew that stance well. It was one that Mr Sowemimo deployed before unleashing his wrath.

He opened the gate and let the visitors in. It was a man

and a woman. The woman shoved some documents into his hands.

"We're from the radio station. According to the contract you and Baba signed, we're meant to get exclusive interviews with you and Baba about his meeting with the Mosquito Man. But you have consistently broken the terms of your contract. I'm the station's lawyer," the lady turned to the man next to her.

"And I'm the airline's lawyer. I'm not here to sue you but to make you understand that part of your agreement with the station was that you would fly with us to Abuja and ensure that the Mosquito Man takes a picture with Baba next to one of our airlines."

Mr Sowemimo roared with laughter and clapped his hands in delight.

"And who said Baba and I signed those contracts?" Dauda said. He's watched enough American series to know that his question was a good delaying tactic.

The lady pulled out her mobile phone. She scrolled through the screen with her forefinger and held it out for Dauda to see. It was a video of him and Baba signing, or in Baba's case, fingerprinting the contract.

Dauda caught himself reminiscing about how life had been uncomplicated in those days.

He shrugged. "So? How do I know that whatever you purported we signed is the same thing that you're now showing to me?"

The lady and the man gave him a look. "Really, young

man. You want to go there?" the lady said.

Dauda wanted to leave Palemo with Morenike and be rid of all this nonsense. That's what he wanted to do.

He folded his arms across his chest. "Fine, what do you want?"

"Nothing. Simply that you keep to the terms of your contract: you and Baba give exclusive interviews of everything you're doing with the Mosquito Man, from now on. And next week, you take this airline to Abuja and make sure that Baba and the Mosquito Man are pictured together, in front of one of our planes," the lady said.

"You better find Baba yourself, because I don't know where he is," he muttered under his breath.

"What was that?" the lady leaned in.

"Nothing," Dauda said.

"Good," the lady said. She nodded to the man standing next to her. "Here's my card. I'm Abiodun and my mobile number is there. From now on, you and Baba should report to the radio station every day at 9am sharp until the day you go to Abuja. And in Abuja, you will do the same. When you report to the radio station, you will tell us what you're doing that day and how your relationship with the Mosquito Man is progressing. We will take pictures and put it on all our social media channels..."

Dauda tuned out. He heard Mr Sowemimo cackle and clap his hands.

"Dauda, the superstar indeed! What a joke!" he said.

"Why, why can't we go to Palemo now?" Baba whined.

"Because there are a few things that we need to sort out," Olabisi said. "We need to take pictures for a few things,"

"No. No more pictures," Baba shook his head. He was not an animal in a zoo. He just wanted to go and sit in the auto-repair shop and talk nonsense all day with Dauda and Dimeji. Nothing changed in the auto-repair shop, whereas life outside of it was moving too fast.

"This is for the airline that is giving us free tickets to Abuja. They want you and Munira to pose with your ticket, so they can put it on their social media," Olabisi said soothingly.

Munira and Baba exchanged a look. Olabisi's warning signal went from green to code red immediately.

"Nothing," Munira said quickly. "Baba is right, though. All these pictures..."

By now Olabisi was convinced that they were up to something. Munira never gave up a chance to be in front of the cameras. She arched her eyebrows.

"What's that look for?" Munira bristled. "It's been a long day. Even I want to go back to Palemo. You rich people and your *wahala*."

"There is no wahala. You're just taking a few pictures. What's the problem?" Olabisi asked.

"Nothing," Munira said.

"Good," Olabisi said, her voice curt. "They'll be here in a few moments. After the photos, then you can go to Palemo. Your new bodyguards should be with us soon."

Munira and Baba sat down without looking at each other.

When she couldn't stand it any longer, Olabisi clasped her hands and put them on the table.

"What is it?"

"Maybe we should be the one asking what the problem is, because you keep on asking questions," Munira said.

"Fine. Be like that. But if I find out you guys have anything..." Olabisi started.

Munira looked away from Olabisi to the wall. Olabisi got the message. She wasn't going to talk.

Olabisi's receptionist knocked and came inside. "The airline is here with the photographer."

Olabisi, Munira and Baba got up. They were done in thirty minutes. "We'll upload to our Facebook and Instagram in a few minutes," the photographer said.

"I just need to do a quick edit to the interview and I'll upload to YouTube shortly after," his colleague picked up after him.

"Very good and thank you," Olabisi said. She ushered them all out of her office and into the reception room. As the people from the airline left, she asked the receptionist how much longer the bodyguards would be.

"Madam, they said an hour at least. There's traffic," the receptionist replied.

"Bring Baba and Munira some food while they wait," Olabisi said.

"Maybe the bodyguards should meet us in Palemo," Munira suggested.

"That defeats the purpose of them protecting you. Your

building will be jam-packed with people now, as will the auto-repair shop, probably. And as much as those area boys respect you, I'm sure they'll be getting restless and wondering why they aren't getting a share of this money and exposure you're getting from the Mosquito Man. Do you really want to risk it by going to your home without some form of protection?" Olabisi answered.

Munira sank back on the chair. She didn't know much about computers, but she knew the power of this "social media", because everybody talked about it. And because it was so powerful, it was only a matter of time before the radio station and the old airline got wind of the deal Olabisi had made with this new airline.

Baba pinched her on the arm, his way of telling her to say something, but she refused to answer him. It was all his fault anyway. If he'd taken responsibility as a man, she wouldn't have had to do all this herself. She brushed his hands away in irritation.

"Leave me alone," she said.

Olabisi watched them both for a few minutes. "I need to wrap up a few things in my office, so you both wait here and I'll let you know when the bodyguards are here," she said.

As soon as she disappeared into her office, Baba spoke urgently.

"Munira, let's just go, please? If she finds out about this airline and radio station..."

"Be quiet. And what will she do? She needs us more than we need her, so she'll spend money to make it go away. And that's all there is to it," she sat back on the chair again and folded her arms across her chest. "We're not sneaking out of anywhere like thieves. People know us now."

An hour passed. Olabisi came out. "The bodyguards are just round the corner. And the airline is also on their way. They said they want to do a quick reshoot with you both. It'll only take ten minutes, they said,"

"No problem," Munira said. "We're in this thing together,"

For the second time in an hour, Olabisi raised her eyebrows at Munira again. She looked back and forth between the two of them, started saying something, then changed her mind. Her mobile phone rang. "You're outside? Oh good."

She was putting away the mobile when it bleeped. "The airline people are here, too. Very good, indeed."

A few minutes later, they heard the lift ping. Two bulky men walked out and headed towards Water for Nigeria's office. They were followed by the airline's photographer and colleague. Behind them was a man and a woman.

Olabisi went to meet them. The man and woman gave their names to the receptionist. Olabisi thought she heard her say that she was suing Baba for breaching his contract with them and the airline, so she went to investigate. In the meantime, she directed Baba and Munira back to her office, to do their interview there.

"I'm Olabisi Thomas, founder of Water for Nigerians. How can I help you?"

The lady turned to her and held out her hands. Olabisi left it hanging. The lady shrugged her shoulders. "Be like that, then," she said. "I'm Abiodun, the radio station lawyer. This here is the lawyer for GWG Airlines, the one that Baba signed a contract with saying that it would take him to Abuja. I'm here on behalf of my client, the radio station. The same one that Baba signed a contract with, granting us exclusive interviews about his adventure with Bono, the Mosquito Man—"

"I have no idea what you're talking about. Baba hasn't signed anything with anyone. He can't even read," Olabisi said.

Abiodun reached into her bag and thrust a sheaf of paper towards Olabisi.

"You can put those papers on the receptionist's table," Olabisi said. "As for you—" she turned to the airline guy. "Baba has not mentioned anything about any deal with your airline to me,"

The guy shrugged. Abiodun brought out her mobile and showed Olabisi the same video she showed Dauda.

Dauda. She should've known. Olabisi seethed. Her office door opened and the photographer came out.

"Madam, we need you to take a few shots with Munira and Baba again," he said.

Abiodun started walking towards Olabisi's office. "And I need you to stop doing whatever you're doing right now, because it is in breach of my client's contract."

GWG's lawyer followed her as she strode towards Olabisi's office. Olabisi wasn't sure what happened next. All she knew was that she saw Abiodun push the photographer away and go marching into her office. She, Olabisi followed and tried to push her out. The two bodyguards got involved and then there was a scuffle and lots of shouting.

Then, the receptionist called the building's security to forcibly remove Abiodun and GWG's airline representative from WfN's offices. And in the midst of all this, Baba and Munira did not say anything, which made Olabisi even madder.

What was it with these two? Why couldn't they be normal? Did they ever think beyond their own selfish desires, she thought.

"Everybody! Calm down and be quiet. Let's settle this like adults. Wande," Olabisi called the receptionist. "Cancel all my meetings for today and cancel your call to the security guards as well. We are all going to the auto-repair shop to settle this matter with everybody involved. And that is all there is to it. Agreed?"

They all nodded. Baba looked away.

GWG of all airlines. The one with the worst track record in Nigeria. They couldn't choose a reputable one. The radio station had conned Baba and Dauda. They had been derelict in their duty to protect them. No wonder they wanted to be photographed with Bono. A single photograph with him, Africa's saviour, in front of the airline plane would wipe out their appalling safety record. They'd been fined a record $10 million dollars by the government and were surely on the brink of bankruptcy.

To date, they'd had four plane crashes in five years. Their

customer service was non-existent. They never kept to time and didn't have Nigerian pilots, because the ones they had swore that they wouldn't put their fellow Nigerians in danger. So they recruited Russians who didn't care.

The 4x4 was silent until Baba tried to speak. "Olabisi..."

"Baba, we shall get to the bottom of this when we get to the auto-repair shop," Olabisi cut him off.

Baba understood and stopped talking.

"You should have some respect for my husband," Munira said. "He's old enough to be your father. Just because you're rich doesn't mean that you can treat us like we're your possessions and disrespect us."

Olabisi turned round to face them as she sat in the passenger seat. She gave them both a look. Munira huffed and sat back in her seat.

The 4x4 rumbled on. Behind them, Abiodun and GWG's lawyer followed in another car.

Dauda couldn't bear it any longer. He had to go and see Morenike. He wiped his hands on a rag and walked over to where Mr Sowemimo was sitting. As he opened his mouth to speak, there was a loud banging on the auto-repair shop gates.

"Baba is not here! He's in London with the Mosquito Man!" Mr Sowemimo laughed again at his joke. Dauda wondered how the joke hadn't gotten thin yet since he'd been saying it for hours.

"It is Abiodun and we're here with Baba and Olabisi. Let us in!"

Dauda looked at Mr Sowemimo and then went to open the auto-repair shop gates to let them in. He looked from one visitor to another: Baba, Munira, Olabisi, two big men who looked like they slept at the gym, and then, Abiodun and the GWG airline lawyer.

"Dauda—" Baba started to talk.

"No, Baba, let Dauda do the talking first," Olabisi said.

Dauda drew in a deep breath. "If this is about the airline tickets, you should speak to Munira. She took them from me. Anything else, I don't know. Now, if you don't mind, I want to get back to work," he said.

Olabisi looked at Munira. "So it is true then?"

"I don't know what you're talking about," Munira said.

"Just tell the truth!" Baba turned to Olabisi and Abiodun. "Yes, it's true. She took the tickets. I think she sold them. She didn't mean any harm. We needed the money," he said.

Mr Sowemimo and Dimeji brought out some chairs. Somehow, they knew that this was one conversation they had to stay out of. Dimeji went to the backdoor. As was customary in this situation, he would stay out there until the crisis was over.

Olabisi refused to sit. "But why? Why did you do that?"

"Do what?" Munira spat. "What good is an airline ticket if you don't have food in your house?"

"You should've said something. Yet, you went ahead and signed the contract with Landis Airlines..."

Abiodun stepped forward. "Well, there's still the issue of the interviews that he's been giving. Legally, we had

296

exclusives to those interviews—"

"Oh, just shut up and let me think," Olabisi held two fingers to her temple.

"But did you both think you would get away with this?" she looked at Baba, who had the grace to look away as if ashamed, and also at Munira, whose demeanour was more defiant. She took in a deep breath and started speaking, as if to herself. "It's okay, the situation is still redeemable. We'll literally buy Dauda and Baba's contract off you. As for the deal with GWG, well, I'm not sure that we can get Bono to take a picture with your plane in the background, but perhaps we can arrange something in which he takes a picture in front of your logo or something. Maybe at one of the summit's after parties?" Olabisi looked at Abiodun and GWG's lawyer. "I think this is fair, don't you?"

The two of them consulted with each other. Abiodun came back. "We all want this to work, so this is what we suggest. You announce that our radio station is your *preferred* media partner, because they are the voice of Palemo and have done a great job in starting all this Mosquito Man business. As for CWG, well, taking the picture with Bono in front of the plane was a long stretch anyway, so we'll settle for a picture of him with CWG's logo placed strategically behind him. That should work," she said. She pulled out her laptop. "I'll write an agreement for the radio which I will request that WfN, Munira and Baba sign. We'll all go to a business centre—there's one three buildings away—to print it out and sign it right there. Then, we can put this whole thing to rest," she looked at Olabisi, Baba and Munira in turn. "Do we have a deal?"

Olabisi held out her hand. Abiodun hesitated, then took it. They all sat down. Only the body guards remained standing.

"If I was you, I would get back to work," Mr Sowemimo said to Dauda.

# 22

Olabisi pulled on her cigarette, hard. She'd given up at university, but somehow she felt like she needed one today, now.

"After all we've been through. They both just stood there and didn't say anything," she cried out to Michael, who was on the other end of the phone.

"Olabisi, are you smoking?" Michael asked her.

"Really? That's what you're asking me right now?"

She took another drag and inhaled deeply. This time, she didn't even bother hiding the fact that she was indeed smoking.

"Okay, I get the message. You can stop with the theatrics," Michael said. "I'll be at your house in ten minutes. What's your new maid's name again?"

"Who cares about the maid. Just come," Olabisi stubbed out her cigarette. She sniffed, blew her nose and went to wash her hands. She then decided to take a shower. Michael hated smokers. He always had. And if he smelled tobacco on her, upset as she was or not, he would give her a lecture.

It had been long day. From the success of the press conference to being blindsided by Munira and Baba, she thought the shower was a good idea anyway. It was searingly hot and she wanted the shower to wash away all the day's events.

Soon after she emerged from the shower, she heard Michael's car pull up her driveway. A few minutes later, he was in her bedroom. She was in her bathrobe. When he saw her, he drew her inside his arms. To her horror, she started crying. Michael gave her some tissue. She blew into it.

"Sorry," she said.

Michael kissed fully, on the lips. "Marry me," he said.

Olabisi pushed him away. "Are you joking?" she asked incredulously. She drew her bathrobe tighter. "Not now, Michael," she said, "I'm exhausted."

"Fine," Michael said. "But know this. One day I will stop asking."

Olabisi acknowledged him with a sigh. "Look, the world will be cruel to our children. People already hate us, they think a Nigerian and a Chinese have no business being together. Can you imagine what they'll do to our children?" she said.

"So you have thought about it," Michael said.

Of course she had, from the first moment they got together at university in England.

"I don't even know why we're talking about this, now," she said.

Michael patted the empty space on the bed, next to him. "Come sit," he said.

She obeyed and put her head on his shoulder. "I don't even know why I'm crying," she spoke softly. She gave him a wry smile.

"It's those two. I thought we were dysfunctional, but

those two are sick. And that's why you're crying, because you don't understand their madness," Michael replied.

They were both quiet, then Olabisi spoke. "They're so devoted to each other, though."

"Because of the madness that binds them together," Michael said. He tipped her face towards his and kissed her again, fully and deeply. Olabisi responded, with tears streaming down her cheeks. She was tired. Tired of it all.

Michael wiped her tears with his hands.

Munira kept looking back at the rear seat at the two men who were supposed to be guarding her and Baba. They'd barely said a word to her, except to say one was called 'A' and the other 'B'.

She tried talking to them in Yoruba to no response. She tried pidgin English and didn't get a response either.

"Madam, they won't answer. They'll just guard you," Kayode said.

"I don't recall asking for your opinion," Munira said.

They continued driving in silence. When they got to their building, their compound was swarming with people. A and B jumped out of the 4x4. One of them opened the door for Munira and the other cleared a pathway for them to enter the building.

When the media surged towards them with open mics and camera, A spoke. "We're not taking any questions today. They've just come back to their wonderful Palemo community to sleep. And we trust they won't be disturbed."

Munira had often fantasized about getting out of a car like those Hollywood actresses. One bodyguard with dark glasses holding the door, while another held out his hand for her out of the car.

The reality was different. Instead of feeling like a superstar, she felt like a hostage with these two strange men.

A and B cleared the path all the way up to their bedroom. To her mild surprise, they hadn't been robbed. She didn't know whether to feel insulted that people thought they didn't have anything of worth to steal, or be grateful that she and Baba had been spared the trauma. She decided that she wished that they had been robbed. At least, then, she could ask Olabisi to replace everything.

Munira put the key in the lock and opened the door.

"I will take up position in front of the building and B will take up position in the backyard entrance" A said.

"All night?" Baba asked.

"Who cares?" Munira said, opening the door. She and Baba went inside.

"Should you offer them something to eat?" Baba said.

"You should've thought of that when we left the auto-repair shop," Munira said. She started undressing. Baba felt himself go hard. He looked away. Munira stood in front of him, naked and forced his head towards her. She made as if to lick her breast, which she knew drove him wild. Baba got off the bed and went to stand by the window.

"You should've just returned the money to the airline," he said. "Did you see the way Olabisi looked at us? As if we were scum."

He folded his arms and watched Munira tie a *wrapa*, around her body. Slowly, his concentration improved. She sat on the bed and clapped her hands nonchalantly. "Everything worked out in the end, so let's leave it there," she said. "And stop feeling sorry for her. She's the daughter of one of the baddest, toughest, godfathers in Nigeria. You saw what she did to that ignorant councillor. Barely an hour after we left the mangrove swamp, I'm told that he was publicly beaten in the market and the policemen just stood there. They did nothing. *Nothing*." Munira sneered the last word. "That's the person whose opinion matters to you, not the wife who's had to do whatever she needed to do to keep a roof over our heads and food on our table." Munira laughed softly to herself. "Dear God, save me from this life."

Baba didn't know if that was a real prayer or not. He and Munira weren't particularly religious. Their village in Ibadan was predominantly Muslim, but people weren't particularly devout. Like a sizable portion of the population, they mixed the old with the new; some Islamic traditions beefed up with others borrowed from juju, witchcraft.

It was all nonsense, Baba thought. He didn't know if he believed in God and he wasn't even sure if Munira herself believed, but he was sure 90% of what Nigerians called religion was called life survival skills. What they professed on Fridays at the mosque and on Sundays in church, hardly, if ever, matched up to what they got up to in the days in between.

Sometimes, he wondered what would happen if Nigerians were less religious. He couldn't prove it, but he was sure that the country would be a better place.

"The councillor wanted to strip her and humiliate her for 'insulting' him. You know that's what these power-hungry people do," Baba said.

"Well, he would never even think about doing that again," Munira said. She looked at her watch. It was 7pm. The cobbler would be at night school. They hadn't really spoken in the last few days and she wanted to find out how he was doing with night school. He always told her that he had nothing to report and she always told him that it didn't matter, that she wanted to hear everything that happened.

There was a knock on the door. Munira went to get it. "This lady here says that she's your niece. Says Jane, the film director sent her," A said.

"Of course," Munira exclaimed. "Come in, come in!" she let the girl in. She closed the door, turned to the girl and gestured for her to sit down.

"Talk," she commanded.

"My name is Stella and I work for Glow—you've seen our adverts on television. Jane is my school friend. I was at her house when your press conference came on and wondered out loud if you would like to be the face of our company. We like to support strong, bold women and you fit our message," she said.

Munira motioned to Stella to stop talking while she dialled a number on her mobile. "There's someone here and they said that you sent them," she said. She listened then hung up the phone. She nodded at Stella, "Keep talking," she said.

Baba watched them and inwardly, he groaned. Munira didn't listen. He doubted she knew how to. He could see where she was going with this and even he could see that it wouldn't end well.

Stella stayed for an hour, during which time Baba was quiet. As soon as she left, he rounded on Munira.

"Why do you want to bring trouble on our heads? Wasn't today's enough? And now, you're going to do a sponsorship deal with this girl. And what is it about a film that you're talking about? Didn't Olabisi say we weren't to do anything without her? Why do you always make life difficult?" Baba sat down on the only chair in the room and put this head in his hands.

"I'm not making any trouble. Besides, nothing is going to happen until after we leave Abuja. They'll come to Abuja, I'll take a picture with one of their lipsticks—"

"No!" Baba said. "No more pictures! Are you all crazy?" he cried.

"Fine. I won't tell you anything then," Munira said, and smiling to herself she went and laid on the bed. Already things were looking up.

Across the room, Baba sighed. Not for the first time, he wished he had never seen the Mosquito Man.

Mr Sowemimo got up from the chair, yawned and stretched his limbs. "Time to lock up," he said, speaking to nobody in particular.

He turned and put his hand on Dauda's shoulder.

"Today could've gone much worse," he said. "Lock it all up and go home. I'll see you all later in the week. And if anybody should ask, Baba has gone to London!" he said.

Dauda stripped off his overalls and went to the backyard to clean himself up. When he re-appeared, he was wearing a pair of jeans and a clean, grey t-shirt. He'd even taken off the gold chain that he normally wore.

Dimeji looked at him in askance.

"I'm going to see Morenike," he said.

"I thought you said her father will kill you," Dimeji said.

"Probably, but I need to find out how she is," he said.

"Call me when you're done," Dimeji said. "I want to know how it goes."

Dauda nodded and saying goodnight to Dimeji, he left and made his way to Morenike's house. She'd pointed it out to him often enough, which was how he and that scum, Muyiwa, could take her there last night.

As he approached her building, his steps faltered, but he picked himself up again. He'd done nothing wrong. Outside a man and a woman sat on plastic chairs. He recognised the father and could see a resemblance in what he could only assume was her mother.

He slowed his steps. "Evening, sir, ma" he said prostrating in front of them, in the traditional Yoruba greeting for males. The man startled, acknowledging his greeting, then looked closer at Dauda. His face hardened at once.

"Sir, I helped to bring Morenike home last night and I just want to be sure that she is okay," he said.

Her father took off one of his slippers and flung it at Dauda, who ducked. "If I see you near my child again, I will kill you! You saw her being attacked by area boys, my ass! People have seen you sniffing around her. If you show yourself around here again, I'll make sure you never satisfy a woman again in your life!" he said, at which point, he started running after Dauda.

It was only after he rounded a corner that Dauda looked behind him. He could see Morenike's mother pleading with her husband to come back to the house.

Muyiwa looked at his phone and held it to his ear again. Olabisi had blocked his number. He fumed silently and tried to pull himself together, as he'd heard those meditation experts say to do. When that didn't work, he went into the front garden and sat there for a while. Whenever he did this, the answer usually came to him.

One thing he knew was that Olabisi would regret ever crossing him. They'd been back and forth over the years, but this was the first time that she had openly declared war on him.

He swore again to himself that she would pay for all the humiliation he'd suffered on Munira's and Baba's story. The swelling on his face had gone down, but the bruises still looked awful. It'd taken every ounce of respect to go to that press conference and watch people look at him. When they asked him what happened, he said he took a stumble down the stairs in the dark, because there was a power failure. On the whole, they'd seem to buy his story. He didn't wait around after. He'd come straight home and filed his report. He also made sure to ignore his manager's calls about the latest update with Baba. As if he knew.

He kissed his teeth. His phone rang. It was his counterpart at Al-Jazeera. "What really happened with your head?" he asked laughing.

Muyiwa kissed his teeth again, wondering why he'd picked up his mobile. "I told you: I fell down the stairs during a power cut. What do you want now?"

He was a fellow hack and never called for pleasantries.

"What do you know about that radio station being their media partner? Don't you think it's a bit strange?" he asked.

He was digging and wasn't even hiding it. "Well, if there was a story there, I'm sure you'll find it," Muyiwa said and hung up the telephone. He'd missed this latest update on Baba and Munira, and right now, he wasn't even sure he cared.

He leaned in his rocking garden chair. Slowly, his sense of equilibrium came back. Michael Li had been at the press conference again, looking pleased with himself.

Muyiwa decided that he had given Olabisi enough time to redeem herself. He had been careful with the emails. His friend was an ethical hacker and had shown him how to disguise his IP, so that the emails he sent to Olabisi couldn't be traced back to him. But, it was time to pull out the big guns.

He'd genuinely thought that Olabisi would do something about her connection with Michael Li and Chino-Centric.

But like all the rich kids, all she cared about was herself. Her little charity was a fraud and he would expose her for the world to see. In the end, she was nothing more than her father's daughter. Look at what she did to that councillor, even if the guy deserved every bit of punishment that he received.

Muyiwa found the practice of humiliating women by stripping them in public distasteful and had written about it at length. It was a particularly vicious tool used by people to lord it over women.

No, he didn't care about the councillor, but he wasn't sure that he deserved being beaten in public and then murdered, his body thrown in the swamp like a dog's. Olabisi's father was ruthless, and it appeared that, contrary to public perception, he'd passed that ruthless streak to his daughter.

All of a sudden Muyiwa was looking forward to going to Abuja. He leaned back even further on his chair.

## 23

Baba hung back feeling sick and dizzy. By his side, Munira preened in front of the media. The cameras were going wild. Thereafter, they were escorted to the VIP section by A and B, with Olabisi marching on ahead of them. Munira glided through the airport. There was no other word for it. He, on the other hand, was desperately trying to hold his bladder together. Suddenly the waiting room careened in front of him as voices faded. When he came to, he saw Munira looking at him with pursed lips.

"What's this nonsense?" she asked him, through clenched teeth.

Baba realised he was lying down and tried to sit up. "What happened?" he asked.

"You fainted," Olabisi said. She looked out of the window. "That's the plane taking us to Abuja. They're just cleaning it up now and then, we'll get on."

Baba felt like he couldn't breathe. He didn't want to get on the plane. In fact, he didn't want to go anywhere at all! He wished Dauda was here with him. The useless boy would make fun of him and tell him not to be an old fool.

"Dauda," he managed to get out.

Olabisi gave him a glass of water. He took a sip. "Baba, there's nothing to fear. We get on the plane and we'll be in Abuja in no time. The Mosquito Man and his people can't wait to meet you and your wife," she said. Olabisi smiled, although the smile didn't reach her eyes. After his and Munira's stunt about the airline ticket, he didn't blame her.

*You and your wife*. She'd never called him and Munira that. He felt rather sorrowful that they'd broken her trust.

Munira shoved Olabisi aside. The two of them had exchanged pleasantries and nothing else since they met at the airport this morning. They weren't friends before, but at least they'd understood each other.

"Baba," Munira's voice was quiet. "It's okay. Just take this before getting on the plane." She opened her hand to reveal two capsules. "Don't worry, it's a new one. The chemist says that people give it to their children before taking them on planes. Puts them to sleep straight away," she said, patting his arm.

Olabisi looked at her in surprise. Michael was right. Munira and her husband were sick people.

"When we get to Abuja—" Olabisi began saying.

Baba saw Munira give her a murderous look. "When we get to Abuja," Munira said firmly, "And not before. Until then, no more talking."

"How long before we get on?" Baba asked.

"They will announce it," Olabisi said. She got up from the floor, where, next to and just like Munira, she'd been hovering over Baba and went to sit elsewhere in the departure lounge.

Away from them, where Wande and the two bodyguards were.

"You'll take the pills when they tell us it's time to get on," Munira declared defiantly to Baba when Olabisi left. She took out her make-up, lavishly applying a fresh layer, even though, from what he could see, the current layer she had on was doing a good enough job.

"You shouldn't use so much of this make-up," he said. "I don't think it's good for you."

"You better get used to it, because it's going to be even more a part of our daily lives," she said.

Baba watched her, and as he did, he realised that everyone was staring at him and Munira. He heard them whispering, "Baba and Munira are going to see the Mosquito Man."

He turned to Munira. "Aren't you scared that we'll die in that thing?" he jerked his head towards the plane on the runway. It looked a lot bigger in real life than it did on television. Munira puckered her lips and shut down her powder case.

"If it's our time, it's our time. We don't get a say-so in how we go. So if it's our time, whether we go in a car crash or bee sting, it's our time. No point in worrying about what you do not have any control over," she said, silently wishing she believed her own words.

She was scared of dying, which was why she fought so hard to survive and to live.

She arranged his agbada. Baba brushed something off her face and they helped each other back to their feet. That intimate moment was captured on someone's smartphone. By the time, they landed in Abuja a few hours later, the image had been shared and liked by millions of people on social media.

Baba felt someone poking his ribs. He made to brush them off, and turned to his side. Then he heard his wife's voice, "Wake up, fool." He opened his eyes, and realised he was on the plane, with no recollection of how he got on there. Munira gave him TomTom, one of the strongest mints on the market to suck on and freshen his overpowering breath. From across the aisle Olabisi couldn't help but wonder again how it was that Munira anticipated and cared for Baba's every need, while at the same time, seeming to loathe him deeply. Maybe there was something she could learn from them. She caught Munira looking at her questioningly and averted her eyes.

Baba popped the TomTom in his mouth. The last thing he remembered was being taken to his seat and him thinking that there was more space on the plane than all his building combined. And it was so clean. Munira had given him the pill and some water. And just when he started wondering how the plane was staying up in the air, everything went blank.

A microphone cleared and Baba heard someone saying that they could all get off. Then, he heard his name. *On behalf of Landis, I also want to welcome Baba from Palemo on our plane. It's a privilege to have flown you here to Abuja.*

The plane erupted into applause. Munira pulled Baba up and together, they smiled, bowed and sat down again. Filing out of the plane, a few people attempted to take selfies with them, but A hurried them along. Finally, the plane was empty and Olabisi came to their seat gesturing that it was their turn to disembark. They were met at the entrance of the plane by the whole crew and they jostled awkwardly to organise themselves as someone took their picture .

When they stepped out, Baba reeled from the sudden change in temperature. The plane had been cool, but the Abuja heat was stifling.

"Wait here," Olabisi said. "We have to take pictures of you coming out of the Landis plane."

Baba looked ahead and saw that there were a bunch of people, some with cameras and a sleek 4x4 waiting for then on the tarmac. Munira positively beamed.

After about fifteen minutes of taking pictures, they were finally in the car.

"I got a message that the governor wants to meet you, so we're going there now," Olabisi said. "We'll be met there by Abiodun and one of the presenters from the radio station."

"What about the Mosquito Man?" Baba asked.

"You're meeting him tomorrow, straight after his meeting with the president."

*The president of Nigeria.* Baba thought that he would rather meet the Nigerian president himself. Somehow, that had more significance than the Mosquito Man.

Munira poked him in the ribs. He knew what she wanted him to do, and yet he squirmed. She poked him again, harder.

"Ahem, Olabisi, can we meet the president too?" he croaked.

Munira nodded approvingly.

"No," Olabisi's voice was curt. "Because I'm not Father Christmas. We're here to work and not to tick off your wish-list," she said.

The rest of the journey was conducted in silence, until Olabisi wound down the window to let in some air, despite the fact that the air-conditioner was on.

Everybody in the 4x4 followed suit. Olabisi didn't need to be told that Baba had farted.

All they wanted was pictures, pictures and more pictures, Baba thought sourly, and he was sick of it. At the governor's official residence, he and Munira had stood, stunned into silence by the opulence they encountered. Olabisi saw their faces and felt some of their pain. She could imagine the questions going through their heads.

Was this how all politicians lived?

Did they *know* how the rest of the population lived?

Did they *care* how the rest of the population lived?

Baba counted at least seven young men surrounding the governor as he spoke about how thrilled he was that Baba was in Abuja.

Who were these boys and what were their jobs?

From what he could see, they weren't doing anything, except standing to attention every time the governor turned to them.

Baba tried to speak and Olabisi put a restraining hand on his arm. "They don't like to be interrupted," she said.

The governor concluded his speech. "And finally, it's

such a pleasure to meet Olabisi Thomas again. I've known her for practically all her life and I'm pleased that she has set out to do what she has said she would do, ever since she was a little girl, which is to help as many Nigerians as she can,"

Munira and Baba looked at Olabisi. She'd never mentioned that she knew the governor.

Olabisi gestured to Munira and Baba to join her. They arranged themselves and the pictures were taken. After that, the governor lost interest in them and spent the next ten minutes talking to Olabisi. When they finished, he gave her a fatherly hug and waved her goodbye.

They got in the car and travelled in silence to the hotel. A and B helped them unload their baggage. Five suitcases, for a two day stay in Abuja. Olabisi gestured to Munira and Baba to follow her inside the hotel, which they did.

Baba looked around him at the glass ceilings. The hotel reception was filled with all kinds of people. It felt like he imagined it would be in a big city, like London maybe. At the reception, Olabisi filled out some papers, and then, finally turned to Munira and Baba.

"It's all done," she said. "The bellboys will take your luggage to your rooms. Try and get some rest tonight. We have a very busy day ahead, tomorrow, so you need to make sure you're rested. A will be staying in the hotel tonight, as well, as will I. We know that you guys want some space from us, so..." she smiled at them both.

"This is not about you giving us space, but about you spying on us. If you were giving us space, you would tell your room number," Munira said.

She was right, but Olabisi wasn't going to admit it. Not to her, anyway.

She gestured to the lift. "Your bellboys are here. Call for room service if you need anything. I need to get some work done, so I'll call you later on tonight," she said. She waved at them and walked out of reception, B trailing after her.

"After you," A said.

Munira snorted derisively and followed the bellboy.

Baba prowled around the room, while Munira luxuriated on the bed. God, she loved this life and wished that she could live it forever.

"Baba, what is wrong? Try and relax. We did it," she said, smiling.

"What if Olabisi finds out about the Glow contract?" he fretted.

"There's nothing to find out because our partnership with Glow will be announced after your thing with Bono, just as soon as we have collected our money from Olabisi, and not a second after," Munira spoke confidently.

Baba sat on the bed. He wished he was back in Palemo. Places like this scared him. They were so clean, so pristine.

"And remember, I'll be the one doing the talking with the Mosquito Man, not you," she said.

"Yes," Baba said. "Olabisi knew the governor. Why didn't she tell us?" he wondered out loud.

"Because, like all rich people, she can't be trusted. I don't even know why we were both surprised that she knew him. For all you know, her father probably sponsored the governor's political campaign," Munira said.

Her phone rang and she picked it up. "Of course," she spoke into the telephone. "Let us meet after the conference tomorrow," she said.

"Who was that?" Baba said when she hung up.

"Peter Omodile," Munira said, her face shining. "He said he would like me to audition for his new film."

Peter Omodile was Nigeria's answer to Steven Spielberg.

"But how did he get your number?" Baba asked.

"He's Peter Omodile and I know it's him, because I recognised his voice. Of course he'll be able to get my number, he's Peter Omodile!" She laughed unrestrainedly and clapped her hands in delight. "He's coming to the hotel now. Says he'll call me when he gets here. I better get ready!"

She threw off her clothes and jumped inside the bathroom.

Too fast, Baba thought. Everything was going too fast. He wanted it all to slow down. For the first time in his life, he wished he knew how to use a mobile phone. That way he could call and speak to either Dimeji or Dauda. The former would tell him, in his calm voice, that everything was going exactly as it should, while the latter would tell him to stop complaining and enjoy the ride.

When Munira emerged from the bathroom, Baba was still sitting on the bed. "I'll come with you to the audition," he said. "You know I like watching you act."

Munira smiled at him. He did. She knew he did.

"What if A finds us?" he asked her, as she got dressed.

"I'm going to an audition. And stop being so scared of everything," she told him. "With the money from WfN, Glow and this film, Jane and I can make our own film. Think like a millionaire, Baba, instead of like a foolish old man."

She finished getting dressed and strutted in front of him, like a peacock. He smiled.

Again, Munira was startled. Baba rarely smiled, and yet, in the space of two days, he'd smiled twice.

She looked at him thoughtfully. "You should smile more," she said.

"You were the one that said I shouldn't smile, because I scared people, that I looked like a dirty old man," he reminded her.

"That's true," she said. She looked around the room. "Shall we go?" she said.

In the lift, she could barely contain her excitement. On the ground floor, they asked for directions to the room number Peter Omodile had given her. When they entered, Peter gave her a wide smile.

"Munira! There you are!" He beamed holding out his hands towards her. They hugged as if they'd known each other for years, instead of a few seconds.

Peter turned towards Baba as if to give him a hug as well. Suddenly, he wrinkled his nose as if he'd decided against it, and stepped back.

"You must be Baba," he said.

Baba nodded unable to speak. He felt that if he did, he

would look stupid and embarrass his wife, which he didn't want.

A ring of five chairs were arranged in a semi-circle. A harassed-looking woman holding a clipboard stood next to a cameraman.

Peter gestured to both Baba and Munira to sit down. They both obeyed, then Peter himself sat down.

"Thank you so much for meeting with me, Munira," Peter began. "I know you must be busy, so I'll keep it brief. I've got an idea for a movie, which you'll absolutely be brilliant in. In fact, I don't even know why you haven't auditioned for any of my films before," he said, giving her a somewhat flirtatious smile.

"I tried. Your casting director called me 'an overweight aunty who should know better than to compete with slim young girls that are half her age'," Munira replied.

Peter coughed. "That's, ahem, a lot to remember," he said.

"I'm an actress. We need to know our lines, so we have good memories," she quipped.

Peter turned to Baba. "And you, when are your meeting, I believe, the Mosquito Man, is what you call him?" he spoke a little too nonchalantly.

Munira's voice hardened. "Is that why you called? To meet the Mosquito Man? You could've at least pretended to watch my audition, before bringing him up," she screamed at him.

Peter flinched back. Fear flitted across his face. Munira

sat back down. There was a few moments of silence.

"Of course I wanted to meet the Mosquito Man, but I also wanted to see you audition. You're right. I should've known better. Here," he handed her a script. "Read the first couple of lines to me," he said, closing his eyes.

Munira read them aloud. She stumbled over a few words. Peter still had his eyes closed. He hummed and ahhed as she read. When she finished, he said, "Very good. Now, stand up and let's act out that scene."

Munira faltered. And then, a calmness descended upon her. She can do this. She thought of all the men in the village and how long it had taken her to get to this room, just to see her name on billboards, and then, she started.

"Who are you," she said, "to tell me that I do not belong here. That I cannot do this?"

The tears fell from her eyes. Her chest rose and fell, and her voice cracked. "I am Shalewa Omolayo and I will not let you do this to me."

The director opened his eyes and leaned forward. The cameraman leaned back as if he'd been hit with the force of Shalewa herself. Munira didn't see them. She was Shalewa, ancient Yoruba warrior queen, about to be usurped by her trusted adviser. With each word, Shalewa's voice rose majestically, her bearing upright. The room faded, in thrall to this warrior queen. Baba watched her, spellbound.

And then, the director spoke.

"That would be all, thank you."

Shalewa didn't hear him. He had to repeat himself. It took

Munira a few moments to let Shalewa go and another couple of moments to come to herself. She turned her shiny eyes to the director.

Peter stroked his jaw. "That was really good," Baba heard him mutter to himself.

Peter looked at Baba and Munira.

"Munira, that was fantastic! Again, why haven't you been in any film yet?" he asked her, not expecting an answer.

"Because your casting agents are fools," Munira said.

Peter got up. "Thank you both." He turned to Munira, "You'll hear from me tomorrow," he said. "What time is the press conference?"

"9:30am," Munira answered.

"I'll be there," he said.

Munira practically hopped to the lift.

"Baba, what did I tell you about things changing for us?" she said.

They exited the lift and headed towards their room. She fumbled with the entry card. Inwardly, Baba wondered how she knew how the card worked and decided that he didn't want to know. Finally, the room unlocked and they went inside.

# 24

Swagger Rafferty pursed his lips while scrolling through the news feed on his phone and read the latest update on Bono Save-the-World, as he liked to call him. Really, the man had no shame, he thought to himself. He noted with familiar annoyance that while Bono's and Angelina's save-the-world antics dominated CNN's and the BBC's homepage, his own event in Conakry, Guinea only got a brief mention in the Glasgow Herald. He supposed it was better than nothing. The Herald had always been good to him, being that he was a child of the city.

He snuggled closer to his wife wrapping his hand around her waist. It was one of his favourite times of the morning, before the chaos of family life reared its head. His wife covered her arm with his and he kissed the back of her head.

As if on cue, an hour later, at 6:12am, his three children, all under ten years old came charging into the room. They climbed on the bed and proceeded to bounce up and down. Swagger and his wife groaned.

"It's okay, hon. I'll handle it," he told his wife. She was taking them away for an extended weekend with her parents. It seemed only fair for her to have a lie-in.

"Come on, kids. Who's up for pancakes?" he said heading towards the bedroom, their two-year-old under one arm.

"You're a legend," his wife murmured, before settling back to grab another thirty minutes of sleep.

A few hours later, amidst teary goodbyes and tantrums, the house was silent. Swagger found himself at a loss. He'd had ambitious plans of catching up on his paperwork and redoing some audio recording of his last film, but when it came down to it, he felt listless, like he could not be bothered. He scrolled up and down his contact list, his fingers hovering over the green dial button every time he came across John's name.

No, he wouldn't, he promised himself that he would stop.

The silence in his house was deafening. His assistant called to confirm some television appearances. Afterwards, he went for a five-mile run. When he got back to his home, he called his wife. Yes, they'd just arrived. Yes, she survived the 75-minute journey, but only just. He could hear his children in the background.

"We love you, daddy!" they chorused.

He told them he loved them too, hung up, had a shower. Afterwards, he dressed carefully, knowing full well what he was going to do, but unable to stop himself.

It was 10pm. He grabbed his keys.

From the outside, the building was nondescript. There was nothing about it that gave an inkling into what happened inside. As he approached the door, which had no handle, it swung open. Another reason he liked coming here. They were discreet. As soon as he entered, he breathed a bit easier, loosening his tie. A man and a woman approached him. He had never seen them before, but he trusted this establishment completely.

He allowed himself to be led to a side room. They pushed him back on the bed gently and began to undress him. Swagger sighed in contentment.

Baba did not sleep that night. What if everything went wrong? What if the Mosquito Man wouldn't take them seriously?

He heard Munira yawn and turn over in the bed. When she opened her eyes and saw him standing by the window, she tutted.

"Have you been standing there all night? Hope you haven't massacred the toilet while I was asleep," she added. He got diarrhoea when he was nervous.

"I don't know what we're doing here, Munira," he said again for the umpteenth time.

Munira flung the bed covers off her body and swung herself to the side of the money. "Not this again. You're not even doing anything. I'm the one doing the talking. All you have to do is stand there and nod and pretend you understand what the Mosquito Man is saying. Then, we take pictures with every fool that's been promised a picture with us, collect our money from Olabisi and that Chinese man and vamoose out of here." She yawned and went to the wardrobe. She picked out his outfit for the day; a black agbada with white trimmings, and laid it on the bed. "Now go shower," she commanded him.

Baba did as he was told. But inside, he knew he wouldn't be at the press conference, because he was going to walk off. The pressure was too much. If he wasn't going to speak to the Mosquito Man anyway, there wasn't much point to him being there. He would find a way to sneak off and let Olabisi and Munira enjoy the limelight. This was their time.

Baba filed into the packed press conference room with Munira and Olabisi. They were directed to a high table filled with papers and some floral arrangements that made his nose twitch.

This was the world of the rich. Wasting money on water for plants, while people in Palemo were grateful for a few drops of water when it rained.

He concluded that the life of the rich was a complicated and wasteful one, and that he couldn't wait to go back to his simple life in Lagos. He noted the doors were manned by bodyguards A and B. He looked around to see if there was another way to escape.

Olabisi tapped the microphone and the room grew silent. "Shall we start?" she said.

"When is the Mosquito Man coming?" someone called out, to laughter.

"As you know, he is a private man, so he has requested a private meeting with Water for Nigerians, Baba and Munira, after which the photos will be released through our media partner, Diamond Life Radio," Olabisi said.

"Baba, where is Dauda, your friend?" another journalist called out.

"We're not taking questions at this point. I'm just going to read out a small statement about WfN, our work in the most deprived communities in Nigeria, and Baba's role in bringing such communities, for example, Palemo to the public's notice—"

"Maybe we should talk about WfN's link to Chino-Centric," a voice said.

"Maybe we should concentrate on the good that is going to come out of this amazing opportunity to deliver water to the good people of Palemo," Olabisi replied smoothly.

"The same people whose councillor was beaten and killed by some unknown thugs last week?" the voice persisted.

By now, there was a silence in the room. Olabisi fixed Muyiwa with a death stare.

"I fail to see what this has got to do with Baba," she said.

"Fine. Then, let's talk about the five manslaughter cases that are facing Chino-Centric in three different African countries. This is a company that has killed 60 people to date in Cairo, Bulawayo and Tangiers, the same company that is now affiliated with Water for Nigerians—"

There was a rustling in the room. Baba wasn't sure what was happening, but he knew it wasn't good, because Olabisi wasn't smiling.

"If you're not quiet, I'll come round and slap you myself," Munira spoke into the microphone.

Someone started laughing, then stopped. The silence in

the room was now deafening.

Baba looked to Munira to translate the English he'd been hearing in the last few minutes to him, but she wasn't looking at him. Her face was set, her mouth in a grim, straight line.

"I do not know or understand the significance of your accusations and I'll be happy to clear it up with you later. But right now, our main focus is on Baba and his wonderful partnership with Bono, which has given visibility to people's need to for water, not only in Palemo, but..."

*Swagger Rafferty*. The name started with a murmur.

Olabisi pressed on. "...in communities all over Africa."

*Swagger Rafferty*.

*Threesome with male and female prostitutes*.

The murmuring had gotten louder. The journalists were now all looking at their mobiles.

"Swagger Rafferty is giving a press conference in London in five minutes!" somebody shouted.

Within five minutes, the press room had emptied, leaving just Olabisi, Baba, Muyiwa and Munira in the room, with a few hotel staff.

They all looked dazed except Muyiwa, who walked up to the table. He was still sporting a bruise on his cheek. He directed his attention towards Baba and Munira.

"Baba, it's only right that you should know the kind of person she moves with," he said.

"Who are you to judge?" Munira screamed at him.

Olabisi didn't say anything. She was still looking at the empty room. She looked dazed. Muyiwa glanced behind him.

"Of course. Swagger Rafferty, the world's number one actor with a beautiful wife and three young children, has been found in a threesome with three prostitutes, who as it turns out were working with a tabloid paper for a sting operation. That was always going to override a press conference about clean water in Palemo," he said.

"But the Mosquito Man is coming," Baba said weakly.

"Not after hearing about WfN's ties to Chino-Centric he won't," Muyiwa said. He turned to Olabisi. "You miscalculated. If the photo-op had been public, you might've still got a couple of leads in some newspapers. But there was no Bono, so they had nothing to look forward to."

Munira came round the table and gave him a hard slap. Muyiwa caressed his cheek and left them in the room.

Olabisi's phone bleeped.

"What is going to happen now?" Baba said worriedly.

"Nothing," Olabisi said, her voice flat. "That was from the Mosquito Man's people. They saw how the room emptied in the press conference. He said to forget about the pictures."

Munira emitted a bloodcurdling wail.

"At least, we can go and eat now," Baba said.

There was no answer from Olabisi. She was staring into space. She sighed and gathered herself.

"I think it's best for you two to go back to your hotel room. I'll call you when things have calmed down," she said. She turned to the hotel staff, "Can you leave me alone, please?"

They all left, leaving Olabisi alone in the room. Suddenly, in a moment of clarity, Olabisi knew what she had to do. She called Michael Li.

"The answer's yes," she said.

"Good. You got your passport?" he asked, knowing full well that she never went to a conference, whether national or international, without it.

"I'll meet you at the airport in two hours," Michael said.

"Where are we going?"

"Montreal, baby."

Of course, Montreal, Canada. Michael's favourite city. Canada was also a safe haven. Nobody would be able to touch him there.

"Don't worry. I've taken care of everything. We will be alright," he said, and she believed him, because he was good at fixing things.

She started crying.

"It's okay. Now, call your dad and tell him what's happening," Michael said. "See you at the airport."

Her father. Of course. He would help her wrap up WfN and divest her assets. She would tell him to recompense Kayode and Wande, the receptionist, handsomely. They had been loyal to her. She sniffed and dialled his number.

"Daddy," she said, when he picked up. "I have to go away. Yes, I know you've heard..."

In their bedroom, Baba and Munira waited for the call from Olabisi. After an hour, their phone rang, causing them both to jump out of their skins. It was the hotel receptionist.

"Your hotel bill is now N200K. How would you like to

pay?" they asked.

"What do you mean?" Munira shouted down the telephone. "Olabisi Thomas..."

"She paid for half of the bill fifteen minutes ago. I think she's on her way to the airport. Let us know how you would like to complete payment—"

Munira hung up and sat on the bed.

"Baba, they said we owe them money. That Olabisi is on her way to London or something..."

She started opening and closing drawers feverishly. At one point, she even upended the mattress. "Gone! Our money is gone! There was N300,000 hidden in various places in this hotel room, and now it's all gone!"

She sat on the bed.

"I don't understand. Gone where? And where did you even get that money from?" Baba cried.

Munira didn't answer. She was punching numbers on her mobile furiously. She listened and threw her phone across the room in frustration.

"That Peter Omodile is a liar," she said bitterly. "He's blocked my calls." Tears rolled down her cheeks. "Glow gave me that money..." she sniffed.

"Look, we'll just sneak out of the hotel," Baba said. "Come, wipe your tears."

Munira did as she was bid. She went to the bathroom to wash her face. Whilst she was in there, she heard Baba open their room door and close it quickly.

"Munira, there are some hotel people outside our room,"

he said.

Munira finished washing her face. So the hotel meant to keep them hostage until they paid? She would show them! After all the humiliation they'd endured today, they wanted to rub salt in their wounds? She would show them, she vowed to herself.

"Come, let's go and talk to them," she said.

They left their room, ignoring the hotel staff that were stationed outside, who now followed them. As they entered the hotel lobby, they saw a few people laughing and pointing at him and Munira.

Baba held his head down, wishing there was a way to spare his wife from the humiliation. They'd been doing so well. He'd even started thinking that maybe when they got back to Lagos, away from the Mosquito Man madness, he would go to night school, and maybe Munira would respect him the way she respected the cobbler for going to night school and doing something about his education.

"Just be quiet and ignore them," Munira said.

They approached the receptionist, who was exactly the kind of person Munira hated. Young, skinny and stupid.

The receptionist smiled at Munira. "Good morning," she said.

Munira recognised her voice from the telephone. "I would like to report a theft," she said loudly. People gave them a few looks and went back to their business. "Someone stole money from our room," she said even louder.

"No problem," the receptionist said. "I can see here that

you have an outstanding balance due. Once that has been paid, we can look into your enquiry."

"I'm not doing anything until you investigated who stole my money," Munira shouted.

*Baba.*

*Mosquito Man.*

The cruel laughter in the hotel reception. Someone went past them.

"Peter!" Munira grabbed Peter Omodile's arm desperately.

He shrugged her hand off. "I don't know you. Why are you doing this?" he said, walking out of the hotel.

Rage rose in Baba. Before he could stop himself, he ran after Peter and kneed him in the lower back. Peter stumbled and fell. Baba stood over him. "Is this how you were raised, you ungrateful boy!" He spoke in Yoruba. "Wasn't it just last night you were applauding my wife in her audition? I've got a mind to kick your butt to heaven and back. *Omo ale, wretched man!*" He then started kicking him. Eventually, he was pulled off by the hotel security.

Twenty minutes later, he and Munira found themselves deposited outside the hotel and being filmed on strangers' mobiles.

A Jeep Cherokee glided out of the hotel. The window wound down and Peter Omodile's head shot out of the window. He wagged his hands, "You're both very lucky I'm not suing you for assault."

Munira took off her left shoe and threw it at his car. The car squealed off. She let her head drop on her chest.

They had no money and no way to get home to Lagos. "It just goes to show that you can never trust rich people," Baba said.

"Oh, Baba," Munira said wearily. "Stop talking."

# 25

They were still in front of the hotel, surrounded by their possessions, when a car pulled up in front of them.

At first, Munira and Baba ignored it. Ordinary people alongside news people had been taking pictures of them all day, revelling in their humiliation. A head popped out of the window. It was the lawyer from CWG airlines.

"Munira and Baba, let's take you home," he said. He got out of the car and helped them pack their luggage in the boot.

At the airport, he took them to a private room, "So you two can be alone and away from this madness," for which Baba and Munira were grateful.

On the plane, they sat in first class, with the entire row free, so no one "would disturb them."

And when they landed in Lagos, the CWG man dropped them in front of their house. As they got out of their car, Munira's phone rang. It was Abiodun, the radio station's lawyer.

"I'm glad you're safe and sound in Lagos. I just want to talk to you about a final, exclusive interview and pictures with us about how everything went so disastrously wrong in Abuja," she said.

Baba saw Munira's face change as she listened to the person on the other end of the line.

"No," Munira said. "No more interviews, or pictures or anything. From now on, my husband and I will keep to ourselves," she said.

Baba heard Abiodun laugh on the other end of the telephone.

The CWG lawyer reached out into his pocket and gave them a wadded envelope.

"Take it and do something good with it," he said. He thrust the money into Munira's hands.

When they went to their room, they were surprised that they hadn't been burgled. As soon as they got inside, they headed for the bed and collapsed into exhausted sleep.

They were woken up by a loud banging on their door. It was the landlord. Munira opened the door. He burst into the room.

"You two owe me, especially you," he turned to Munira.

"I don't owe you anything. How much is the rent outstanding? How much?!" She took the envelope CWG's lawyer had given them and started counting. "Here, is N300K enough?"

She brushed past him and banged on Mama Jide's room. "Come out! I know you're listening anyway!"

Mama Jide came out and Munira dragged her to hers and Baba's room. "Here, be a witness. Today, I have given the landlord N300K, and from now he will leave me and my husband alone," she said. She thrust a mobile into Mama

Jide's hand. "Video it. Send a copy to me, to Dauda and to Mr Sowemimo, the garage owner, and don't pretend as if you don't have his number, because I've seen you with him," she said.

Mama Jide started filming. The landlord took the money. As he was leaving the room, he paused by the door, as if he wanted to say something, but then changed his mind.

Mama Jide handed the phone back to Munira and scrambled out of the room. When she left, Munira burst into tears.

The cobbler waved at them both as they left the building. Baba was looking at his wife as if with new eyes. As they walked to the auto-repair shop, they were stopped several times by some area boys thanking her for helping them out.

"So that was where the money for the plane ticket went?" he asked her.

"Those boys are thugs, but I also know that they want to go to school. So I helped pay their fees for night school. They want to leave their criminal lives, they just don't know how," she said.

And all the while, he thought they respected her because of her brash nature.

The sun was getting hotter. The traffic was still as terrible as ever. A few people hailed him as they walked, but for the most part, they ignored him, and he wasn't sure how he felt about that. Fame was fickle, he was finding.

Mama Seyi smiled at them both as they approached the auto-repair shop. "I'll bring you both some dundun and akara as soon as I get set up," she said.

Dauda and Dimeji were just opening up the repair shop gates. There were hugs all round.

Baba sat in his favourite chair, while Dimeji pulled out another one for Munira. Dauda turned the television to BBC World Service. There was still talk about Swagger Rafferty's threesome.

Someone knocked on the gates. "Come in!" Dauda shouted. "Baba is NOT in London!" he said, laughing to himself. He stopped laughing when he saw that it was Morenike, carrying some steaming dishes from Mama Seyi. She smiled shyly. "I finally managed to convince my father that you helped 'fight off' those men and that you weren't a 'useless boy,'" she said.

Dauda smiled back at her.

On the news, the Mosquito Man came on. "Bono has announced that he will be going to Cairo to help the victims of the Chino-Centric building..."

"This man should learn to mind his own business," Baba said.

## THE END

# Acknowledgements

Massive thanks to Valerie Brandes and the Jacaranda team for believing in Baba and bringing him to life.

# About the Author

Abidemi Sanusi is a former human rights worker, now, author. Her book, *Eyo*, was nominated for the Commonwealth Writers' Prize. You can find out more about Abidemi at baldglasses.com. She runs online creative writing courses at abidemi.tv.